To Mhirne

CW01429879

SHE'S NOT THERE

F E BIRCH

Let Right Be Done!

Stac x

Copyright © 2023 FE BIRCH

The right of FE BIRCH to be identified as the Author of the Work has been asserted by him in accordance with the Copyright, Designs and Patents Act 1988

All rights reserved. No part of this book may be reproduced, stored in or introduced into a retrieval system, or transmitted in any form or by any means (electronic, mechanical, photocopying, recording or otherwise), without the written permission of the publishers.

This edition published by Wire Books in 2024.

This book is a work of fiction. Any resemblance between these fictional characters and actual persons, living or dead, is purely coincidental.

Prologue

It was in the man's eyes as he looked into hers, and she knew. Men like him spotted kids like her because it was there, always in their eyes. Men like him knew when they'd found one and wouldn't let them go. It was always telling, in the eyes.

'Come with me, pretty,' he said, grabbing her puppy-fat hand in his rough paw.

She imagined his hand as a glove because it didn't feel like any hand she knew. It was hard and bumpy on the inside in that bit where his fingers started. Bumpy like speed bumps, sleeping policemen who never woke up, who could never rescue her. They couldn't stop him, wouldn't stop him, and she would feel his long, long fingers touching her forever. She would feel his calloused hands upon her for a lifetime.

He took her by the swings, near to the shuggy horse with the metal handles which were too hot to hold on a baking summer day, gusseted in a gold sheen that looked like a pool of fabric draping the beast.

The expressionless gardener, a sullen man who wore no other face, didn't glance or bother to see. He'd seen it on similar days with similar girls. Different faces, but all had the same eyes. He turned away, closed his own eyes and his mind, and left the park, leaving her alone with him.

'I don't like the bushes,' she squealed, tugging away from the man as he pulled her into an area where white flowers with thick petals hung with a perfume that clogged up her nose. A magnolia tree.

He squeezed her hand tight and she gasped, couldn't breathe as she felt her pulse in her wrist and her head, thump-thump, thump-thump, like she might pop, burst like a balloon, and fritter away in the wind, scattered like the petals.

He grabbed her thin arm above the elbow, and gripped it like a mangle, twisting, pressing the blood from her limb until it tingled with a thousand pins.

'Ouch! You're hurting me!' she squealed, a tinny tiny mouse-squeak.

He showed her his yellow horsey teeth, lips parted with a smile that wasn't a smile; a door that wasn't a door, but an entry to another world, a different place, somewhere behind the white-petal bush. Somewhere like a Narnia through a wardrobe but not. Somewhere she knew she didn't want to go, didn't have a choice but to step into.

He bent down, his face to hers, and he breathed sour cigarette breath at her. She saw his thick tongue, a slimy slab of ham, wet, with a smell like a taste that made her gag.

'My little warm dumpling child...you...you will do as I tell you. Naughty girls like you deserve all you get.' He turned her around and pushed her in the low of her back above her school skirt waistband.

She juttered forward, stuttering steps into the soft dark earth with her black gym plimsolls. He pushed her down, palm flat on her shoulder so her knees buckled like one of the collapsing donkey toys her granny had bought her for Christmas, all jangly joints held taut and tight until she pushed up the little round bottom base to make the poor donkey quiver and wobble and fall.

And she fell.

Like donkey.

Her round, pudgy, baby-fat knees pushed into the soft earth, two little dimples like the dimples in her cheeks and two little dimples in the small of her back. She knew she'd go home dirty and mother would have to Brillo pad her in the bath to make the stains disappear from her knees. And she'd have tears in her eyes as mother told her off. Again. For playing in the bushes. But she couldn't, mustn't, tell because it would all be too bad.

The man told her to turn around and lay down, so she lay flat on the soft earth. As he touched her with his bumpy lumpy hands, she imagined his fingers leaving prints on her skin. She was six now, a big girl, not a baby anymore, even though she still had baby rolls. She was a big girl who knew about fingerprints because she'd heard mother say that's how they caught the burglar who stole Mrs Fraser's television and ornaments and money from the secret biscuit tin she kept hidden in the coal house. The burglar lived over the road from them; an incomer who mother said had been to prison and had come to their village to hide. But mother said there were no secrets in their village, and it was no place to hide.

The man squidged her cheeks to make the kissing lips so he could put his tongue into her mouth. When he'd finished kissing her, he did other things. Other things she wouldn't want to remember, not ever, so she closed her eyes to not see and closed up her nose so she couldn't smell. She lay on the soft, brown, clumpy earth like it was a princess bed scattered with long white petals. She sniffed the air that wasn't full of him and she smelt soft talcum smells from the flowers. She dreamt of floating away on a blanket of earth with white flowers in her hair and wearing a pretty dress made by her mother with baby butterfly stitches, barely seen.

As the man did his thing, she listened to a bird singing a song, an old lament, an inquisitive tone, just like the robin who sat on their gate in autumn, cocking his head, watching, twittering, and trilling some more.

When the bird stopped singing and the man had finished, she opened her eyes. He dragged her up by her curly ponytail and pulled up her laddered school tights. He pulled down her school skirt and said, 'You made me do it. You made me do this thing. It's your fault. Don't you forget. It's your fault. Say nothing. Nothing. You know what will happen, child. Don't you? Don't you?'

He poked his horny-nailed finger into her face. She looked up at him from under thick eyelashes. She looked into his eyes. It was there in his eyes. And now it was in hers. The telling was always in the eyes, if you knew to look there.

She nodded, trying not to let him see her wet eyes, trying hard not to let the wet drip down her ruddy face. The bird watched, cocked his head, flew off. She would see him another day, she was sure.

Chapter 1

Jed landed face to face with a smack, straight onto the skull, squashing his cheek against the decomposing body. He heard the squelch and felt the sponge of decaying flesh as the gut-wrenching stench seeped up his nose and into his mouth. His arms lay outstretched, redundant, unable to help him in the moment between seeing the remains and tripping over them. His brain screamed. I've killed her! I've killed her!

He scrabbled in the earth, trying not to touch the bones. He spat bile and earth and slime. No! No. No, he hadn't killed her. Sharp air stung his chest and he caught his next breath in a coughing fit. He hadn't killed her. Not this one. Not this body, this person, whoever they were.

That was Cassie.

Cassie.

Like a cliché from one of his books, he'd stumbled upon a body while walking on the hillside, a jaunt aimed at clearing the alcohol-fug. The tree with flaking bark, and dead branches, and defiant budding leaves, half-dead half-alive, beginning to bloom, uprooted but not yet fallen. The bulge in the earth at the foot of the tree looked inconsequential as he strode up the hill and he hadn't seen the protruding roots. Until he tripped.

He brushed down his trousers, smearing the mud on the knees of his jeans. He hand-washed his face and spat out bits of earth and rotten flesh. He bent down and gripped onto his kneecaps to help steady his ankles, so he didn't slip a second time. The damp earth mingled with sodden bark, and Jed couldn't shake the reek of death nor blink it away. He stared at the carcass, saw the decomposing skeleton half-buried, half-sheeted, left to the elements, and exposed to beetles, rodents, birds and other creatures. He saw a body long abandoned and presumably forgotten. Tweed material mimicked a two-piece, and from what he could see without touching, it had been a skirt and matching jacket, one flat black shoe, lace-up with a rounded toe, size small, much smaller than his, the other one missing, and a necklace, a broken silver chain with a locket. Female, then, he presumed.

Rex, Jed's crossbreed terrier, bounded over to him from a dead bird he'd been scavenging. The dog cocked his leg against the tree trunk, spray-back reaching both Jed, the body, and the dog as he nosed in the wet earth. He crouched.

'Rex! No!' Jed reached for the dog and pushed him away, stronger than he'd intended. Rex yelped, sniffed again, and scratched at the soil with his back legs, bullets of earth flying behind him.

Jed stood upright, slapped his hand hard against his thigh, firecracker loud, but lost into the air as the dog persisted in digging up clods like coins spewing forth from a jackpot win; three lemons and a gold bar.

'Come on, boy. Come on, Rex.'

Jed had hit the jackpot, all right. A coil of anxiety started in his groin as he deliberated running, simply packing up and disappearing. He was good at that, going on the run, mingling in crowds, hiding in plain sight, vanishing. Why? Why now? Why him?

Why not?

Lethargic clouds teased, scuffing the sky, grey and sullen. Jed felt the first few spits on his face and closed his eyes. Pinpricks dotted him, sharp darts stinging his cheeks, blurring his eyes, his cheeks beginning to burn as the rain came. It was the first time he'd cried since Cassie. An involuntary shiver covered his shoulders like a shroud and he tried to shrug it off. He rubbed his face again and whistled for Rex. This time the dog came, obedient and eager. Jed grabbed his collar, his hand hesitating, eyes red-rimmed and hung-over.

As he hovered over the remains, he knew he couldn't do it, couldn't leave this woman. He had to do the right thing. She was somebody, someone who had a life, and someone must be responsible for her. Her story wouldn't be a good one, it never was, and whoever she was, she didn't deserve a shallow grave. He dug into his combat jacket for his phone. He checked it for charge and a signal, shaking it as if it might prompt a connection. One bar. Oh, how he wished he could be in a bar right now, anywhere in the world, anywhere but here.

He pressed nine three times.

It was supposed to be paradise, a beautiful place to grow up, if you were fortunate to be born, or move, there. It was a palliative place to retire if you were lucky enough to afford it. Jed Gillespie loved places like Glendargie, with imposing pines and proud Munros. They'd called to him like a mermaid's lament ever since he'd visited one lost summer weekend. He'd been passing through on his way somewhere, anywhere, then a few months later upped bags from his flat in the Borders and took himself and his dog, Rex, to become members of the Glendargie community.

The tiny, two-bedroomed cottage was tucked up on the estate of a family called Struan. The paint on the rotting door was flaking, like the paint on the walls inside, slivers of eggshell cracked that broke away when touched. The little house smelt of damp, and mice, and soggy rotten plants that had been allowed to grow unbidden in the stone walls and through the crumbling window frames. Bats had made the belfry into their personal roost, up in the eaves above his bedroom window and, as they were now a protected species, regular visits from the Bat Conservation Trust meant they were there to stay. Unlike him.

Jed, settled for now, savoured the space, the quiet fresh air, unfiltered as it came through the many cracks in the stone house. He'd had to buy oil for the heating, and a thicker duvet for his bed, but he liked the quirky place. Despite the pitfalls of a sudden move, Glendargie was a beautiful place with stunning views, and it gave him somewhere to rest his head, lay himself down, try to forget. None of the problems with the house mattered. He'd put it right and make it a home, in time, and he had plenty of that. Time enough to forget.

A rush of flames from the open wood burner gushed as he walked into a bar of friendly faces. No hushed silences here, not like the last place, where a stranger was a stranger until you'd lived there fifty years or more. Jed was being given a good welcome, embraced by natives who'd done their research on this stranger. They wanted to know who walked among them and who could blame them? He hadn't reckoned on that and he didn't usually confess to anything, but when they wanted to know where he found inspiration for his bestselling novels they'd read from the public lending library that still existed in their tiny town, and when they filled him full of praise, Pale Ale, and the best malt, he coalesced.

Bolly, the pub cat, sauntered over and coiled himself around his legs, black and white fur brushing around him as he stretched out by the fire. A few minutes spent eyeing him up was enough and Bolly strolled off to curl up with Rex, who lay at his master's feet and didn't flinch other than to cock an eye, letting him know who was boss, a warning flash not to try anything.

For a while Jed was a local celebrity, supplied with kind words and plenty of drinks by locals who warmed to him, this tall, strange stranger who wrote books for a living. They embraced him and he returned the compliments, tot after tot.

It was the next afternoon, a couple of hours after waking late, three cups of black coffee, and a pounding head he deserved, that Jed and Rex took to the hillside behind the cottage. The path was supposed to lead up into the high trees that shielded the big estate house, but he never got that far. The weather was foul, cold to the bone; the air hanging with ghosts. Jed blamed the hangover.

He wondered where the path would lead, if it would peter out somewhere at the top of the woods or wind back on itself and disappear into the woods where no one trod and no one heard the sounds. Would he discover some place different? He was enjoying the discovery. It had been a long time since he'd felt the freedom to walk, to think, to explore something new. He told anyone who would listen that he'd retired from writing but perhaps inspiration would kick him after all. Fresh air nipped across his cheeks like summertime midges, and the fug began to sweep from his head.

Ten minutes later the discovery of a decomposed body meant Jed couldn't stay; not in this town, not now, despite the friendly faces and free drinks. It was another reminder there's nowhere to run. He should have known better. He'd now exposed someone else's secret and knew there would be plenty more of them with this discovery. Someone else's secrets, he scoffed, as if he didn't have enough of his own. It had taken only three weeks for the shine to tarnish. Three weeks was all it had taken for him to be embroiled in what he knew would be a full-on police investigation.

Jed returned to his cottage once he'd finished giving his statement to a young, uniformed officer. Slivers of ice rattled in his fat whisky tumbler, a present from a crime writing conference back when he topped all the credible book charts. The malt tinkled into the glass, generously covering the ice. He blamed himself, it was his own fault, he'd gone looking for escape. He was always looking for escape. It's what he did for a living. A professional escape artist, piss artist, a man who wrote about other people's lives, other people's problems, and what he knew, or should have known from experience, was that a small place is no place to hide.

SHE'S NOT THERE

So why did he keep trying?

Because there was always the thought of a paradise out there somewhere.

Chapter 2

Kat Dubois reached into the back of her car for her boots. Pristine and too tight, they nipped at her heels as she pulled the laces taut. She'd been back in Scotland for a month, and it was only her second week in the job. This was her first dead body. She hadn't expected one so soon.

There were ten murders a year in Tayside, roughly. There were many more suicides, and plenty of road traffic accidents, or collisions, as they now had to be called. Accident implied no blame but there was always someone to blame, as the persistent and annoying television adverts for compensation solicitors confided, like a well-known secret. Gun crime and knife crime was plentiful in the East End of London but here she was expecting drugs and petty gangs led by big fish swimming in a small pond, who Kat knew wouldn't last a weekend on the harsh streets of Hackney, Whitechapel, or Forest Gate. Twenty years at the coalface had given her plenty of experience and knowledge and although knowledge was power, police fought a battle that would never be won until society changed, and so did some police officers.

Where once she'd thrived, enjoyed every day on the job, she'd become fed up with persistent cases of mundane murders, gang warfare, and relentless battles on streets that bred attitude. And when one lynchpin was taken down, there were five vying to take the helm. She knew the minute she thought of a murder as mundane, she was becoming hardboiled, and she didn't want to be that sort of cop.

SHE'S NOT THERE

The last murder investigation was tough, and enough. A girl, just sixteen, had been stabbed at a party. As she lay dying a youth had sex with her, turned on by the rush of blood from her wound and the rush of blood in his head and between his legs. He stood in the dock and wept, a pathetic creature whose only remorse was for himself. He hadn't killed her, he wasn't the one who wielded the serrated knife that had stabbed and twisted her in the gut, but he hadn't helped her either. Instead, he'd taken advantage of the dying girl in the most horrific way. The jury couldn't decide if he was evil and sick, or a liar, or as he protested, an innocent youth who just didn't realise.

'She said she wanted to be my baby-mamma. We had a thing, man,' he told the jury of five women and seven men. 'She wanted me. An' I wanted her. She was pretty. She tol' me to go upstairs wiv' her in five. I wen' up and she was on the floor. She called my name. "Kez. Kez." She said over agen', "Kez." So, I did her and she was groaning and makin' this noise and I though' she liked it. I din' know she bin stabbed 'til I'd done ma thing, man, and then I saw the blood, but I din' know it was from her belly. I jus' though' she was likin' it. I din' know.' He wept.

The jury couldn't reach a verdict on the charge of rape. Kat walked away from court knowing she'd done her best but it didn't feel enough.

The sharp barristers had earned their money and reputation at Snaresbrook Crown Court, the court with the highest acquittal record in London, if not the UK. The murderer of Miah Siad was still out there and although they had a suspect, they had no substantial evidence. It wasn't the first time Kat had dealt with this scenario, the inability of the jury to decide, or the charge of a youth who raped a dying girl. It seemed to be the thing to do these days. Who knew what was next? She had no doubt that Cock of the Walk Kenzie Abbott would leave court, strut his stuff, and become invincible. He'd carry

13

kudos, his crocodile tears wiped away as he flew up the strata on the streets. Someone would take him out, take his place, and up the stakes, and it would all start again.

Kat knew it was time to move on, her time in London done. Let some other detective inspector take the reins of a flogged horse because it was a race she didn't want to run anymore. For her, the race was run. She'd been there, done that, knew the well-worn track. She didn't care for colour or creed, nor cruelty, only people, and helping to make it right, whatever and whoever they were. Justice came in many forms and it was time she tried something different, learnt new games, new faces, with different boundaries. She'd known it would happen sometime and knew she would know when.

That time was now.

The day after the hung jury let Kenzie Abbott walk free, Kat sat at her desk flicking through the latest police orders. She saw the advert for Police Scotland calling for experienced officers. Good remuneration package for the right people, it said. Pension transferrable. All ranks considered. All skills acknowledged.

It was time to go home.

In no time at all Kat found herself standing on the edge of the Glendargie community shivering against the wind and lashing rain. Kat ran through the script in her head. As the detective sergeant, a rank she'd had to accept upon transfer despite the initial promises, it was her job to stand in for the DI, a job she was more than familiar with. Her expertise would serve her well, the DI had said, as he gave her directions to the scene of crime. She wasn't sure how many dead bodies buried in the woods he thought she'd dealt with in London, but, she surmised, a death is a death is a death.

Kat could see the crime scene investigators busy taking photographs, collecting samples, and logging each scrap of information just in case it should ever become evidence. A uniformed officer was taking a first account statement from a man Kat presumed was their witness. She scanned the countryside with house-to-house enquiries in mind. There were cottages dotted in the distance but there didn't appear to be any immediate neighbours. She had no doubt it would be a case of hear no, see no, speak no, something she was used to, but here it would be because there was nobody to hear, to see, to speak.

Kat stood by her car for a moment to admire the scenery before setting off up the hillside. It was cold and windy as she strode up the narrow footpath. The damp and tangy wood smells of a wet spring day brought back long-ago memories. The farmer's fields were vast, flocks of sheep peppering the landscape like dots on a map. The foot of the small but dense wood began halfway up the path. Tractors had created their own lines around the edges of the fields, frozen tracks thawing with the rain. The previous three days had brought a prevailing and blustery north-easterly wind and Kat had forgotten how it crept into your bones, biting and persistent. Down south she'd rarely felt the cold and southern weather was nothing like the callous Scottish winters, more a tantalising wink of cool autumn sun by comparison. The summer in Scotland was heady for a few weeks only and today was the weather she remembered, not hot hazy summers and droughts. Kat stepped towards the cordon where the makeshift tent had been erected.

As the wind whipped around her head, flying her wet lazy curls any which way, Kat watched the CSI standing over the body work his camera. He was meticulous. Intense. This case would be extraordinary for the team. It wasn't every day they had situations such as this, their usual scenes of crimes being drug dens, street crime, assaults, and burglaries. Kat rubbed her chin between the forefinger and middle finger of her left hand, the way she always did when thinking. With her right hand she pushed wayward curls behind her ear and pulled on her ear lobe as she stood watching the work going on in front of her. She didn't immediately hear the call behind her.

'Ma'am? Ma'am?'

It took a few moments for her to realise the uniformed officer was talking to her. It was always 'guv' or 'guv'nor' where she came from.

She turned. 'Sorry. I wasn't ignoring you, I was concentrating, lost in thought.' She stepped toward him and held out her right hand to the PC. 'DS Kat Dubois. I'm covering for the DI. Sorry, I don't know your name?'

The officer hesitated. 'I'm PC Pritchard, Ma'am. Tom Pritchard.' He took the offered hand, unsure, giving Kat a low handshake. 'I've got the statement from the witness, Jed Gillespie. He's wondering if he can go now?'

'You got his details? Mobile phone, house number, all that stuff?' she asked, taking the sheaf of statement papers from him.

'Yes, Ma'am.'

'Sarge will do fine, Tom.' She smiled at him.

'Okay... Sarge. Yes, Mr Gillespie's details are all there.' The officer leaned forward and whispered. 'He's that writer. Y'know, the Gillespie guy who writes crime novels.' He gave her a sharp nod as if she should know him.

Kat leant forwards to match him and whispered, 'Is he? Never heard of him.'

That's all she needed, a crime writer, an amateur sleuth. No doubt he'd think he could solve the case. Or worse... write about it. Kat shuffled the papers to find the personal info page. Jed Gillespie. Age – forty-five. Mobile number only. Address – Burns Cottage. She'd find out soon enough where that was.

'Tell him he can go but not to leave town. Tell him I'll be in touch, probably tomorrow.'

'Righto, Ma... Sarge.'

'Before you go, what did he write? Anything I'd know?' She didn't expect so. She didn't read crime fiction, had enough of it at work, the real stuff, without reading about fantasy serial killers and clichéd cops. Nor did she watch any of the crime shows on television. What was the point? She'd only end up arguing with the box. Police procedure didn't translate to television for her. Cops were usually alcoholics who bent the rules and never got caught. Mavericks. Of course, there were clichés because clichés exist for a reason, she knew many of them, but did she really want to watch them for entertainment? Busman's holiday. She knew too many clichéd cops, most too lazy to be maverick and go out on limb for the cause. Most cop work was boring as hell and who would want to watch all that stuff? Then she remembered the reality shows that filled the extra channels. Real CSI and what was the other one? Killer Cops? She chastised herself. Stop being so bloody cynical, Kat. You came here, for a fresh start, new beginnings. Stop it.

'He wrote Blood Letting, For the Dead, Dope Dog... oh, tons of stuff, he's written maybe a dozen or more. He's good. Gritty. Interesting. Different take on stuff if you like to read it. Not done much for a while though, I don't think.'

'I'll have to look him up. Before you go off duty will you please leave your own statement on my desk, Tom?'

She didn't want to be chasing him around for three weeks while he was on days off and on night duty.

'Of course, Sarge. Never wouldn't.' He doffed a finger to his forehead.

Something told Kat he meant it. She looked over to Jed Gillespie. He'd have a following, a fan club full of people who loved to read about murders and bent cops but she doubted he'd find inspiration in Glendargie. The rich landowners and country houses and small streets with stone houses, a handful of cottages and the estate council houses, all of it rooted in Scottish history with a scattering of rogue incomers, were hardly high stakes in criminal underworlds. Not of the sort he no doubt wrote about.

Maybe things had changed in her absence? What did she know about Glendargie, really? Or writing? All her energies went into

17

proper policing, the real stuff. She should read more but when did she have the time or opportunity? It was a luxury to read a book. Oh, the irony. Grumpy cops and she was being the epitome of one. She made a mental note to do a bit of research on Mr Gillespie.

Her phone pinged. She slid it from the back pocket of her suit trousers. It was a text message from DI Munro, telling her the undertaker was en-route to the scene to remove the body to Dundee mortuary for post-mortem. A second ping read – Press release? Was he seriously asking her to prepare a press release? Wasn't that his job? Kat was versed in speaking to the media because the Met made their senior officers and special investigators take media courses. She'd lost count of the times she'd spoken on TV, on the radio, and to journalists. There didn't seem much in the way of media interest up here though, not yet. She'd have time to cobble something together on the way back to the station. The forty minutes, or longer, drive back down to Perth would give her plenty of time to work out what she was going to say but there was nothing like being thrown to the wolves before she'd even made her desk her own.

Kat slipped the phone back into her pocket and turned her attention to the activity by the body and the crime scene investigators. Oh, for faux confidence and winging it. There were so many people to get to know. She watched as the long-legged author strode off with his little dog jumping up his shins. He bent to pick it up and the wriggling creature was all paws and wiry hair, not unlike hers. The dog lapped at his owner's face like the excited puppy he was. Kat wondered what part he'd play in this story, how he'd fit into the investigation.

As if he knew he was being watched, Jed Gillespie turned and looked at her.

She watched him watching her.

SHE'S NOT THERE

He saw her watching him. He wondered...What sort of cop was she? And something more pressing...How soon can I leave town?

Chapter 3

Kat had left the engine running so the car was warm when she climbed back in. She opened the policy log and folded the front cover back, creasing the spine so it was easier to write on the first page. Every decision, every conversation, every single movement would have to be accounted for. Too many mistakes, presumptions, and assumptions, by people who thought they knew better, now meant everything had to be justified. At least now if you got it wrong, you could justify the decision. A justified sinner. Less likely to be sued. Or if you were, you had your own evidence trail.

Dave Partridge floated back to her like a bad smell; he was something she couldn't shake that easily, the stench of bad memories involving maverick bosses. She'd known a few. They always tried to justify their deeds by carrying out them out in the name of the job. She'd learnt a lot from Partridge, a lot about how not to do the job. When they caught up with him, he was an almost-retired cop and because of their misplaced loyalty, he took a few down with him. So much for the handshake squad and jobs for the boys. They'd finally been rumbled. He was bad and instead of taking demotion, or being kicked out, they let him take retirement. She knew Partridge and his team liked to sleep with prostitutes, sexual favours in exchange for information and tip-offs given on both sides. It was general knowledge in every nick he'd ever blessed. Kat had a good and decent working relationship with the street girls from when she'd been involved in sex offences, the SOS squad. She'd learnt to keep her distance from the likes of Partridge, a small but powerful man with lap-dog followers hanging about for his scraps. Fewer female officers were as ruthless though some had egos and temperaments just as difficult to deal with. The only thing worse than a bad male boss was a bad female boss.

Kat scrunched her eyes to clear the images of bad bosses and sordid cases. It was different territory now. Today she might have a juicy investigation, something tangible to quench her thirst and prove her worth, but she also knew it involved somebody's loss. She never lost sight of the tragedy and the grief when a body was discovered.

The pristine policy log with its smooth pages waited, tempting Kat to write the first entry. She flicked through the white blank leaves. What would it reveal when it was finished, when the investigation was complete? Fait accompli? Maybe. Maybe not. She hesitated, clicked her pen, again and again. Flicked almost-dry curls behind her ear. Stroked her chin with her left hand. Kat did all the displacement she usually did before beginning to write. What would help in this investigation? What resources would she need? She'd have to grab an ordinance survey map of the area and she'd need the coordinates of the location of the body. Perhaps the helicopter would come and take aerial shots? India 99, the Met Police helicopter, would be up taking photos at the first opportunity, but she wasn't sure on the guidelines or budgets of Police Scotland. So many hurdles. She was back to a novice again, the potential of disaster a searing pain and too real, so she had to get it right from the start. It was annoying to be a newbie. She didn't like it.

She was deep in thought and didn't notice the CSI approach. He opened the driver's door and leant his arm across the top.

'Hi, Sarge. I'm Gary, Gary Liddle. I'm in charge of the team and we're just about ready.'

He smiled, his face a tad too close to hers, and she leant back. 'Good to meet you, Gary,' she said, extending her hand to his. Firm, strong, determined. Good to know.

'We've uncovered the whole body now and I've got one of the lads sealing up the evidence bags. Wanna come see?' He cocked his head towards the tent.

She flung the policy log onto the front passenger seat, glad to ditch it.

'You bet!' She felt the familiar tickle inside her tummy, the dread, anticipation, and fascination, not wanting to see but unable not to look.

The rain had stopped, the temperature dropped. One of the junior CSIs was erecting a light. It would be dark in the next hour or so. Kat strode along the public footpath behind Gary, her boots still nipping. They approached the blue ticker tape, an ineffectual barrier and psychological fence that prevented the public from gawping. There was no need for it up the hillside as there were no passers-by, except the wandering crime writer, but procedure was procedure, and the area was cordoned off in an attempt to protect against the elements and contamination.

Kat took the white booties and suit offered by Gary. Once she was zipped in, she stood by the makeshift grave. The body, an almost-skeleton, decomposed and exposed, bones jumbled just a tiny bit out of normal order, the skull to the left, twisted at an angle, possibly separated from the spine when Gillespie fell on her. She'd read in his statement that he'd heard a crack as the skull shifted beneath him. He probably broke her neck, decapitating her. The bones of tiny feet lay to the right as Kat stood looking at the remains. Tree roots protruded from the earth, having lifted the body as the tree altered its position, moving with the heavy rains and shifting earth. Kat could make out a sheet like some sort of shroud wrapped beneath the skeleton.

'The sheet is beneath her, and was half covering her lower half. We think it's moved with the tree as it uprooted.'

Kat nodded in agreement. Totally plausible and likely.

'We took photos to show how she was found and then moved the sheet to get to the rest of the body. It'll all have to go to the morgue, of course,' said Gary.

It wasn't a random burial. Kat knew whoever it was had been buried there, in that spot, on purpose. A deliberate location. A sort of designer grave. Perhaps because it was hidden from the main road, the snaking A9? It was off the main track and out of view, way out of the way. Was it a significant place? That good old gut feeling was considered passé and bosses now insisted it was not to be relied upon as apparently there was no such thing as a 'copper's nose' anymore. Hard evidence was the thing for a conviction should there ever be a trial, and she knew that, it was always the way, but gut feelings were rooted in something so what was it that gave Kat the impression this was a deliberately chosen spot? What were the subliminal signs?

She believed in instinct and worked to prove or disprove, not to blatantly disregard. Instincts struck for a reason. They weren't always right, she knew that, but any serious investigator developed and honed those senses beyond the usual five and she wasn't going to dismiss them. This body must have been in situ for some time, but she wasn't a forensic anthropologist and had never dealt with a case like this. She hoped the experts in Dundee, the nearest forensic mortuary, would be on hand to assist. Did they automatically become involved? Was it in the budget? Or would she have to sell her soul for them to take a look?

Gary waited until she was ready.

When she turned to him, about to speak, he jumped in. 'Looks like the body was wrapped up in the sheet and buried here specifically. The earth is naturally peaty. The tree is dying off, you can see by the dead branches and the bark. My thinking is the persistent rains and winds, all the terrible weather we've been having lately, has caused the earth to move. It's sodden, waterlogged in places, and it's caused the tree to shift and the body to surface.'

Kat nodded. She couldn't disagree. What did she know about peat? Or buried bodies in the wood? Her usual bag of domestic murder, overdoses, drugs, suicides, gun and knife crime, and gangs had never involved this. It was first, a body in the woods. And now it was her body in the wood. An earthy damp dead body smell, like old sour cheese, caught in the back of her throat, added to with a hefty dose of rotting tree. It didn't make a great flavour or taste. She coughed but it was still there, stuck up her nose refusing to budge.

She looked around the fields, at the wide-open space leading to the denser wooded area. 'Whose land is this?' she asked.

'Part of the Struan Estate but a lot of their fields are rented out to local farmers. Struan owns most of the land up here, including majority of the property. The old man is a recluse, hasn't been seen for a for a long time, so his son does the estate management,' said Gary. 'Beyond that, you know as much as I do.'

Local knowledge was vital. Somebody always knew something, even if they didn't know they knew it. Someone back at the nick would know the farmer who rented this particular stretch of land. Licensing might be the place to start. Farmers have guns that need to be registered and the licensing officer would be indispensable, a good place to start to gather some information before putting her size nines into something she knew nothing about just yet, and in the meantime, she'd try Struan's.

'You had many cases like this?' she asked.

'One or two similar but this is a first. There was a dead girl we found buried fifteen years or so ago. She'd been reported missing and everyone thought she'd had some sort of accident. The Tay had burst its banks and she'd been walking along the footpath, a shortcut home. She was buried in the landslide over by Strathtay way. The other was an unidentified body, probably a wanderer, but the body was too far gone and there was no ID and we couldn't confirm who it was. Not back then. Maybe we could now but I'm talking early 90s. Once old folk go wandering and lose their way, they end up anywhere. Happens all the time, especially with dementia. We found one old guy in a burn. He'd left the care home and rambled off. Found him three days later face down in the water. None deliberately buried like this one though. Nobody goes missing and falls down dead wrapped up in a bed sheet, do they?'

'Deliberate, I agree. The sheet, the position, buried under, not dumped on top. How long do you think she's been here?'

'Dunno.' Gary shrugged. 'It'd take a while to be fully skeletonised, that's my guess, but I'm nay expert. Weather's been a bit braw, freezing. Ice and snow could delay decomposition, but you're asking the wrong chap.'

Kat wondered if she could get the pathologist to come up to the scene. Although she regularly liaised with pathologists, doctors, barristers, and such, she knew protocol here was different. She didn't have the network or connections, so was working blind. She also knew there was no way the DI was going to authorise aerial shots. It would be standard procedure all the way unless she had something substantial to tell him and right now, she didn't. She reached for her mobile. She'd see what he had to say without it looking like she was after his advice. The last thing she wanted was for him to think she didn't know what she was doing. It had all been friendly-friendly so far but this was her first test and she didn't want to mess up. She tried to dial his number three times.

'Ahh, yes,' said Gary, smiling at her. 'You're lucky if you get a text through up here. Should have warned you about that, Sarge.'

Kat looked down at her new upgraded smartphone. No Service. Gary laughed.

Kat looked at him, perturbed. Did he think this was funny? Was he laughing at her? She needed to get to know these people and quick.

As if reading her thoughts, he said, 'I'm not laughing at you. I'm laughing about our crime writer. He managed to get us up here using an old analogue. You can spend a tenner and get a better reception than you can with a five hundred quid fancy phone.'

Kat smiled back at him. Of course, old, tried, and tested was often best. And yes, she mused, Jed Gillespie seemed just the sort of guy to have a burner phone.

'Guess we'll have to wait for the undertakers then, Gary. You can fill me in on who's who and what they do while we wait.'

By the time Kat returned to the station her head was buzzing with titbits, gossip, and a list of names she knew she'd forget by the end of the week, if not the night.

She thought of the visit to the Struan House before she'd turned down the A9 and back to the station. The reticent housekeeper claimed she was home alone apart from old Mr Struan who was incapacitated and in bed. 'He'll not be answering any questions, m'dear. He barely kens his own name these days,' she'd said.

'How about Michael, his son?' asked Kat.

Michael Struan, his son, wasn't home. 'Ach, but he'll be at the estate office in the morning, hen, if you want tae catch him there.'

No, the housekeeper didn't know who farmed what land, though Kat suspected she knew exactly what was what and was choosing to plead ignorance. She'd left her card and a message to please inform Mr Struan, junior, that she'd be in touch the next day.

As she approached the police building it was shrouded with shadows from large bare branches of trees hanging down over the entrance. The front doors were barely illuminated by the dull Police Scotland lamp. In the moonlight she saw a row of cars in the visiting bays. They told her the front office was still open for business on this late Sunday evening, not closed like many of the outlying stations. She pulled up in the bay reserved for the top boss, confident he

26

wouldn't needing it at this late hour.

The foyer belied the silence of the exterior, and like every police station ever, the reception hosted the usual clientele. Miscreants sat huddled in a corner, no doubt waiting for their pals to come out of police custody. A young guy was holding a smashed car wing which was either evidence of his damage or belonged to the car which had hit him. A young couple stood in a state of distress, huddled together and crying. A large middle-aged lady was sniffing into a tissue as she made a report of losing her handbag which she'd last seen hanging off the back of her chair in a local restaurant.

The waiting room had the familiar smell of stale and sadness, of dirt and body odour and tobacco, with an added whiff of fancy perfume. Kat heard the woman say that the bag contained her house and car keys. The front desk clerk handed the lady a telephone to call her husband to come and collect her, but judging by the awkward conversation, he hadn't expected her to be in Perth.

While this was going on around her, Kat struggled with the security buttons on the door into the non-public part of the station.

A voice called from behind the screen. 'You the new guv'nor?'

She looked over and nodded as she retrieved her warrant card from her coat pocket and flashed it at the female civilian clerk who immediately came round to the door to let her in.

'Kat Dubois,' she introduced herself. 'DS, not quite the guv'nor. And I thought you all said boss up here?'

'Ach, we do, but I used to be in the Met, so you know...'

'An ally!' said Kat, as she walked through to the warmth and brightness of the main building.

'I used to work in the CAD room as a civilian operator, when they used to have them. My husband was a PC on the same shift, and we transferred back up home about ten years ago. So yes, it's still guv'nor to me. I'd heard we were getting a female DI. Keen to meet you. Boss.' She returned Kat's smile.

Kat shook her hand and clocked her name badge. Sue Kinell. 'Well, it's good to meet a friendly face, Sue. Is your husband still in the job? Is he stationed here?'

'Oh, we got divorced a few years ago. You know what the job's like. He was shagging a probationer on his shift. Not a female, either, but hey ho, that's life. The kids don't mind, and neither do I. Everyone's much happier all round.'

Kat didn't know what to say, not because of the revelation, but by Sue's relaxed openness.

As if mindreading, Sue said, 'If I didn't fill you in, someone else would, so I like to be upfront.'

Kat nodded, thinking of Gary and his gossip. He must have missed this, or perhaps he didn't think it was newsworthy.

'I best get back to the counter. If you fancy a drink some time, let me know. I think you live near me. Catch you later!

'Thanks, very kind. I don't drink much, but a night out would be good. I appreciate it.'

It was no surprise that like bad news a new face was gossip that spread quickly. That was going to be her for the next few weeks until she became a familiar face and someone else came along. Everyone would want to know who she was, why she'd transferred, why to Perth. They'd want to know her secrets and her skeletons. She hoped Sue wasn't expecting her to divulge her life story though she had no doubt somebody would have been tasked with finding out. It was a common tack to contact an old adversary who knew someone, who knew someone else who knew her. The police family was a small world and she'd come to an even smaller place, but curiosity would settle, and they'd soon lose interest when they realised there was nothing, no juicy gossip. None they would find. Kat was tempted to create something salacious just to see how far it got. A few gins and she might just do that – if she could be bothered.

True to his word, PC Pritchard had left his statement and a bundle of paperwork on her desk. It had been a long day, though an interesting start, but the reality of lone working hit hard. Tomorrow she'd be assigned someone but standing in the desolate CID office, computers shut down, desks tidied, blinds closed, she felt more isolated now than she had done when driving up the A1 behind the removal van.

Kat had settled comfortably into the house. It was relaxed, cosy, bright, and airy. Her accent had made her less of a stranger and more of a returner, even though it had been many years since she'd been back. After her mum died, the house had been looked after and rented out by an estate agent who duly completed all repairs and redecoration without bothering Kat, other than to pay the rent into her bank account minus their commission. Kat wasn't bothered with any of the details, happy the house was being cared for by long-standing tenants. She'd intended to rent somewhere else for herself and had found a riverside apartment in Perth. It was serendipitous that the tenants in her mother's house had decided to leave before Christmas, moving further north to the Black Isle now their children had grown and gone.

When Kat moved in, she knew she was home, somewhere she was meant to be. It was the place her mother bought after Kat moved to London, so she'd never lived in the house herself but that didn't matter. It was quaint and though it wouldn't have been her choice to live so far from work, she concluded, why pay rent when she had somewhere of her own?

She was debating the wisdom of that decision as she sat at her desk, having just driven forty minutes from Glendargie to the station, and was now going to have to do a return trip, and a bit more, to get home. Then in less than ten hours she was going to have to come back again. The flat by the riverside was tempting…

Sue Kinell appeared in the doorway. 'Don't suppose you could hang around half an hour and give me a lift could you, Sarge? Someone's done my tyres and I've got no way of getting home unless

I get the last bus at midnight. I can get the car sorted tomorrow, I'm days off, but it would really help if I could nab a ride.'

Kat looked up from her desk. What could she say? 'Where do you live?'

'Dunkeld.'

'Why not? I could use the company.' She didn't know if she could or not but there was one way to find out, and she could do with a friend.

Chapter 4

Gary Liddle was waiting for her, sitting at her desk when she arrived at 8 a.m. He swivelled round to face her as she walked up behind him. 'You didn't fancy a drink last night then, Sarge? Me and the lads waited for you, in the… boozer.'

Boooza. He'd added a mockney drawl to the word which made Kat's shoulders prickle.

'I'm sure you can fill me in, Gary.' She looked at him. 'Or are you Danny Dyer this morning?' She added a smile, not wanting the heckle to be obvious.

Gary looked back, eye to eye, and bit the side of his cheek. A moment, no more than three seconds, then he smiled. 'Don't worry about it, I'm sure there'll be plenty of other times when you can buy me a drink, Sarge.'

Brushing it off, Kat said, 'Are you coming to the mortuary? Need a lift? I've a few loose ends to gather up but I was planning on leaving once the DI has my update.'

Gary nodded, looked about to say something, but Kat continued, 'I'll give you a lift. And dunnae worry, I'm as Scottish as you are, hen, never doubt it. Born, bred, and dispatched south at such a young and immature age. Didn't think I'd ever be back, but things change, eh?'

Gary closed his open mouth. Opened it again, then shut it.

She gave him a proper smile, not wishing to make an enemy of him, or anyone. 'I've a feeling we'll be working together a lot in

31

the future, so plenty of time to get to know each other.' Like ping pong, like all new beginnings, it was as much about her insecurities as a newbie as it was about him seeing how far he could go. Push-me-pull-you and boundaries, the social interactions that would set the scene for their future workings together were about to be set. 'Now, what can you tell me about the morgue?'

Gary stood up and leant against the desk. 'Scheduled for eleven but if you want to chat to Palmerston first, I'd be there early. He needs three teas before he's ready to talk to anyone. And take biscuits. Garibaldi's.'

Kat gave him a look. 'Really, Gary? Garibaldi's?' She looked at his hairless pate.

'I know, I know.' Gary shook his head. 'Please. Don't. I've heard it all.'

They looked at each other and laughed, the last strands of tension broken.

'Well, you can take me to a Garibaldi's boozer for lunch when we're done, sans booze, of course.'

'You're on. And I know a little shop on the way out of town that stocks the biscuits so we can get them en-route.'

DI Munro was more than agreeable for Kat to take charge of the investigation. He told her he'd allocate a DC to her to assist and said he had every confidence she'd have the matter dealt with in a timely manner because cases like this were unusual and therefore quicker to solve, unlike the spate of whisky robberies at a series of distilleries around the central belt and the Highlands that was causing a lot of consternation and expensive investigation. Resources were being thrown at it for tracing and tracking the gang involved and Munro informed her she was to be seconded onto it as soon as she had this rogue body sorted.

Kat couldn't bring herself to be excited about whisky thefts but knew it was high priority. The theft of a barrel of Dewar's Aberfeldy at two and half grand a tot was big bucks. Kat preferred dealing with bodies, alive or dead, but knew priorities were priorities, especially in policing.

The drive to Dundee took much longer than she'd remembered. The road there was as patchwork as it had always been and not yet earmarked for improvement, unlike the A9. It was over twenty years since Kat had visited the city and the changes were impressive. It was much cleaner and held a sense of purpose that had been lacking in her youth. It was less industrial, though a few oil rig constructions were being built by the riverside. Dundee, the city of jute, jam and journalism, always had a different atmosphere to other Scottish cities but like them all, it had an underbelly: the ruling gangs that infiltrated schools, the dealers with a variety of drugs, pay-at-home women who sold their wares on the 'net, and everything else that went on behind city gates, everything that made it the city with Scotland's highest crime rate in recent years.

Today, in the bright spring light, the city shone with a prosperity and positivity that Kat hardly recognised, the rot well hidden, disguised with spotless streets and well-kept roadsides, and just like a dirty habit, all hidden away beneath a frock with no knickers. It was a harsh city, but the new museum and a flourishing university had encouraged it to become more diverse and welcoming. She made a note to come back another day, for pleasure rather than business.

The mortuary at Dundee University had recently been named after the prestigious crime writer Val McDermid and Kat was eager to see it. She hated that someone had died to provide her with the opportunity for a trip there, though she'd much rather be in a modern up-to-the-minute building than somewhere like the old Poplar mortuary, ramshackle, cold and ancient. The important thing in a sudden death was the subsequent investigation and Kat surmised that the dead hadn't had the best of times, so they certainly deserved the best in death.

Kat always liked to know who she was working with so had done her homework on Palmerston, the home office forensic pathologist. He had been involved with some high-profile cases in his time and had some association with the Lockerbie disaster of '88. His reputation preceded him and if he was anything like the previous pathologists she'd known, she was expecting a character.

Whatever Kat had anticipated, her stereotype couldn't have been further from the truth. She'd imagined a man of rugby player proportions, wild wiry hair, glasses, wide features, big feet; a man of bulk with a brash nature to match. What she got was a man at least six inches shorter than her, almost but not quite a dwarf, slim stature, and tiny hands. His skin was cracked and peeling, a sign of long-standing eczema. For a short man he walked with a stoop, each step like a trot and she noticed he had a small hunch behind his neck. His pinched face held a pair of glasses taped together in the centre, but the most striking thing about him was his eyes. They shone out, bright blue and lively, showing more life than his body implied. His receding hair gave him a prominent widow's peak, much longer than any she'd seen before. He wasn't dishevelled so much as mismatched.

Palmerston offered Kat his hand. 'Welcome.' The shake was solid, hearty. He indicated for her to take a chair on the other side of his desk. 'You on your own?'

She detected an Irish lilt. 'Gary Liddle, the CSI, is just parking my car. I thought he'd be here by now.'

'Ah, Gary.' Palmerston nodded. 'He always finds the right place to park. I trust he'll have brought Garibaldis? A bit of a standing joke. Can't stand them really but he always brings them. Never fails. The staff in the office enjoy them, though.'

Kat thought of the two packets she had in her handbag. They were definitely staying there.

Palmerston said, 'You must be the new girl from the south?'

'You've heard about me then?' Kat sat down where he'd indicated, the arms of the chair wide and the seat lower than she'd anticipated.

'Of course. I like to do my research, know who I'm working with.' His eyes smiled at her. He hopped into his own seat on the other side of the desk.

Kat liked him. She could tell a lot by eyes. Personality was there, always in the eyes. She felt like a schoolgirl in front of the headmaster, waiting for a sticker rather than a shouting match. She had expected glossy, silver, metal, white, not quaintly old-fashioned. The room was more of a study than an office, two walls with floor-to-ceiling bookcases rammed with tomes nobody read, and on the floor, a carpet that looked dusty, well-worn with a faded pattern, typically tartan. The rounded bay window looked out onto greenery, burgeoning trees, and gardens. Kat wasn't sure from where she sat where they looked out and made a mental note that they were two floors up. The weak sun was warm where it fell through the glass onto her left side, lighting up a streak of carpet, not so dusty pink and green. A clock she couldn't see ticked, solid and mechanical. The burr of a phone sounded through the wall and she heard light chatter. This wasn't so different to what she was used to, and it could be 1990 or 2020; everything had a timeless feel, airy yet consumed with purpose.

She had just finished taking Palmerston through the case, as she knew it, when Gary knocked and entered the room.

'Right, we're off,' said Palmerston, setting his computer to stand-by mode. He reached down for his briefcase, the light brown leather as flaky as his skin.

Kat took his cue and the three of them set off along the corridor to the morgue, Palmerston leading from the front.

The smell of putrefaction had long gone from the body. Apart from stray remnants of skin and fleshy protuberances here and there, the remains were skeletal beneath what was left of the clothing – a grey-green tweed two-piece, cream blouse with tiny black buttons like watching eyes, a once-white silk petticoat, waist-high elasticated pants to hold in the non-existent belly, pale nylon tights, albeit not much left of them, black, a flat lace-up shoe, the other still presumed missing, like a castaway at sea. The sheet had been rolled around her, encompassing her body, rips and tears where it had been pecked and bitten and gnawed. Every item of clothing was soiled, and chewed, little nibbles that left teeth marks caused by scavenging wildlife.

Gary diligently took photographs, logged the samples as they were taken. Kat felt guilty for calling him out earlier that morning.

An hour and twenty minutes later, Palmerston muttered, 'The uterus, nearly always the last to decay.'

Female, as she'd suspected but couldn't take for granted. If someone went to the lengths of burying a body, they might dress it in women's clothing, for fun, for confusion, for any number of reasons that made people do the bizarre things they do. Kat had learnt a long time ago not to presume, or assume anything until proven, nor to take things on face value, but to question everything. She supposed that made her a cynic, someone who didn't trust, but she knew she did trust, it was just buried, like this body, surfacing only when she was sure.

'Any idea how long she's been dead, sir?' Kat asked.

Palmerston didn't immediately acknowledge, but Kat knew he'd heard. She was used to asking questions in such circumstances that elicited a pause. He was thinking and she didn't want to rush him.

'I'd say, given the level of decomposition … that she was in a shallow grave exposed to the elements and the animals… hmm…' He paused and stood back, gloved hands raised as if in surrender. He cocked his head. 'I'd say… two years maybe? That's a generous estimate. Bearing in mind the weather, it's been well below freezing on many occasions before and after this last Christmas, and that would have slowed things down somewhat. What are we now? End of

March? I'd say a couple of summers but let me think about it, get some of the results back and I'll have more of an idea. As for cause of death…' He looked at Kat.

She returned his gaze, waiting.

'You were going to ask me that next, weren't you?' he queried with a turn of his head, just like a question mark.

Kat wanted to laugh but didn't. 'Yes, I was, yes.'

'I can't tell you that.'

Kat frowned. 'Why not?' She crossed her arms, legs weary from standing for so long, with an aching knee and a hip that she suspected was giving in to early arthritis. She waited.

'I can't find signs of any trauma, there's no head injury… nothing typical that you might expect to find in a case like this.' Palmerston walked around the metal gurney. 'There's a few missing bones, a couple from the foot, some from a hand, two ribs. They might have been missing from birth, some people have extra bones, some have less, an inconsequential finding really. Animals carry off bones when they're feasting. I'd expect to see that in these circumstances.' With a gloved finger he beckoned Kat forward.

She moved closer to the body and Gary joined her, camera poised.

Palmerston pointed to the right cheek. 'See this, the striations?'

Kat's eyes widened. She sensed rather than smelt the body, pungent, earthy, woody, cloying with decay, not fresh like a recent deceased would be.

'Some sort of rodent feast, see the teeth marks?'

She wished she hadn't. 'Hm,' she murmured through closed lips and clenched nostrils.

Gary's camera silently snapped the image, but Kat wouldn't need a photo to remind her. It was the minutiae, the things like the rodent teeth marks, that stuck in her head, not the stabbings, the shootings, the vicious assaults, but the personal intimate details, like the baby with the whack marks of a stick across the soles of his feet when he couldn't yet walk; the smashed frenulum of his bottom lip when he couldn't yet toddle and fall that proved it was caused by a bottle jammed into his mouth to make him gag; it was the soiled pants of a mother strangled, incontinent at the time of death. It was all these things that stuck with Kat, not the bodies themselves. It was these things that made them real, that drove her on in her investigations, that fired her belly to push her to find the answers. These were the things that flashed back at her in the shower, when she was dropping off to sleep, and came to her in her darkest moments and they were the things that gave her purpose.

'What I can tell you...' said Palmerston, hesitating, 'is that I think this lady had malignancy. I can see it in her bones. I can't be certain that's what killed her, and of course, we need to carry out whatever toxicology we can, but there's no obvious insult or injury. I don't suppose that helps, but that's all we have.'

He was done.

Chapter 5

Jed was too hungover to eat. He searched his bathroom cabinet for the prescription pills he'd picked up because the old painkillers had started to make him itch and feel ill. His new GP seemed on top of things and had prescribed something different. His records had come through and Jed had been called to the surgery to discuss his ongoing treatment for his recent diagnosis of Multiple Sclerosis. Apart from excruciating headaches every so often, everything seemed steady, all on track. Overindulging in alcohol didn't help, but he really hadn't thought he'd had that much last night. Perhaps his tolerance was weakening, a side effect and probably not unexpected. It was the same with his medication. The consultant had said this might happen, things he was used to suddenly becoming foreign to his body, causing intolerances, or allergies. He'd hoped alcohol wasn't going to be one of them. Cutting down maybe, but not cutting it out. He didn't want to cut it out any time soon, and even though he was struggling emotionally, it helped.

Depression. Another side effect. His dark thoughts had often helped his writing but now he couldn't even do that. Oh, how he used to mock those who complained of writer's block. Now it was his turn and he was a believer, like a convert consigned to the blank page, it was punishment. Perhaps he'd try a short story later, if he felt up to looking at the screen, if his headache subsided.

If.

SHE'S NOT THERE

It was always If, but today he was eager to find out if he could make a few sentences go somewhere other than into the bin. If he didn't produce something soon his publishers might forget him completely, or worse, his readers, and then he'd be consigned to chauffeuring cars for a living... if he still had his licence. The royalties and his savings would soon run out unless he produced another book, or at least promised one, but living on a promise didn't earn money.

As he brushed his teeth, he remembered the policewoman said she would call him today. He didn't know what else he could add. At least he wasn't a suspect. Was he? In one of his books a jogger taking an early morning run had stumbled upon a body on the railway tracks and he'd written him up as a potential murderer. Which book was that? Which one? He washed his face and rubbed his eye sockets, fingertips massaging his eyelids, then out to his temples. Was it just a fuzzy head because of too much drink or was this a development, a new deterioration?

Hydration. He'd have a pint of cold water, and then some coffee, which he knew he shouldn't really have. Despite his banging head he really needed decent coffee. He swallowed two of his pills with a gulp of fresh water direct from the tap, fresh from the running stream. Delicious and cold and refreshing. Except for last week when it had rained non-stop and the water turned brown with peat. He'd had the runs for a few days afterwards. Damn his bloody oversensitive body and its reactions. He'd have to stock up on shop-bought water over winter, if he was still here.

He checked his watch and then his image in the mirror above the mantle, the glass as tarnished as he felt. Damp spores spread out behind the glass like little jellyfish.

He checked his watch again, looking but not seeing. The edges of his brain were tickling him, a deep-rooted itch he couldn't scratch, interspersed with low-grade discomfort, letting him know the pain was still there despite his attempts to ignore it. He needed a hair-of-the-dog. They did good visiting ales down in the Open Reach, the pub

40

down by the River Tay and his mind wandered to the one he hadn't yet tried, Angle Root. Woody, dark, and sombre. Tempting …

By the time Kat Dubois called he was on his third pint. No, he didn't have any other information to add. No, he didn't have another number for his landlord, Michael Struan. No, he didn't know the farmer who worked the land where he found the remains. He didn't know much about anything and most of all, he didn't know how long he was staying.

When she asked him if he would make sure he was available for the coroner, and said, 'It'll be a similar process to the last time you gave evidence at an inquest,' he knew she knew about Cassie.

She clenched and unclenched her left hand, pudgy fingers making a fist, anxiety and nausea rising as she watched him walk towards her. She felt her right hand tighten around her mother's clasp as they faced him, head on.

One step.

Two step.

Three.

Four…

Then he was there. There. In her face, horsey teeth smiling down on her, a shadow bigger than any cloud, like a big bad wolf about to gobble her up, to eat her whole.

She blinked.

She looked at her ma. She was smiling at someone or something. Not him, please, not him. How could she? What sort of bad dream was this?

With the next footstep they turned, and her little body was swept behind her ma like a ragdoll, sweeping her out of harm's way, and in that one deft movement she found herself looking into the window of Woolworths, huge thick glass, cool and solid, somewhere for her to place her outstretched hand, the other still in the cupped comfort of her mother's grasp. She steadied herself and could breathe. She hesitated, took a little gasp, then a deeper breath. Deep breath. Safe. For now.

His last words – 'fine for a fuck' – leapt around her head like a bad bouncy ball she couldn't catch. She had been frightened she might crack and confess and tell everything in one full breath of badness. Fine for a fuck.

Fine for a fuck. Fine for a fuck. Train on a track, train on a track, train on a track.

It was a bad word. A big bad word that mustn't be spoken, that mustn't be heard. She didn't know what it meant but she knew it was like him. Bad.

Whoosh, her mother was off again, and there she was, facing a leather corner sofa with a price tag she knew they could never afford. It was brown, dirty, and dark like the earth in her hair, the dirt on her knees, the stain in her head. A big bad brown memory. She didn't want a brown leather settee, all soft and squishy that would swallow her up like a hole in the ground. White. She liked white. White that smelt of magnolia and jasmine and pretty things.

She squeezed all the light from her eyes and said hello to the darkness, a welcome friend. She squeezed her ears tight too, blocking out the chitter-chat of her ma and the shop man trying to tell her all about payment plans and money and other things she didn't understand or need to know. The noise in her ears, like the wind on the hillside, and the darkness in her eyes like the darkest night, filled up empty holes in her head. She thought she might burst, pop like a blood blister on her hand when she played on the swings, holding onto the chains for too long and too tight. Like blood from a blister trickling down her finger, a tear trickled down her cheek. She couldn't stop her eyes from leaking, her thoughts from shouting, her mouth trembling.

She was bad. A big bad little girl and ma would be so so cross with her if she knew that she was fine for a fuck.

SHE'S NOT THERE

Chapter 6

Once back at the station, Kat tried calling the two numbers she had for Michael Struan. One went to voicemail, the other was disconnected. She tried the office for the estate, and left another message requesting that Michael Struan please call her back as soon as he received this message.

Kat sat at her desk, mulling over the case, flicking through less than useful statements, looking for inspiration. Guy Lynn, her allocated DC, had appeared and was making coffee and being very noisy about it. Kat had seen him dotting about the office, dealing with the daily overnighters in the cells and had been impressed with his workload. Unless he was one that always looked busy, but she didn't think so. All she knew about him was that he seemed an affable chap, had a young family and a pregnant wife, and looked like he'd been put together in a hurry. He had one shoulder higher than the other and he strode with a lollop, the eagerness of a keen detective in his eyes. Long may it continue, thought Kat, as she watched him clunk the coffee down. He rattled the teaspoons in an old pickle jar and selected the least-stained one.

'How are you getting on, Sarge?' He hollered far too loud across the office.

'Hmm. Not so great to be honest.' She curled her right leg up beneath her and leant over paperwork that was scant and hopeless. 'The witnesses can't add anything extra and I've been given the run-around by Michael Struan. We're going to have to go up there. I was thinking of calling in on my way home.'

'Any news on an ID?' asked Guy, pouring sugar straight from the bag into a cup.

Kat shook her head. 'No sugar for me, thanks. And not yet, no, but someone must know her around Glendargie. It's hardly bursting with people.'

Kat knew she was irritated and knew it was showing. The persistent rain pattered on the windows, the central heating was too hot, every noise was annoying her, every sense on overload. She was tired. She hadn't slept well and the drive up and down the A9 was getting to her. The roadworks, whilst essential and something she wholeheartedly agreed with, were causing mayhem during peak hours. Very often she was driving much earlier or far later than the typical 8 a.m. or 5 p.m. and the road was dark, with no lighting, and required full concentration. It was a different drive from the one in and out of London along the A13. That had been something entirely different. Kat loved the fresh Scottish air but without days off she wasn't enjoying much of it. She needed a day at home, doing nothing, a luxury lazy day, but there was always something that ate at her time. She closed her eyes. It was three o'clock. She hated slow progress, even though it was technically still only day two in the case of Jane Doe.

'The pathologist was quite certain on a few things though, wasn't he?' Guy stirred his coffee, splashing it down the metal drawers of the makeshift tea station.

'Yeah...' Kat looked at the sheets in front of her, hoping to see something she'd missed, looking for inspiration. 'Definitely female, almost certainly white, aged seventy to eighty...perhaps. He was fairly sure it wasn't a recent burial, more likely a couple of years, given the state of decomposition. Birds, insects, wildlife have all had a great feast.'

'Ugh,' said Guy, plonking down a cup of too-dark coffee in front of Kat. 'No evidence of murder, though eh?'

She looked up at him. 'None he could detect. No broken bones, no trauma. Likely some sort of cancer but cancer doesn't bury you in a field under a tree.' She rested her arms behind her head and stretched out her back, feeling her right leg tingle beneath her as she sat on it. 'Toxicology is a pain in the butt, the length of time it takes. Maybe that'll give us something.'

'Perhaps she was poisoned?' volunteered Guy. He slurped his coffee.

Kat grimaced, leant forward, and closed her eyes. She reminded herself he didn't know he was annoying her. He didn't know she had sensory overload. He didn't know how to drink a bloody cup of coffee! Could she get away with chucking hers down the sink? She held her head down. 'I have a loose theory. If Palmerston is right about the cancer … and there's no reason to suggest he isn't, he's seen thousands of corpses … maybe she was overdosed, on purpose or otherwise. A sort of dignity-death, her choice, rather than let the cancer take her. Or perhaps she was demented, and the family overdosed her and did a granny dump. Whichever, whatever, someone out there must know because someone buried her.'

Guy slurped again.

Kat squeezed her eyes and squeezed out her ears to make a thunder rush. She held it for the count of five. And again. And again.

Something touched her shoulder. She jerked up. 'Woah!'

'Kat? Are you all right?' Guy stood next to her with a look of concern. 'I didn't mean to startle you.'

She struggled not to fluster, to keep calm. 'I'm trying to concentrate but it's too warm in here and I'm tired. Thanks for the coffee.' She picked up the cup and took a sip. It was strong, bitter, and she could taste the chicory of cheap coffee. She focused on slowing her breathing and took another undelightful sip.

'I said, did you hear me?' asked Guy. 'It didn't seem like you did. I said – hair strands. There were some found, if I remember right?'

'Yes. Gary's sent them off to the lab. And we're checking dental records too.'

'Hair is only of use if she's already in the system though, DNA wise.'

'Quite,' said Kat, taking another sip, wondering how soon she could go to the ladies and ditch it. 'We can ask for it to be tested for various drugs, the generic ones, unless we suspect something specific, but where do you start? And if she'd been on cancer treatment it won't prove a thing. I'd expect morphine and the like, so I don't think it will tell us much, just that she'd ingested it, whatever it was.'

She remembered a young girl who'd been given methadone to keep her asleep while her parents went out partying. They'd done it before, were complacent. On the night she died they'd dosed her up a bit too much. They'd denied it, but her hair proved otherwise. It showed up in toxicology, a whole six months of persistent use. They then argued which one had given her it, both blaming the other, but in the end, there was enough evidence to convict them both.

It wasn't Guy's fault he was annoying her, and she'd have to tell him she didn't like being touched, even if he only did it do it to get her attention. She shrugged her shoulders around to loosen up her neck.

'The forensic dentist is an option, as is facial reconstruction, but I'm not sure the boss has the budget. You can always ask? I have these ideas but I'm always told no. He might go for it if you ask,' said Guy.

'In my experience, probably only as a last resort.' Kat unfolded her leg and stood up, stretching it out to relieve the prickle of pins and needles.

'He might give you a ticket to ride you know, because don't forget Dundee is a teaching university and there's always students eager for a project. Worth an ask?'

'Hmm.' Kat mulled it over. She hadn't thought of that. 'When's the guv'nor back?'

'Wednesday.'

She looked at him. 'And who's in charge in his absence?'

Guy looked at her and laughed. 'Why, Sarge, I'm guessing that'll be you. Haggis has the hump, which is why he's out on enquiries all of the day. Sour grapes if you ask me.'

"Haggis. Bob Harris?'

'Yes, the one and only.

'Why's he called Haggis?'

"He was nicknamed after a burglary victim kept calling for DS Haggis. Even though she was constantly reminded he was Harris, she still insisted on calling him DS Haggis, and the name had stuck.'

Kat thought of him and if anyone looked like a haggis, or the perception of one, it was him: rotund with a thin neck and thin legs, puffed-up belly and unhappy.

'He hates it but it's there to stay, just like his desk over there.' Guy pointed to the corner desk in the office, tucked out of the way of the main door.

'Right then, I'll discuss it with Bob, if he ever returns.'

Guy slurped. 'Suit yourself, Sarge, but he won't be interested. I'll bet on it.'

'Then he can't say he wasn't included, can he? If I get challenged on it, I can always say I discussed it with DS Harris.'

Guy laughed. 'I like the way you're thinking, Sarge!'

'Stick with me, kid, I've dealt with a lot worse than Haggis.' Kat placed both hands on the low of her back and stretched.

A voice boomed from the doorway. 'Have ya now?'

Kat turned to see DS Bob Harris glaring at her. 'Hi! Bob … glad you're here. I was just saying to Guy that your experience is invaluable. You could give me some of your worthy advice.'

Harris looked at her and frowned. He dumped a black briefcase and tatty carrier bag onto his desk. 'Yeah? Is that so?'

'Yes. I wasn't sure how easy it is to get permission for the forensic team at Dundee to do facial mapping from my dead body and I thought you would surely know how to go about it.' Kat smiled at him, pulling herself up to full height and still only reaching his shoulders.

'Well, little lady, I don't know why you thought I'd know. There aren't too many unidentified dead bods that turn up around here.' Harris grunted as he pulled out his chair and fell into it. He opened the carrier bag and took out a squashed supermarket sandwich and a bag of prawn crisps. He tipped the rest of the contents onto the desk. A bruised tangerine and an apple rolled out, followed by a plastic bottle of water. He diverted his interest to the food, not forthcoming with anything else as he ripped open the sandwich. He coughed, spluttering as he took the first bite, a sliver of tomato squeezing out from one side of the bread and a slice of chicken covered in mayonnaise from the other.

'Want a cuppa tea, Bob?' asked Guy.

Harris looked up at him and grunted. 'Yeah, but don't make it pishy.'

Kat tried again. 'So, any idea where I can start? With the boss away it's me and thee so if you've anything at all to help me out, I'd appreciate it.'

Harris grabbed his bottle of water and took a long swig, then another large bite of his sandwich. He folded over the remaining piece and popped it in his mouth. He scrunched the carrier bag, flung it into a waste basket by his desk, and reached for the other half of his sandwich.

Kat pushed out the inside of her ears again as he smacked his lips and half-heartedly attempted to disguise a burp. 'Nope. But you'll work it out. And when you do, I've got a Blue Peter badge waiting for yer.'

49

'Charming, that is, Haggis,' said Guy, putting down a steaming mug of builder's tea. 'We're only asking for a little help here.'

'What do you think I am? Ask the audience? Phone a friend?' He shrugged and squeezed the crisp packet until it burst. He picked a large crisp from the centre of the bag and popped it in his mouth. 'Look, I dunno,' he said, crunching. 'I'm off oot soon anyway. I've got a lorry driver's statement to take about that armed robbery at the distillery in Crieff. At Glenturret.' He looked at Kat. 'You were supposed to be giving us a hand.' He glared. 'So as soon as ya sorted with ya murdering crime writer,' he turned to look at Guy and nodded at him, 'you or him can jump aboard.'

'Okay, nae bother, pal.' Guy raised his eyebrows and turned back to Kat. 'Can't say he wasn't asked, ay? What now?'

'I don't know for the moment, Guy,' said Kat. 'It's all a bit like flat-pack. Looks great and easy and straightforward, but the minute you start to unpack it, everything is in the wrong place and you can't see how it all fits together, and you just know it's going to take forever. Munro said there's pressure from above. They'll no doubt want me to sack it if we can't move it along because we've got jobs coming in thick and fast.' She held up a pile of crime reports. 'There's this lot for a start, aside from the distillery thefts. And where's everyone else from this office?'

Guy started to tell her about court cases, annual leave, and a myriad of other excuses why the desks were empty, but Kat had zoned out.

An hour later Kat was on the A90 on her way to an appointment with the Forensic Anthropology team at Dundee University. She checked her phone for messages and saw Unknown Caller ID on the unanswered call list. Another missed call. Damn. No voicemail. That was three in three hours, ten in two days. She'd have to keep the volume up because whoever was trying to call her wasn't leaving a message but they were persistent and she didn't think it was Struan. He'd leave a message, not keep ringing, she was sure.

Chapter 7

Dr Lesley Grey was keen when Kat took a punt and phoned her. She had eager students to teach and impress who would want to know all about the body under the tree. Lesley Grey was a warm and welcoming lady, someone who didn't look like she worked with the dead for a living, but did any of them, thought Kat. She was like a friendly mum who would make you eat something before you left her house, the type who would insist you rang the moment you got home after a long drive. Lesley Grey reminded Kat of her mum, only thirty years ago. Smaller than Kat, rounder than Kat, but fit and active, and smiley and kind. The women hit it off straightaway. Kat could have, would have, talked for hours but Dr Grey said she had a class in less than ten minutes. 'The thing with cases like this, DS Dubois, although they're unique, there's usually something significant about the resting place.' 'Oh please, don't call me DS Dubois. Kat is fine. And yes, I agree, but the problem is, there are very many people who pass through Glendargie every summer, heck, all year round, and there are many who probably feel it's a special place for them. It's not like it's hidden away. It's a tiny village but the service station is without doubt the best known on the whole of the A9 stretch between Perth and Inverness. I have no idea how many people stop there daily, never mind yearly.'

The doctor nodded. 'Yes, I know it quite well myself. It's our regular stopping point, a gorgeous tourist trap with the Glendargie Falls, and children love the wishing well.'

'Then there's the truck stop.' It suddenly overwhelmed Kat to think of the traffic and the people the little place must court every year.

'I think you'll find this one is closer to home than you think.' Dr Grey checked her watch, a worn silver band with numbers that stood out, purple and luminescent.

Kat became aware of people gathering outside the lecture room and took the hint. 'Do you think you can help?'

'I'm sure of it. But it's going to take a little while.'

'We don't have that much time,' said Kat. 'Pressure from the boss. And budgets of course.'

'Don't worry about that, I have my own budgets, and projects to undertake, I may be able to help you there. Leave it with me.' The doctor smiled. 'It's lovely to meet you, Kat. I'll give you a ring tomorrow once I've sorted the logistics with Palmerston's team. I'll hopefully be able to give you an update on timescales, too.'

They both reached out to shake hands at the same time, and for the first time in the investigation, Kat felt a shimmer of assurance.

It was a long drive back up the road from Dundee to the Struan House. As Kat pulled up into the gravel driveway she noted the expensive cars, a jag, top of the range land rover, and some sort of sporty number that would have an equally sporty price tag. The house was in darkness and she guessed she'd be given the same response as the previous night. She pulled out her phone, noted it was 7.11p.m. and she had no service. Neither did she have a notification of any text, email or missed calls. Struan hadn't bothered returning any of her messages and neither had the No Caller called again.

She stepped up the weather-worn stones to the front door and a security light flooded the grand entrance. She clanged the knocker and pressed a button doorbell that she didn't hear sound. Eventually, two attempts later, the housekeeper answered.

'I passed on your messages. I'm not his PA, I only look after his father. It's almost bedtime so I'm busy, I dinnae have time to chat.

Michael is in Perth, at some meeting or other. I'll tell him you called. Again.'

'What time will he be back?' asked Kat.

The housekeeper scoffed. 'No idea, hen. He might not!'

'Is his wife home? Maybe she could help?'

'Divorced. And I doubt it. Depending on how much vodka she's necked since lunchtime.'

'Oh, I didn't realise. Where does she live?'

'If she's not in one of the pubs, I'd say try her tomorrow. She lives in one of the social housing flats in Kendollich. But if it's about that body ye found, she'd not be able to help ye.'

'How so?' queried Kat.

The woman scoffed again. 'Marion Struan knows nothing about nowt, always drunk. Best thing he did was get rid, now I really do have to go and see to the old man, sorry.'

She attempted to close the door but Kat reached out to stop it. 'I'll call tomorrow. What time is best?'

'I've told ye, I'm not his keeper. I don't know his schedule though he's usually around mid-morning. That's the best time to catch him … but dinnae bank on it.'

This time the door shut with a clang. As Kat climbed back into her car she wondered what vehicle Struan would be driving as he obviously hadn't taken one of these. She'd have thought they'd be garaged, especially at his time of year. If they were his. If they didn't belong to visitors that were cosied up somewhere in the house with Struan. Was four expensive cars a lot for a man like him? She made a note of the makes and registration plates on her phone. She also made a note of Marion Struan. She might come in useful. Drunks had a habit of having loose lips – and loose lips sank ships.

Chapter 8

Kat drove to work frustrated. With having to wait on forensics, lab reports, and nothing forthcoming, things were going nowhere fast and what she didn't understand was the lack of urgency from upstairs. It was a dead body but also a life, someone's life. She was used to running a team around an investigation but there was hardly any team and not much forthcoming for an investigation.

Her morning didn't fare any better. As the only available detective in the building, she'd been given the task of interviewing then charging a thug for a random attack on a squaddie who as a result of the altercation had been given a broken cheekbone and cracked rib. Kat sat at her desk and mulled over the case file she now had to type up and send off. She cast a glance out of the window, pleased to see a peak of sun instead of the rain again. She reached for her mobile, fed up with waiting for a call, any call, that might help because there had been nothing from either Struan or Dr Grey.

The phone rang in her hand.

'As if by magic! I was just thinking about you,' Kat said.

'All good I hope?' said Dr Grey.

Kat trusted the reassuring tone in the doctor's voice meant good news. 'Of course!'

'I think we have something. Can you call over this afternoon? I have a lecture at three on your case and I thought you might want to be here for it. If you've the time.'

She had an appointment with Gary, the scenes of crimes officer, to go over the records. He could wait. It was now

approaching one o'clock. She had time to grab a bite to eat and a coffee on the go. 'I'll be there by two-thirty?'

'Great! See you then.'

When Kat arrived at the university, there wasn't a soul about. The streets looked squeaky clean, a stark contrast to the streets of London, which were filled with chewing gum, raggedy pigeons, and belching bus fumes. Far from being paved with gold, they did have flashing lights of siren blue every minute of every day. Maybe the crime capital Dundee knew something she didn't.

Dr Grey gave a great welcome. She shoved an iPad into Kat's hand as they walked the corridors to the lecture hall. Outside the lecture hall, the doctor asked Kat to scroll up the screen.

There it was - a face staring back at her. An aged lady's face with sunken eye sockets and sallow cheeks and a quiescence that only the dead carry. Surely someone, somewhere would know who she was? Where she came from? What secrets she held?

'…you'll see more when we go through to the lecture theatre. This is just the computer imagery. We need to peg the sculpture and work on the clay head, but you can see from the images that we are able to see the lower jaw malocclusion. It's quite distinctive. These days craniofacial surgery would take care of it, but this lady wouldn't even have had braces. You can see how defined her cheekbones are, and with a wide forehead you can see she would have been quite handsome, rather than pretty. I haven't run the image through the database yet, I thought I could leave that for you to sort out.'

Kat was blown away by the face before her. Her head was spinning. So much to take in, such a lot of information to process. If only there had been access to this sort of technology and information and resource earlier in her career.

'Come through. You can see her for yourself on the big screen,' said Dr Grey, leading Kat through to the lecture hall.

There she was, waiting for them, a full cinematic screen filled with a woman's face.   'What do you think?' asked Dr Grey.

'Wow. This is beyond anything I've come across before. It's marvellous,' said Kat in total awe of the face with green glass eyes, proper facial features and almost, but not quite, a personality. 'How long did it take?'

'I worked with the forensic artist and we finished today. We've still got the sculpture, 3D image, to work on but that will be the student's work. I hope you've got enough to go on for now. I can't tell you how grateful I am that you called. It's come just at the right time for my class.'

'I think I've just broken the Police Scotland budget,' said Kat, feeling suddenly weary.

'Don't worry about that. As I said, this is just the sort of project we've been looking for. I'm confident we can fund it. We help out with lots of investigations with various policing and security agencies, and our European counterparts too. This is perfect for us.'

'Tell that to my boss, please?' said Kat, taking a stool by the lectern. Now the lady had a face, she was alive. A real person. A woman with a past, with ancestry and descendants, and as soon as she had a name, Kat could get started on properly getting to know her.

The theatre began to fill up, a buzz of activity, eager students gliding down the aisles, filling the seats at the front and back first. The room was fully airconditioned and delicately cool. One of Dr Grey's assistants, newly qualified and eager, came to the lectern to assist in the delivery of the session. The room was over half full and it struck Kat that over seventy per cent of the audience were women.

SHE'S NOT THERE

The hour disappeared in a click of Dr Grey's fingers and she magnetically held her audience until the end. A lot of the technical stuff passed Kat by, but she was extremely interested in the accuracy, the precise work, and the diligence of the staff and students who were working on the project.

Dr Grey looked both invigorated and exhausted. When everyone had filed out, she turned to Kat and said, 'There's a little more. I took the trouble to look at the cadaver.'

Kat hadn't heard the word 'cadaver' for a long time, and felt she was slipping into another dimension. Not since training school, more than twenty years ago, had she heard that word.

'When I say cadaver, I mean the skeleton, of course. I was interested in the bones. I know Palmerston has already given his initial report, but I like the other touches. I looked at her clothes too, and I'd say the lady made her own. The blouse at very least, if not the full suit. I don't know if it helps you any.'

She said suit like suet and it made Kat smile. 'It just might, thank you. We've had nothing back on forensics yet. No news on either the sheet or clothing. Or the locket.'

'Och! I didn't know about a locket. Very interesting. I'm keen on this case, Kat. Please will you keep me up to date?' She reached out and placed her hand on Kat's arm.

'Absolutely. I can't thank you enough for everything you've done. Can I arrange for photos, some sort of images, and we'll get them out there as soon as we can. Hopefully get a positive ID.'

'No need. It's done. They're all packaged up in my office. We did arrange it earlier and I printed them this afternoon so they should be ready. I've also sent you the computerised images by email so they should be there when you next log on.'

'Marvellous! Thank you.'

'Dinner on you when it's done and dusted, then?'

'Absolutely.'

'And bring your crime-writer friend, too... I'm sure we have a few people in common. Unless he's a suspect, of course.'

A bemused Kat left the university armed with a package of photos, a blank invoice, and a dinner invitation. Of course, she smiled to herself, Dr Grey would know about Jed Gillespie. He was one of the UK's bestselling authors a few years ago. And he had found their body. Why wouldn't she be interested?

She looked at her phone. Another missed call from a withheld number. She hated missed calls. Why wouldn't they leave a message?

Chapter 9

The next morning, as Kat drove down the misty A9 to Perth, she wondered what Jed was writing about. This was a writer's cliché, and if that wasn't inspiring for him, she had no idea what would be. She didn't care for armchair fiction, had enough of her own real-life investigations, and then came this, a rare gem, something a bit different to investigate. She pulled into a vacant parking space and saw a young lady totter out of the police station in diamante-studded heels that weren't becoming at eight thirty on a Wednesday morning. She looked like she'd been crying. Some things never changed. Every police station across the land all had similar clientele.

Kat grabbed her bag and iPad and made her way into the station, almost tripping over an abandoned training shoe. A taxi pulled up alongside her and the driver poked his head out of the window. 'You for Stanley, lover?'

'Not me,' replied Kat. 'Might be that lassie over there.' She pointed to the young woman wobbling on her sparkly shoes.

'Ahh, Ms Tottering Heels,' he said. Then he shouted to Kat, 'You've dropped an envelope, lover!'

She looked down. Damn! It was the envelope was full of the prints of Jane Doe.

'Cheers,' called Kat, panicking as she hurried to pick it up. Tottering heels climbed into the back of the taxi, the driver gave a wave and drove off.

SHE'S NOT THERE

Sue Kinell was stood in the foyer trying to see outside. 'Did she get in the cab?'

'The lassie in the heels? Aye, just driven off. Going to Stanley?'

'Yeah. I'm worried about her. She's been sat here for the last six hours. I came on at seven and gave her a cuppa. She seems to think her boyfriend was here somewhere, but I assured her he wasn't. She said he'd left his pills behind and she had them in her bag.'

'Why would he be here? Did you check the pills?'

'Course I did. Common anti-depressants, but no matter how much I said he wasn't here, she didn't leave. Apparently, he'd said to come here. Strange sort of meeting place. When I asked for the fifth time if she wanted me to call her a cab, she said yes.'

Kat lost interest. 'Hey, Sue. You know a lot of people and a lot of places. Could you take a look at this.' She handed Sue the envelope.

Sue led them through to the back office. 'This the body you're trying to identify?'

'Yeah, I've got the facial reconstruction photos. Long shot I know, but once we get them put out to the media, I'm sure someone somewhere must know who she is.' Kat slid the photos from the envelope. The face was etched into her memory. She'd spent the previous night staring at her. Seeing her again this morning gave her the buzz she felt when close to a breakthrough. 'A name would be good.'

Sue didn't know her. 'Ain't it amazing what they can do now? Not like when we started, eh? I bet by the time she's been on STV and shared thirty thousand times on social media, you'll have her. Bingo. Job's a good 'un.'

She handed the prints back to Kat. 'So, when are we going to have that pub crawl then?'

'Let me get this little lady sorted and we can go out to celebrate.'

'I'll hold you to it.' Sue turned her attention to a group that had piled into the front office asking for directions to the train station.

Kat took the stairs up to the CID office, looking at the face in the photo. Not long now, she thought, not long, and we'll have you.

The media had whipped up a storm. And so had the DI.

'What the hell have you been doing? Who gave you permission for this circus?' DI Munro spluttered as he sat down at this desk. 'Kat, this isn't high drama, it's not bloody TV, and not how we do it here.'

'Sir, I rang the university on tentative enquiries and the professor was more than eager to help. It was just the thing she was looking for, something like this, for the students. There's not going to be a cost. It's pretty much pro bono.'

'Yes, well, she says that now. Wait until we get the bill. Even pro bono can break the bank. You never asked me, Kat. It's not good enough.'

'When I called her, she invited me over the same afternoon. You were off until today. I did run it past DS Harris.'

Munro grunted, which turned into a coughing fit.

Kat frowned at him, concerned. 'You okay, guv?'

'Damn pesky cough, hasn't shifted for weeks.' He waved her away. 'We'll talk about it later. For now, deal with the press, Dubois. I understand you've got good training on that front, at least.'

'Sir.' Kat edged out of his office and shut the door behind her as Munro took another coughing fit.

She needed as much publicity as she could get. She had an appointment with a television journalist at two-thirty. The release onto social media had been authorised in Munro's absence by upstairs and it had been picked up and shared far and wide across Twitter, Facebook, Instagram, and other apps Kat wasn't familiar with. The nationals would have it by teatime.

SHE'S NOT THERE

It wasn't long before the office phones started to ring and she realised that she hadn't really thought it through.

Guy called to her from his desk. 'Hey, Sarge, I'm not a one-man bandit! They're coming in thick and fast and I can't keep up. I've called the PF's office and they're going to try to get them diverted from our switchboard to theirs. This is the number for you to call them.' He slid a piece of paper across her desk with the number of the Procurator Fiscal's office. 'Some dudes in some office somewhere will take the information and sort through it. We maybe should have had a plan of action before releasing the photos.'

Kat bit the inside of her lip. She knew Guy was right. Classic junior error, in too much of a rush and now it was information overload. Far too much work for just two of them, just her and one detective. She stood, tapping her fingers on her desk. She looked at the pile of paperwork. Thefts, assaults, deceptions, general CID fodder. And an unearthed skeleton that had taken over her world. Bloody Glendargie. It had to be bloody Glendargie.

'Kat!' shouted Ken Munro from his office door. 'Good news. The PF's office has set up a small enquiry team. They reckon you'll have an ID by morning.'

Chapter 10

With the phones manned by nameless faceless personnel elsewhere, and butterflies building a lepidoptera in her tummy, Kat wanted to trek back to Struan's. 'Guy, grab your coat. You're coming with me.'

Kat drove round to the back to the estate yard and parked up. 'Fancy a walk around the grounds. Get a feel for the place?'

'Think we're allowed?'

'What do you mean, allowed? We're not in the property, we're not searching, we're just looking, having a wander. And we are the police. We're on legitimate business, an investigation. Never cased a drum before?'

'A drum?'

'A drum. A house, a gaff. Spinning a drum... executing a search warrant. Checking it out before you do so, casing the joint. Professional burglars, blaggers, that'll be armed robbers to you...' She looked at him, laughing. 'Casing a joint before doing a job. Two sides of the same coin.'

'Yeah. Right. Get it. You can stop jibbing me now. It's side splitting.'

The classy jag she'd seen the other night was parked up alongside a couple of general runners, and a working jeep, parked haphazardly, was blocking the exit for the other cars. A row of dilapidated outhouses stood off far to the right. She could see the one furthest away housed large farming machinery. They climbed out of

64

the car and Kat expected a farm dog or two to come bounding over, barking at them, but there was only calm.

'Are there any conservation issues around here?' she asked Guy.

'Not that I know of. The estates usually keep themselves pretty much sorted and the general public don't fear to tread anywhere near them, so who would know? I think there's various grants and things they can apply for. Those that can afford the upkeep do so, and those that can't, well, they fall into disrepair and either get sold off or left to rot. You can buy a castle for next to nothing but you'll be bankrupt by the upkeep. Way off my pay scale, but if you have something to sell in London, you could maybe afford it.'

'Ha! I'm not rich, trust me. What do you know about the Struans? Are they aristocratic?'

'Michael Struan? I wouldn't have thought so. Old money, for sure, and his da' may have thought he descended from some sort of Earl or Laird or something, but I don't think Michael junior subscribes to it. He's posh, an' that, but from what I know, he's down to earth and mixes with us commoners, hands on with the land and the estate properties. Drinks with the gamekeepers in the local, that sort of thing.'

Kat pointed to a low dense black cloud moving towards them. 'What the hell's that?'

'A swarm of flying ants by the look of it. It's been raining non-stop hasn't it? It's the weather. I've seen them before at different times of the year. They won't harm you.'

'I don't plan on finding out.' Kat walked over to the outhouses. 'If anyone asks, we're looking for Michael Struan.'

There were four outhouses forming an L-shape. In the first one a work bench, more than a foot deep and etched in woodworm, ran around the inside edge. Clamps, anvils, and a myriad of rusted tools covered the surface. Thick metal twine hung low from the remaining rafters where menacing metal hooks hung from the ceiling.

'For the wildlife,' whispered Guy, looking up. 'Rabbits, hares, birds.'

Kat imagined shiny black crows hanging down headfirst, beaks skimming the neglected lathe, and rabbits strung up waiting to be skinned. A cloud crossed the sky and chilled the air and mood and goosebumps peppered the back of her neck and down her arms. She rubbed at her sleeves and took in the outhouse crammed with farming artefacts, rotting wood, iron implements, the discarded detritus of years gone. More recent were dumps of food rubbish, either tossed or blown in: Pot Noodle cartons, empty crisp packets, biscuit and chocolate wrappings, a rotting cauliflower and a heap of neeps, and pages of newspapers that, when Kat checked, were from the local gazette earlier that year. Hardened bags of plaster had split, scattering light-pink dust across the floor, and a pile of lobster pots and some thick netting sat beneath the bench, tucked into a corner.

'I wonder what's in the other outbuildings,' said Kat, whispering.

'Sarge?' hissed Guy.

'What?'

'What are we whispering for?'

Kat laughed. 'I dunno!'

They walked into the next building, which housed a derelict combine harvester rusting away in the elements. In the third a home-made bivouac looked messy in the corner with a soiled and decaying mattress with springs and stuffing exposed on the cobbled stones. A dark blue sleeping bag, open and ripped, had been discarded on top of the mattress. Porn magazines poked from beneath it. Guy kicked a plastic bag. An empty aerosol can rolled out. A small box of condoms flipped open.

'I wonder whose den this is,' said Kat, staring at the crude makeshift area, also wondering if it was for sleeping or for sex purposes. Possibly both, she mused.

'Excuse me.' A male voice boomed from behind. 'What do you think you're are doing on my land?'

Kat and Guy swivelled. A man dressed as a gamekeeper, minus the hat but complete with cocked shotgun, faced them. His thick eyebrows fell down to his top eyelashes and his bushy beard covered every inch of cheek and chin making him appear ageless and dishevelled.

'If you've got a dog, I've every right to shoot it,' he warned, snapping the shotgun closed.

As if surrendering, Guy put both arms up. Kat knew she'd rib him for eternity, but now wasn't the time.

Kat reached into her back pocket and brought out her warrant card. 'Nothing to worry about.' She waved at him to put the gun down. 'I'm DS Dubois and this is DC Lynn. Mr Struan, I presume? I've been trying to get in touch with you.'

Guy dropped his arms by his side, said, 'No Kat—'

Kat turned to him. 'I'm sure Mr Struan will invite us in.'

'No, Kat. He's not Struan.'

'Aye, the kid's right,' growled the gamekeeper. He lowered the gun. 'I ain't Michael Struan. He's not here. And he warn't like ye poking your nose around his land, I can tell ye.'

'When's he back?' asked Kat.

'What is it ye wanting?'

'Just a chat.'

'That tells me sweet FA, so if ye want more frae me, then I need a bit more frae you, ye ken?'

'Fair enough.' Kat relented. 'Can you please ask Mr Struan to contact me at his earliest of convenience. It's about the body that was found on his land last Sunday. I need to talk to him.' She handed him her card. 'Your name please, sir?'

'Fergus Campbell. Gamekeeper. An' I cannae promise. Struan daes as he likes but aye, I'll let him know.' He looked down at the

67

card. 'Kat Dubois, eh?' He looked at her again and squinted his eyes. 'Kat… Dubois, ye say?'

Kat's arms pimpled up again as she nodded, and despite having no knowledge of him, she saw recognition cross his eyes.

Chapter 11

Kat had taken her coat off and kicked the chair out from under her desk to sit down when Guy shouted, 'Sarge, there's a phone call for you in the boss's office.'

'Is it—'

'Yes, Procurator Fiscal.'

They'd beaten her to it. She was planning on calling them first thing. She had no idea how it was all going to work, if they'd let her keep the job herself or if it was going to be passed over to the Sudden Fatalities Investigation Unit, the SFIU, an acronym she struggled to say as well as remember. If they were anything like the Murder Investigation Team, or the MIT, which was far better to roll off the tongue and recall, they'd be asking her to keep it, to work with a local team. She hoped they would, although there was no local team as all the detectives she'd met so far had their own very important jobs to deal with. Plus, like the MIT, the SFIU would have too much work and not enough money, and a whack of a lack of interest in anything that wasn't sensational or away from the norm. She was quietly confident they would back heel it to her.

Kat hurried across to the small office built within the main CID office. It had a double window looking down to the front of the station and across the parking bays, and a double window looking into the office and at the team. The door was full-length glass and both door and windows had the advantage of horizontal metal blinds to block everything out, should the occupant wish. In the DI's absence the door had been permanently open, though the office was left in shadow with all blinds drawn.

She snatched up the receiver. 'DS Dubois.'

A broad Glaswegian voice replied, 'Hello. I was trying to get hold of DI Munro, but I understand he's absent today. It's about the body in the woods by Glendargie.'

'Yes. I'm dealing with that one,' replied Kat. 'I've been waiting on your call.'

'Wait no longer, lassie. I've got news for you. Bit of a shocker.'

'Do I need to sit down?' She feigned surprise. Were there any surprises left when it came to a dead body? The examination had seemed straightforward enough. Palmerston had been fairly convinced of the fact that the recent bad weather and interference from animals had brought her to the fore. All enquiries seemed to be heading that way. So what was the surprise?

'We have an ID on the body…' Silence.

'Let me get a pen,' said Kat, reaching for the pot of biros on the desk. She scrabbled around for a scrap of paper. She opened the bottom drawer and was pleased to see some habits were the same across the land. A bottle of Dewars, two-thirds full, stood to attention at the back, out of sight but not quite hidden. Something to bear in mind for when the time came to celebrate. In the absence of writing materials in the drawer she slid a sheet of blank A4 from the printer on the shelf behind the desk. 'I'm ready. Go on.'

'Your mystery lady is Rosemary Fraser, 29.10.1940. Last known address 10, Fortingall Crescent, Glendargie.'

Kat nodded, yes, local then. She'd thought, in principle, that it was a case of granny dumping, but that theory was now not likely as the address was less than half a mile from where she'd been found.

'That's not everything…' the officer said.

'Yes?'

'Rosemary Fraser was certified dead over two years ago.'

Certified dead? Okay, so what did that mean? A 'proper' death but no proper disposal? Kat rubbed her chin between finger and thumb. If she'd been certified dead, why hadn't she had a funeral? Had austerity come to this, that people couldn't afford them anymore? Was it more a case of dead granny dumping?

'You still there?'

'Yeah, just thinking, sorry,' replied Kat. 'So, we have a death certificate then, yes?'

'Well, yes, but there's more,' he said.

'More?'

'Yes. You might find this hard to believe but...'

Kat waited. He was expecting a prompt, prolonging the reveal. She gave it to him. 'Okay then, spill.'

'Rosemary Fraser was cremated in Perth one week and a day after her death, on twenty-second January 2020.'

Chapter 12

Kat watched DI Munro moving around in his office. He'd opened all the blinds, hung up his coat on the stand in the corner, reached for his post, and shifted through the envelopes. He picked up his empty cup, sniffed it, then placed it back on the desk. She still hadn't worked him out. Irascible? Occupied? Disinterested? He seemed pleasant enough, polite without being curt, to the point without being abrupt, and he didn't pester for updates or information, which was always good in a boss, but she knew something was going on with him. Maybe he was always like this, maybe he was biding his time to retirement, but she'd done her homework and knew he had little less than six years left before he could retire, which was far too early for him to be winding down.

He looked up and Kat caught his eye. He smiled, as if he knew he was being observed. He raised his cup and mouthed, 'Coffee?'

Kat nodded and reached out to kick Guy Lynn sitting opposite her.

'The guv'nor wants coffee. Did you bring that machine in?' she asked.

'Yeah, but the coffee's strong, not sure you'll like it.'

Kat looked at him.

'All right! I'm on it.' Guy had finally brought in a coffee machine he'd been promising since Kat had arrived. His pregnant wife had gone off both the smell and taste of coffee and had switched to tea, making the machine redundant.

SHE'S NOT THERE

Kat gathered up the paperwork for the Fraser case and took it with her to the DI's office.

Ken Munro was stood looking out of the window. It was raining, again. Without turning he said, 'Did you know, Kat, that if it rains on a Monday it will rain for the next three days?' He turned to look at her. 'Or is that three weeks?'

'Not heard that, sir,' she said, taking a seat in the far right of the office, leaving the other one for Guy when he brought the drinks.

'Don't think it's true, but when it rains, it sometimes forgets to stop. You're from around here originally, aren't you?'

He took his seat, a much more comfortable chair than the others, his made of leather, or faux, not metal and red hessian like the rest of them in the CID office.

'I am, sir. Well, farther up than Perth, just past Pitlochry, not that far from Glendargie as the crow flies, but worlds apart in how the people live their lives. Each town, village, they're all different, unique in their own way, aren't they?'

'Hmm.' It was if he hadn't heard or didn't want conversation, as if small talk was irrelevant.

Kat saw a worried man. She didn't know what he looked like before she arrived, but she saw it in his face and in his eyes; he looked like a man with a problem. His slender frame was more akin to a footballer than a rugby player, or perhaps a golfer, one of the three sports most policemen favoured. His office didn't have any of the usual trophies many bosses' offices displayed. There were just two items of personal props: a passing out photo of his CID course, and a silver frame on his desk with a photograph of a woman who Kat presumed was his wife. She was smiling, light-brown and blonde-streaked hair flicking behind her as she leant to one side; a pretty woman, around Munro's age, early fifties or so, Kat guessed.

'I'm sure you'll find things a bit different, but the job's the same, so I've found, whichever station or department you're in,' said Munro.

'Sure,' said Kat, not really sure.

Guy brought three cups into the office and gave the door a kick behind him so it closed with a bang, rattling the partition wall. He placed the cups onto the desk. 'There you go.'

Each took the cup nearest to them and Munro sat back in his chair. He looked at Kat. 'Have you got the records from the crematorium?'

'No, sir, not yet. I've made an appointment for one o'clock this afternoon. Guy knows one of the operators, or operatives, or whatever they're called. Cremator, maybe. Said they'd have the information ready for us.'

Munro slung an arm either side of his chair and tapped the edge of his desk with his fingers. 'SFIU have said they aren't going to take it. Not yet anyway. They want us to do the donkey work and I've to get back to the Chief Super by Monday. They've got a triple murder in Dundee which is keeping them busy and their budget is stretched. A witchcraft thing or something. What's the current state of play here?'

Kat shrugged. 'I pulled the information together straight after the call.' She shuffled through the papers. 'In summary, Rosemary Fraser's remains were found by a dog walker. He's new to the area, a crime writer. He tripped, face-planting the skull. Post-mortem states she likely died of a malignancy, probably cancer, and now confirmed as such by the death certificate. No signs of injury or assault or any other cause so far as can be seen. We're still awaiting toxicology. Initial thinking was that she'd gone for a walk, collapsed, died, but she was found a bit too deep, buried in the earth. And it looked like a specific burial spot.' Kat took a sip of the bitter coffee. Guy was right, it was too strong. 'However,' she continued, 'that doesn't account for the body being wrapped up in a bed sheet. She was dressed, likely

SHE'S NOT THERE

Sunday best, or what you might dress someone in for their final journey. In their coffin.' She was thinking of her mother, and the outfit she'd chosen for her cremation. It was the outfit she'd worn for Kat's wedding. The most expensive clothes her mother had ever bought. Stupid really, but Kat knew it was what people did for those they love, to try to give comfort, to make sure they looked good for a proper send off, fitting for the occasion. Her voice cracked. She hadn't been emotional about her mother for a long while and the power of the sudden feeling shocked her. Grief over her mother had been overtaken by another, one that she was still coming to terms with and she still hadn't got used to the term – widow. It didn't suit her.

She continued. 'As you can imagine, like the body, the clothing was in various states of disintegration and decay. Pretty much as you'd expect after two years underground.'

Kat paused and Guy continued. 'We retrieved a silver locket from the remains and assume the deceased had been wearing it. There's a faded black-and-white photograph of a man and a woman inside. Maybe it's her, maybe her parents, we don't know.'

Kat read from the papers. 'She died January fourteenth and was supposedly cremated on the twenty-second. We know who she is, and probably the cause of death, but not the other hows, wheres, whens, and whys. I'm going to do a bit of research on her family tree because there's nothing obvious on our systems. We haven't spoken to the direct family yet, that's scheduled for tomorrow. We're at the crem this afternoon. We've yet to contact her GP, that's on the list today. There's only the one surgery in Glendargie. Then we need to see the undertaker when we find out who they are from the crematorium. I've spoken with Jed Gillespie, he can't add anymore to his statement, but we'll keep in touch with him, and we've yet to speak with the landowner, Michael Struan, who is proving elusive. I've called a few times, both on the phone and in person, three times now, but he hasn't returned my messages so I'll try him again later, maybe pop up there on my way home tonight.'

'Maybe he's keeping a low profile,' suggested Munro. He looked at them both and said, 'Sounds like you have enough to work on so go and get on with it. Keep me informed, Kat. I know you know what you're doing. I'll need you on the whisky job asap. Don't forget, we don't have the endless budgets here, you know.'

The reality was the Met's budgets were even tighter than the rest of the UK, but instead of saying that she replied, 'Sir.'

'And I presume Dr Grey is still keeping to pro bono now we have an ID?'

'I'm hoping so, sir.'

She was met with a nod to signify they were dismissed.

Upon returning to her desk she saw that her phone, which was on silent, showed yet another missed call, number unknown, no voicemail.

Chapter 13

Kat shifted in the uncomfortable chair. It didn't matter that she was there for work rather than personal business, she didn't like crematoriums. The building was pleasant enough for a place of death, vases dotted here and there bursting with unassuming fresh flowers. A faint hint of orange and violet hung in the air, an astringent tang of disinfectants. Like a connoisseur, her senses were stuck on overactive. Bland pastel walls were decorated with light oak framed prints, copies of scenes of peaceful countryside and misty riversides, and photos of random swirls and twirls of colour, everything inoffensive to eyes that didn't see and minds that desperately wanted a distraction but couldn't be disturbed from grief.

Kat shifted again and looked over to Guy Lynn. He seemed fine, at ease, slouched in his chair with his arms folded and eyes everywhere.

She turned to the older gentleman seated behind the desk. He was English, but she couldn't place his accent. She wasn't sure exactly what his job title was, other than he was the person in charge today.

He removed his glasses and hesitated, looking at Kat as if expecting her to start the conversation.

She took his lead. 'Thank you for seeing us today, Mr Carr. We appreciate your time with this unusual enquiry.'

'Fire away.' He shook his head. 'Please, no pun intended.'

'I didn't notice, honest.' She hadn't. 'We're making enquiries about a body we believe was cremated here. Can you tell please tell us if your records show a service on twenty-second January for a Rosemary Fraser?'

'I took the liberty of checking both computer and paper documents ahead of you coming today when you sent over the details. I can confirm, yes, our records show that she was,' he said.

'But how can that be? That she was cremated but her body turns up elsewhere?' Kat asked.

'That's the question, isn't it? I have no idea. I can only assume it was a problem with the undertakers. There's no way we could make an error like that. We would never proceed without a body.'

Before Kat could ask her next question, Guy leant forward, 'Can you tell us about the cremation process, please?'

Kat flashed him a look, but he continued, 'There's a lot of supposition isn't there, I mean, do you stack them up and wait until the end of the day, are people done together, how do you know you've got the right ashes... that sort of thing. So many questions.'

Carr arched his back. 'Yes, it's confusing to the lay person, isn't it?' He cocked his head at Kat. 'I get asked these types of questions all the time. It's quite straightforward, really. And there's absolutely no confusion over ashes. It's important that everything is right. The procedures are very ethical.'

Kat didn't want to know the finer details. The thought of cremation, of hair starting to shrivel, of skin and flesh melting, starting to burn, of bones disintegrating into ash, made her shudder and want to weep. Not many things got to her like this. Even death itself wasn't as abhorrent.

'I'm sure that it is completely ethical,' said Guy, not looking at Kat, not picking up her cues as she waved her hand across her knee, trying to signify 'no'.

He continued, 'How do you know if there's a body in the coffin at all? Do coffins even go in the cremating machine? Do they get recycled?'

'My dear man, dismiss all those thoughts. Every crematorium operates the same, and no, certainly not, coffins are not recycled, nor the brasses taken off. It's highly regulated. Staff train for the BTEC diploma in cremation. Trust me, I would know if there was anything not right with any of our systems.'

Kat could see the teasing glint in his eye. He was going to have fun enlightening them but she wasn't up for a science lesson, or physics, chemistry, biology, or whatever field cremation fell into. Her snatched sandwich at lunchtime was dancing in her stomach. She didn't want to go quick-stepping off to the ladies but she might have to if they kept this going.

'If you could give us a brief idea of how it works, we can see how it fits in, or not, with our enquiry and we can take it from there,' said Kat, relenting.

'I can do that.' Carr pushed himself further up his chair and leant forward onto the desk, hands clenched in front of him. 'There's two options to start with. The first, the undertaker brings the coffin to us ahead of the allocated service and sets it ready in the chapel. Not too early, or we'd have a backlog of coffins. Second, the coffin arrives with the mourners and is brought in by the pall bearers just before the congregation enter, or is brought in when they are all seated, family choice. We then host the ceremony, which is usually half an hour, though some families elect the hour slot. Bedlam in the car park for the bigger funerals, but I digress.' He paused. 'Once the committal is done and the gates are closed, everyone leaves the chapel. The coffin travels along a short conveyor belt to take it to the back room where the cremating machines are housed. We have two here in Perth. Others have three, or four, but not us. We cover a large area and as you know, many people come to our beautiful area to retire, so we have a higher death than birth rate. We're constantly busy. Busier than PRI maternity unit, which of course, has now moved to Ninewells in Dundee.' He chuckled.

Kat's stomach danced with a flip and a flop.

Guy turned to Kat. 'Pitlochry is sixty-eight per cent pensioners these days. Locals call it the true waiting for god ground.'

'I'm aware…' said Kat.

Carr continued, 'You can imagine how busy we are in the winter months.'

Kat rubbed her chin and tucked a curl behind her ear. This was going to take some time. From the corner of her eye, she saw Guy stretch out his legs. He was settling in for the long haul. It was okay for him, he was interested, but Kat certainly wasn't. Her focus was the investigation and one specific aspect of it, but she supposed they needed to understand the process in order to understand how the body ended up not being cremated.

'Can I get you a coffee? Tea?' Carr offered.

They declined in unison and Kat said, 'Mr Carr, can you explain what happens when your staff collect the coffin at the back of the chapel please?'

He paused as if considering her question, or prolonging the attention, she wasn't sure, but she was sure he was enjoying his reveals.

'It's placed on a large trolley and conveyed to the cremation machine. The temperature has to reach six hundred and fifty centigrade before the coffin can be inserted. Now then, let me explain…' He spoke with his hands, left one way, right the other, twirling them round. 'The gurney has wheels along each side to move the coffin along.' He moved his arms, parallel, forward and back. 'Once the gurney is lined up to the door that opens up at the rear of the machine, it slides along the gurney and straight inside, then the door shuts. The hatch at the back is open then very quickly closed. There's no room for two coffins in there, not at all, it can't happen. The operator observes the cremation through a set of small porthole windows at the front of the machine to ensure everything is working as it should. They also monitor the temperature, which must be maintained. It can't be too high as the body will burn too quickly, nor too low as it would take hours to complete. Too fast and you get a whoosh of black smoke from the chimney and that's never good, especially for any straggling mourners outside to see it. Not good at all.'

Kat looked at Guy. He was into it, really into it.

'So, the coffin gets burnt with the body?' he asked.

'Oh yes. Of course. You can't reuse a coffin.'

'Handles and adornments, too?'

'Absolutely, despite what you may hear to the contrary.'

'How long does it take? For it all to burn, body and all?' he asked.

'A straightforward cremation should be an hour and a half, but that's not the end of it. There's more to it than that.'

Oh, no, thought Kat. Please, no more. I really do not want to know.

'What do you mean? Do you have to put the fire out?' asked Guy.

'There's no fire. For example, cancers take a longer time to burn, and the amount of fat on a body can make a lot of difference, so it varies on timings. Once everything is burnt, the remnants are raked through a small hatch in the side of the machine. Everything is scraped into a hopper beneath. This includes the ashes of both body and coffin. Sometimes there can be larger pieces of bone that haven't quite... erm... diminished, shall we say.'

No, we shan't. Kat's stomach was not good. Her face drained, the blood seeping away, and palpitations were making her head swim. She felt herself weaken and knew the blood had left her face as she leant her head into her hands and rubbed her eyes. She was on the verge of a faint. Deep breaths. Deep breaths.

'When it's all in the hopper, everything cools down as cold air is blown across the ashes. The heat is immense...if you can imagine embers from a dying fire,' continued Carr, oblivious to Kat's distress. 'After sixty minutes or so, when everything has cooled sufficiently, the hopper is taken to the cremulator, which is a large machine, not unlike a tumble dryer, industrial size, of course.'

Of course! Kat pushed down the bile.

'The contents of the hopper are poured into the machine where it's ground down further with the aid of large marble balls of varying sizes. They help to granulate it all. When it's finished, everything will have been reduced to fine fragments, the end product, as it were. The ashes. And that, in a nutshell, is how we cremate a body.' He sat back, pushed his glasses further up his nose, and gave a satisfied smile to his audience.

'So how hot does it get then, inside the machine? And what happens to the jewellery?'

'Guy, as interesting as this is, I'm not sure it's relevant at this stage,' interjected Kat. He could ask those questions another time, when she wasn't there, as no doubt they'd be back.

'Our next service isn't until three o'clock. Would you like to come through and you can see it for yourself? There's more information I can add, if you want?' Carr looked from one to the other, and half raised himself from his seat, palms on each side of his chair.

They echoed each other.

Kat, 'No, thanks!'

Guy, 'Yes, please!'

Without giving Carr an opportunity to respond to either of them, Kat said, 'I have a few more questions.'

Carr sat down. 'Go ahead. Happy to answer anything, as long as we aren't the ones in trouble here.'

'We're purely making enquiries at this stage. Thank you for explaining... erm... it all.' She swallowed. 'Would you know if there wasn't a body in a coffin when it was cremated?'

'Yes, for sure. No doubt.'

She looked at him, waiting for further clarification, though it had been a definitive answer.

He took her silence as a hint. 'The person doing the cremation would instantly know if the coffin was empty. They'd be monitoring the burn, watching it to ensure there were no problems, the right heat, etc., It would be over in no time at all if it was an empty coffin and it would be obvious there was no body because the wood burns very quickly. You see the body as the coffin burns away. The operator would definitely know, yes.'

Tick, one down. 'Thank you. How would you know if it was the right body inside the coffin?'

Carr frowned. 'We don't check it, the person in the coffin, if that's what you mean? That's down to the undertaker. There was one occasion, many years ago, when they brought the wrong coffin and we held the service with the bereaved family. We started the cremation only to discover the coffin was the one due for a service later that day. The coffins had been mixed up at the undertakers but the bodies themselves were in the right coffins. The undertaker checked. It was purely the service that had been mixed up. The same funeral company dealt with both and the person who should have been cremated in the morning was the one for the afternoon service, and vice versa, if you understand me. Heads rolled over that and procedures were tightened up massively. Never happened since.' Carr shook his head. 'Not here. Touch wood.' He smoothed the top of his desk. 'Dreadful for the families. For all concerned. Truly dreadful.'

'I can imagine.' Kat could well imagine. 'Does each operative know the name and details of the person they're cremating?'

'We have checks in place for that. Each coffin has a plate with the person's name and date of birth, and it's checked against our records for that day. It's checked at every stage, from handing over to the end of the cremation.'

'But could you tell during the cremation process if the body in the coffin was someone other than who it should be?'

Mr Carr stared at her, concentrating. He pushed his glasses up his nose for the umpteenth time. She could almost hear his brain ticking. An air freshener squirted loudly behind her, making her jump. An essence of ghost. She shivered, her shoulders jittery. Orangey violet floated around her.

Carr still pondered.

'I think' – he started, then paused again – 'I think… if we had a man, six-foot six, weighing twenty stone, instead of a slim young woman of five foot say, that might be noticeable, or a child when we were expecting a grown adult, maybe, possibly, but you get small adults and large young adults. I'm not sure how to put it…' He faltered. 'My operators obviously don't know the people personally, and if they do, they will declare it and they wouldn't be allowed to cremate a relative, so no, they wouldn't know the person, or what they looked like. Unless there was an open coffin, but that's a rarity these days… And the usher and undertaker would close the coffin before it went through to the machines. By the time the coffin has burnt, the body is unrecognisable so I guess… no, there's no way we would know if they were the person they should be.' He shrugged. 'Again, that's a question for the undertaker.'

'So, to clarify and confirm,' said Kat. 'You would know if the coffin was empty?'

'Yes.'

'If a body inside the coffin was other than the intended one, you wouldn't know?'

'Um, probably not.'

'And you trust your staff to bring any discrepancy or problem to you?'

'Absolutely, yes. Integrity is the essence of this place, Sergeant. As I told you earlier, it's a very ethical process.'

'Thank you, Mr Carr. I think you've answered everything for the moment. We just need to check your records for that date, please?'

There was a perfect entry for Rosemary Fraser, 29.10.40. All details correct. The time of the service was listed as 11 a.m. on twenty-second January with Graves, the undertakers from Kendollich. Details of next of kin, Mr Drew Fraser, deceased's nephew. Kat made a note of his address and phone number.

'Please keep these records, Mr Carr. We may need them,' asked Kat. 'Do you know who carried out this cremation?'

'Yes. It's written here, the operator was Ross Thomas. He's been with us a couple of years now. I trained him personally. But you can't speak to him today. I'm afraid as he's on leave until next week.'

'Any chance of seeing him at home?' she asked.

'Anything like that would need to be done in works time, I'm afraid. The records would be here, so…'

As frustrating as it was, she surmised Ross Thomas would have nothing additional to say but she'd still need to speak with him and get his statement. Likewise, the elusive Struan.

And as if will made things happen, her phone rang with a number she was becoming familiar with, having called it quite a few times in recent days. It was the Struan Estate.

The man across the road died yesterday. The ambulance came and so did a lot of people. A black van arrived, and men were in and out of the house. Ma dragged me away from the window and made me stay in the kitchen for ages and I couldn't see what was happening, but I knew when I saw the black van because the same van came when Mrs Smather died last year. I saw them bring her out all wrapped up and her son was in the street crying, jangling his car keys like he didn't want to be there, like he was in a rush to be somewhere else. I couldn't help but look at him. I hadn't seen a big man crying before and I knew it must be something bad. He was standing outside our house where I was watching, seeing him, a bit like a conversation you can't help but hear because people are talking where you are. When Ma had finished with me helping her sort out the tins in the cupboard, Mrs Smather's son had gone. I thought he might still be crying.

SHE'S NOT THERE

Bad things happen all the time. They happen lots where I live. First Mrs Smather and now the man whose name I don't know. Lots of people must die here but not because it's a small little place but there is a funeral shop in the High Street. It's called Graves. I think it's really right that the man who owns the funeral shop has that name. Da' told me he's an undertaker. I know it's not really true that he puts people under the ground so they can be taken to meet God, but I like to think it happens. I don't think heaven can be a real place because of all the bad. The bad people don't just go straight off to be good, carried away to heaven on a rug like Aladdin flying off to Persia. There are too many bad people and too many bad things and when I grow up, I want to make sure that bad things don't happen. If that's a job someone can do.

I need to stop thinking of the big bad thing. I try hard not to think about the big bad thing. I have to crunch my eyes tight together to stop it being in my head and behind my eyes. Now that the man across the road has died, it has made me think of the bad thing again. If I'm not a good girl, and I know I'm not a really good girl because I do bad things, Ma or Da' might die just like the people in the street. I think he might be making the people in my street die to make sure I'm good because if I'm not, it might be Mammy next. I must do as he says, and I mustn't tell Ma anything because if I do, she will be next.

Chapter 14

Kat had forgotten how cold the real cold could be. Growing up in sub-temperatures hadn't left any permanent damage to her psyche because she realised she hadn't dressed for the weather. It had been blitzed from her memory. It had taken fifteen minutes for her car to warm through. The 7am ice displays frosted onto windows might be picturesque, but when she was in a rush and her car was a piece of old crap that should have been scrapped long ago, fifteen minutes was too long. As she scraped away the ice she saw no beauty in the patterns on her windscreen, only frustration. The car heater blew cold air and would do so until she arrived in Glendargie, about ten minutes from her house on a clear run, as the morning traffic had yet to build. She really needed to upgrade her motor, especially with the miles she was doing, more in a day than she used to do in a week.

She met Guy in the car park of the off-road motor café where a dozen or so vintage cars were parked up. Of course, she thought, remembering the yearly rally, amazed they still did it, and reassured some things never changed. She remembered the year when she'd almost been run over by an ancient red Bentley racing around the bend on the country lane leading up to the school. Such a long time ago. A different lifetime. Same cars, though.

She spotted Guy standing against his smart new Renault and gave him a desperate look as she watched him pull on a pair of floppy wellingtons. Even she knew walking boots were almost essential in rural Perthshire, especially at this time of year, so why did he think wellies would do? He's so obviously a townie, she thought, pulling into a convenient space next to him.

'Just in case,' he panted as he pulled the green rubber up his leg. 'Like bloody Cinderella's slippers, these things.' He stood up, bent his knees, and stamped the ground to push his toes further into the boots.

'Well, I haven't brought mine, but then I'm not looking for a prince,' she said.

'Not what I've heard, Sarge.' Guy looked up at her and winked.

'Then you've heard wrong.' She felt a prickle around her neck. She'd have to put the brakes on that gossip. 'Let me assure you, DC Lynn, I'm not on the market.'

Her tone silenced him, and an awkward pause followed, which she deftly broke. 'What are we hoping to discover this morning?' It sounded more of a test than a question.

Like a recent recruit, he replied, 'When you draw a blank, go back to the beginning. Start again. See what's been missed, what's different, what we can disprove as well as prove.'

'Ahh, you were listening. Good stuff. Then let's go.'

They set off up the incline, weaving their way along the hard, frosted footpath, up towards the cottage where Jed Gillespie lived. Tall rich-green pines lined the top of the path, heavy with mists that hung in the top branches, now starting to lift as the day came alive. Woodsmoke filtered into the crisp air from cottages dotted along the hillside. The temperature gradually rose by one, then two degrees, as the day emerged. Crows cawed as the detectives strode, disturbing their scavenging beaks. Doleful sheep stared as they walked on by in silence. In the undergrowth wild animals rustled and scuttled away as they tramped on. A few feet into the woods they came across an exhausted campfire. A collection of dumped rubbish told tales – an empty bottle of vodka, two of Jägermeister, half a dozen crumpled and burnt cans of fruity cider, and a couple of used condoms, crisp packets, fag ends; typical adolescent debris of kids trying to escape their dull and boring lives in suffocating small towns and surrounding villages.

'Wonder if the kids knew about the body when they were here?' said Guy.

'The minute she'd been taken away. In my day teenagers would be itching to get up here to do the sleeping-out-dare thing, getting drunk, scaring themselves senseless by making up daft and ludicrous stories, the more gruesome and wackier the better, a la Stephen King. You seen Stand By Me?'

Guy shook his head. 'I'm not a horror fan.'

'More coming of age than horror. You should watch it. Better still, read it.' She'd loved his books as a teenager, likening Castle Rock very much to Glendargie.

Gary raked around the makeshift camp. 'That's about right… teenagers. Doesn't look like a homeless shelter, does it?' He snapped a few photos on his smartphone. 'Just a few pics… in case, you know.'

'Good thinking. Hand your phone in when we get back and we'll get it sent to the photo unit to retrieve them.'

'What? I can't give my phone in. I need it.'

The look of horror on Guy's face made Kat laugh out loud. 'Joke. I'm teasing. Yes, they might be useful, good idea.'

'Humpf.' Guy kicked a discarded black bag.

Kat could see a half-smile beneath his pretend sulk, proving he was still smarting from earlier. She'd been grumpy, irascible and well aware her colleagues weren't sure of her yet. Guy didn't know how far he could take it and didn't know how she'd react. They were still at the testing of boundaries stage, their working relationship yet to develop, to settle into a professional camaraderie. It didn't hurt to keep things close, keep herself to herself, for now at least. He'd get used to her and she'd try harder.

They left the camp and walked further up and off to the right, to the path weaving towards Jed Gillespie's cottage. Light smoke coiled from the chimney, either the remnants of a very late night, or the beginnings of an early morning. As the path turned to the left it took them to the tree where the remains had been found. Frost had kept the ground hard and Kat noted that unless it was boggy further up, her walking boots were a far better choice than Guy's wellingtons and told him so.

She stopped and turned to look down at the small town at the bottom of the hill. In another month spring would bring the landscape alive. Glendargie was growing. The populace had been three thousand strong when she left but it must be nearer five or six now. Housing estates had expanded, and new ones had been built. The town was now attractive to families, not just retirees. She must visit soon, a proper tourist trip to see the developments for herself. So many memories, so many different lives, such a long time ago.

Guy, walking ahead, stopped and turned. 'Admiring the view, Sarge?'

'Something like that,' she said, swathed in a chill. She shivered.

He lost interest and turned back up the path.

'Ghosts,' she said to nobody but herself.

The remnants of police tape hung around the tree like a sash. Signs of a disturbance of sorts were there if you knew to look for them, otherwise, it was just an old uprooted tree, teetering but held firm. All signs of a burial and a body had gone. The tape flicked around the trunk and Kat was tempted to pull it away but thought better of it. She wasn't sure she'd remember the way again, should she need to revisit. Someone else might remove it but she'd take the chance.

'Guy, take a photo please. Just in case I need a reminder of where it is. Context, you know.'

'Sure,' he said. 'What time are we meeting Struan?'

'8.30am at the house.' She looked at her watch. 'We have fifteen minutes.'

'Grand. No time to speak with our writer friend then?' Guy nodded over to his cottage.

SHE'S NOT THERE

Kat glanced up and saw Jed Gillespie watching them a few hundred feet away, a bit too far to shout a hello.

'No,' she said. 'Not now.' She watched him watching them and remembered she still needed to complete her research on him.

The detectives stood in the large working kitchen of Struan House. The housekeeper had informed them Mr Struan wouldn't be long and asked if they would like refreshments.

Kat usually declined such offers, but her fingers were so cold that she had accepted and asked for coffee. Guy chose tea. She had thought it would be a good idea to go to the scene before seeing Struan to get some perspective, both of his land and his influence. When he'd said he had a few minutes this morning to see her, she felt obliged to comply, not least because it meant she could start her day off closer to home. She hadn't banked on freezing for the cause.

Struan strode into the kitchen, a man who carried his presence leaving you in no doubt who was in the room. 'Good, you've got a cuppa. Follow me please.'

An instruction, an order to be obeyed, so they did, like puppy dogs following a master, a man who not only wanted to be in charge but who had neither the concept nor the will of things being any other way.

He took them to an office two doors down the plush hall. The room was lined with bookshelves crammed with books, artefacts, ornaments and trophies, all packed in. The desk was vast and imposing, rich mahogany and old, perfectly placed by the leaded window to overlook a section of well-kempt gardens. Papers and files spilled across the desk beneath a computer screen not much smaller than Kat's television. The screensaver was of a young woman in her late teens clinging onto a sailing mast and smiling. The family resemblance was striking.

Struan's eyes caught Kat's and he said, 'My daughter, Lydia. She's away, travelling.'

'Where is she?'

'Australia. For now. I haven't seen her in over two years. We keep in touch though.' Struan leant over and set the computer to sleep mode and the girl flicked off the screen. He turned back to Kat. 'Sorry if I've been elusive, officers. It's been a busy time. What can I do for you?' He waved an arm, indicating for them to sit down. He took a seat in a worn leather office chair that fitted like it had been made especially for him.

A pair of dining-style chairs next to the desk looked placed just for them and they took the cue. Kat looked for somewhere to place her cup but couldn't see anywhere suitable, so held onto it.

Struan held out his hand for handshakes. 'Sorry, forgive me.' His hand informed them he was in charge, on his turf and on his time, the strength firm and brisk, in, out, no lingering, business like.

'We'll need a statement, Mr Struan.'

'I don't know what I can say.' He leant back in his chair and shrugged.

'I presume you know why we are here?' she asked.

'Yes. Of course. The body that was found on my land. But... I don't know how I can help you.'

'Did you know her?'

'I did, yes.' He nodded. 'I saw the reports in the paper, a lady from the village. It's hard not to know people around here.'

True, thought Kat. 'Is that part of your land farmed? Who is responsible for it?'

'Well, there's the thing. The estate has properties on the land, and some of the tenants farm the land. We rent it in acreage, for crops or sheep, or whatever they wish. We no longer farm ourselves. Some of it is... how can I put it... waiting for development opportunities. The rest of it is public access. Like the footpath up to the woodland where she was discovered. Anyone, everyone, has access.' He splayed his hands wide before bringing them back together in a clasp on his thighs.

'So that particular area is not rented by anyone?'

'No. Not at the moment.'

'What about two years ago?'

'We farmed it until the 80s. The recession led to streamlining and it's been left barren ever since.'

'Nobody manages it?'

'We do, as part of the estate, but we don't farm it. We allow the public access. We rent out the houses nearby, but that particular area, it's open land.'

'And anyone has access.'

'As I said, yes, that's right.'

'Do you know how Mrs Fraser ended up buried on your land, Mr Struan?' she asked, her eyes never wavering from his.

'I can't help you, officer.'

'Can't... or won't?' She wasn't sure.

'I don't like your implication, officer. All of this is rather unfortunate for us at the moment, having this on our doorstep. Do you have any idea how long your enquiry will take?'

'None, Mr Struan. Have been up there to have a look?'

'No, I haven't been. Not yet. Don't see why I need to. I've been rather busy, running between Perth and Inverness. I suppose I should take a look really but I haven't had the time. I can't imagine there's much to see and it's all rather inconvenient,' he repeated.

She looked at him. 'Yes, I suppose it is. Is there anything you can add, that you can think of, that might be helpful?'

Struan shook his head, pouting his lower lip. 'Nothing. I don't know how I can help.'

'What about the gamekeepers? Might they know something?'

Struan scoffed. 'Fergus?'

'He'll know the land as well as you do, I'm sure. If not better?'

'Ask him. Feel free.' Struan stood, pushing his chair behind him. 'Is that it?'

'For now. We may need to speak with you again though, Mr Struan. Thank you for your time today.'

They were dismissed, meeting over. 'Thank you. Hope you liked the coffee, officer. Best beans from Columbia.'

She had enjoyed it but a good instant would have sufficed. As she stood, she said, 'Oh, one more thing. How well do you know Drew Fraser?'

She noticed a flicker in his eye and then it was gone. 'He's a chap from the village.' Struan hesitated. 'Of course, yes. The old lady is related. I didn't immediately make the connection.'

Oh yes, you did, thought Kat.

Chapter 15

The dozen houses that made up the crescent were uniform in style and once council-owned, the front doors now painted to the owner's taste, no longer local authority blue. House-to-house enquires had proved futile but Kat always liked to check things for herself. Now they had a name and next of kin to work with, Kat wanted to focus closer to home.

After being swiftly dismissed by Struan and told that Fergus Campbell was out of reach and out of contact for the day, there was time before lunch to make a start knocking on some doors.

They walked up the path to 5, Strathtay Crescent. A flimsy chain-link fence separated the neighbour's palisades. Unkempt hedgerow spilled through the gaps, and an overgrown and dying clematis draped down over the door, dried-up purple flowers reminiscent of blooms that once shone.

The house looked empty, unlived in. Dirty grey nets hung at the downstairs windows, the upstairs bare. Damp spider webs weaved across the doorframe and around the lock. The broken letter box was stuffed to overflowing with leaflets for pizza, bargains in the latest-but-long-gone sales, and all the free local magazines.

Guy rapped on the front door. 'You never know.' Half a minute later he knocked again.

The neighbour's front door flew open. A woman, bushy-haired and frowning, stood on the step. Kat placed her mid to late sixties and watched her as she slouched against the doorframe and folded her arms.

'You the new tenants?'

'No,' said Guy. 'We're looking for people who live here.'

She looked them up and down. 'You the cops?'

'Why d'ya ask?' he said.

'I can tell by your ya bobby's knock. I thought you were bashing on my door, you made it rattle through the hoose.'

'We're making general enquiries,' said Kat. 'Do you know the people who lived here?'

'Is it about the body that was found?' she said. 'I went to Rose's funeral. What a funny do, her turning up like that.' She cocked her head. 'Aye.'

'Did you know her well?'

She laughed. 'As well as you know anyone around here. Aye, I knew her. Lovely woman. How the hell she ended up on the braeside, phuff, I dinnae ken. An' if it's the Garvey's you're looking fa, they moved oot a while back. She moved abroad, got a job in Dubai or somat. The middle east somewhere. They've all gone over now an' the hoose is up for rent. Lorna at number eleven might know. She keeps in touch with Isla.'

'Isla?' asked Guy.

'Isla Garvey. The lassie from next door. Their mothers used to work together at a kids' nursery down in Perth. Don't know how she got that job abroad coz she was always shouting at her own kids. Not someone I'd want looking after mine, if I'd o' had any tha' is.'

'The funeral. Anything stand out? Anything different?'

'No. Other than she wasn't in the coffin, wae she?'

'Apparently not,' said Kat. 'Was it well attended?'

'As well as anyone of her age, I guess. Not like she was a bairn, eh?'

'Anything strike you as odd?'

'I'm not a bleedin' professional funeral-goer. What's odd? I dinnae ken.'

'Okay. Thanks for that,' said Kat. 'Your name, please? Just to record we've had this chat, you know.'

'Me? I've nothing to do with it.' She held up both hands. 'Leave me oot of it. I know nothing, me.' She turned her back and shut her door, leaving no doubt she wouldn't be opening it again, no matter how hard DC Lynn knocked.

When they came to 11, Strathtay, Kat knew someone was in because she'd seen the front window blind move to the side. It took until the third knock before the door opened.

A teenager frowned at them. 'Yeah?' She stood, hand on the handle as if she might shut it any minute.

'Are your parents in?' Kat asked.

'Who are you, like?' she said.

'I'm DS Dubois, and this is my colleague, DC Lynn.'

'What do you want to speak with him fa?' Kat heard the panic in her voice.

'Can we come in? It'll be better than talking on the doorstep.' She smiled, giving the girl a little nod to encourage her to open the door further. Kat stepped forward.

'Get lost. Just fuck off. We don't want no coppers 'ere.' She tried to slam the door, but Kat's foot was just over the lintel, stopping it from closing.

Her foot jarred but she'd had worse. 'Nothing bad, we just need to speak with your dad.'

The young woman stood in the small gap between the door and frame, anger palpable. 'He's not 'ere. I telt ya, so you can go now.'

She tried to shut the door again and this time Kat had her leg in the gap. The girl shot off and Kat saw her fly up the stairs two steps at a time. A younger girl came from the front room, maybe fourteen or so. She looked at the detectives and stood, one arm across her body, fingers nervously picking at her school cardigan sleeve. She invited them in.

'Please excuse my sister, she's not always disrespectful or rude.'

'When will your parents be back?' asked Kat.

'Err…I'm not sure. They've gone to Perth to do some messages and a big shop. Mam likes to pick her own fruit from the supermarket because she says they only give you rubbish on the delivery. They could be home anytime, dunno really.'

Kat felt her worry and saw anxiety in her face and knew she shouldn't question her too much without her parents present. She looked around the room and despite the light grey décor, the house felt heavy, something not quite tangible but certainly emotional. Two teenagers could do that, she surmised. The house looked clean and tidy, a standard 42" TV, dark velour suite, an over-full magazine rack with newspapers and celebrity rags spilling over the top, coffee table with correspondence on the shelf below the glass top. A box of toys in the corner and a small child's wooden table and two little chairs beneath the window. A typical busy family sitting room, lived in. A large photograph was framed and hung above the fireplace. It was the two girls, about ten years earlier, standing on a grassy bank, laughing with their hands outstretched either side of a small waterfall. Glendargie Falls in an apparently happier time. Kat glanced into the kitchen. The back window was clean, but dust lay smudged on the windowsill and she could just see the sink with plates and cups and a pan stacked on top, probably one of the girls' jobs that they'd had yet to motivate themselves to do before their parents came back. Just a regular family home, so why did she feel so uneasy about it?

The girl's eyes followed Kat's and she said, 'I've got to hoover and wash up before they come back. And put the dinner on. Lorna's not feeling well so she's left it for me to do. Have you got a card I can give my Da' when he gets back?'

Guy reached into his back pocket for his wallet and pulled out his contact card. Kat gave one of hers first.

'Can you ask him to call me on my mobile rather than the office, please? Best to reach me on that.'

The girl nodded.

'Thanks for letting us in. What's your name?'

'Mary, I'm the youngest one, I'm Mary. My sister, Lorna, she's eighteen.'

'Thank you, Mary. Hope your sister is feeling better soon.'

Lorna. Lorna Fraser. The name wasn't familiar, but Kat couldn't shake the feeling that she'd met her before, but how could that be possible?

In the safety of the car, out of earshot of nosy neighbours and troubled teenagers, Guy asked, 'What do you think, then?'

Kat looked out of the side window as she held onto the armrest. Guy was rushing them through the country lanes towards Kendollich and a café for lunch. A dead cat in the road caught her eye. Too many HGVs and fast boys in smart cars paid for by their parents. Locals knew to avoid roadkill, except for mad pheasants who, in a panic, ran into cars rather than away from them.

'Do you have to drive so fast, Guy?'

'It's not that fast, Kat. I'm familiar with the roads, is all.' He took a bend at least ten miles faster than she would have. 'You're just not used to the drive.'

'Yeah, city driving is more like move a mile in ten minutes. It's making me queasy, is all.'

'You're not pregnant, are you?' joked Guy.

'Not a chance. But –' she paused, 'I'm thinking she is.'

'Who?'

The surprise in Guy's voice made Kat laugh. 'Lorna. Lorna Fraser.'

'You got all that from a stroppy teenager?'

'When the Old Bill rock up people often act strange. You can tell when there's something they're not saying.'

'You'll have to enlighten me, Sarge. You a psychic cop or something?' Guy laughed.

'Don't start saying that, people will think I'm strange or something. If they don't already. No, it's nothing weird, sometimes I have a feel for something. There's always a reason for it, something subliminal. Might be relevant, might not, but I'd rather not dismiss it. And if I've noticed something, sure as, someone else will have.'

'What makes you think she's pregnant?'

'She was anxious. Agitated and defensive. Mary said she was sick. They were definitely edgy.'

Guy slowed the car as they approached the corner with the village shop. A boy racer sped past, exhaust rattling as he took the bend. 'They'd know someone would rock up and ask questions though, surely.'

'Yes, they would, but don't suppose they expected to be speaking with us rather than their parents,' said Kat.

'Plus, it's a bereavement.'

'What, Rosemary Fraser? She's been dead two years. Not like this is fresh news. What would make Lorna Fraser panic?'

'Dunno, but why hasn't someone in her family been in touch asking us what's going on?'

'And that, DC Lynn, is a bloody good question.'

After a quick lunch in a quaint café run by an irascible older woman who looked like she didn't want customers and treated them the same, they returned to Strathtay Crescent.

Alison Fraser wore an old duffle coat with a striking red-and-black dogtooth. It looked expensive. She was mid-twist in the door lock when she turned and frowned at the detectives walking up her garden path.

'Can I help you?' she snapped.

Kat smiled at her. 'Sorry to bother you. We called earlier but your daughters said you were in Perth. We left our cards but thought we'd try again on chance you might be in this afternoon.' Kat showed her warrant card and introduced herself and Guy. 'Could we come in, please?'

'If you must but excuse the mess.' Alison Fraser left the door open behind her. 'I asked the girls to tidy up but you know…' She bent to gather post from the floor. 'Bank statements,' she said, as she dumped the envelopes on the hall ledge beneath the mirror.

Kat could see Alison's reflection as she shuffled off into the front room. The woman wore defeat like a badge.

They followed her into the sitting room where they'd stood less than two hours earlier. A dozen or more silver paper doves lay scattered across the settee. Alison brushed them aside as she sat down and opened up her coat. 'An untidy house is a working mother's guilt.' The lines on her forehead and creases around her mouth, the exhausted look in her face, the wrinkled and hard-working hands, and the sigh of resignation, made Alison Fraser appear a spiky wife, an impatient mother, a worn-out woman too old for her years, as if her lifeblood had drained away.

'We were hoping to speak with you and your husband,' said Kat.

'He's working a late shift. He's gone up to Aviemore and won't be back until late. Is this about Rosemary?'

'It would be best if we could speak with him, too.'

'Sorry, I can't tell you when he'll be back.' Alison leant back further into the settee and closed her eyes as she asked, 'What can you tell me, in my husband's absence?'

It was a judgement call. Kat didn't want to set something in motion that might escalate out of her immediate control. Would it make any difference? She fiddled with a curl, pushing it around her ear, mulling it over.

'Just a routine enquiry, Mrs Fraser. Given the circumstances.'

Alison sat up and started to take her coat off. 'Rose? She died of cancer, nothing suspicious about that. You seriously don't think we bumped her off? Really? Drew said he thought you'd think that.' She looked up at Kat. 'The community nurse was there when she died. It was respectful and very expected. She died at home. Her home. I'm sure the GP will tell you that.'

'I'm sure they will. As I said, the questions, they're just routine.' Kat handed her one of her cards. 'Just in case Mary doesn't give you the one I gave her. Is Lorna feeling better?'

Alison frowned as she took the card. 'Better? It was Mary that pulled a sickie this morning.'

'Yes, Lorna. She rushed off upstairs when we came earlier.'

Alison turned the card around in her fingers, corner by corner. 'The baby is due in September. She's not coping so well. Still a kid herself, with a kid already.' She shrugged. 'Spends all her time knitting, drawing, making things, when she's not looking after Cam.' She picked up one of the silver paper doves. 'Like this.' She threw it like a paper airplane, and it landed by the television.

The woman's despair was palpable. There were a few secrets behind this door, Kat was sure.

'They'll be at the park. Lorna usually takes him there around now. Mary must have gone with them. She's a good kid, helps out looking after the bairn. Saves me doing it all.' She stood up and let her coat drop to the settee. 'Rosemary was an old woman who gave a lot to her family. We miss her, her straightforward no-nonsense approach. More like our mother than aunt. She always knew what to do.' She looked Kat. 'I'll tell Drew you called, get him to give you a ring to sort out when's best to come back. He's got a few questions of his own, not least how his aunt came to be buried when we cremated her. I hope you're going to give us some answers.'

Kat and Guy returned to their respective cars just as her mobile rang. It was the DI calling from the office.

'Kat, that crime writer, your witness, rang to say he's moving on. Don't know what his game is, but have we finished with him?'

'Yes. No. I'm not sure really, sir. I have his contact details and I don't suppose we can stop him.'

'Can you give him a call? And you might as well book off. The roads are gridlocked because of a suspicious package at the train station. Turns out it was nothing, a backpack nicked by a hitchhiker from a trucker and he chucked it onto the train line, but bomb squad were called. I've just this minute heard they're finished but there's no point you coming back down here to turn around and go back in an hour. Sure that you've some work you do from home.'

'Yes, Guv, thanks. I'll see if Gillespie's home, pay him a visit, see what he's up to.'

'See you next week then, Kat. Don't work too hard over the weekend, we haven't got the budget.'

There it was again. She regularly put in more unpaid hours than paid and it had become the sort of expected thing to do, unless it was a bank holiday but Police Scotland didn't pay double time and she never claimed for all the overtime anyway, or her full expenses. 'Okay, Guv, have a good weekend.'

Ken Munro grunted and the line went dead. He didn't like 'guv' and she resolved again to try harder.

She arranged to meet Guy the following Monday morning, assuring him he didn't need to accompany her to Jed's house.

'Only if you're sure, Sarge? I'd hate for something to happen.' He looked at his watch. 'Though we did have an early start and if I leave now, I might get through the traffic to pick the girls up.'

'Get on with you. I'll be fine with the writer on my own. See you next week, don't be late.'

As she left the car park she turned right, instead of left. There was somewhere else she wanted to go before Jed Gillespie's.

Chapter 16

Kat drove to the rear of Burns Cottage. There was space for about four or five cars but there was only one parked up, a large black Rover, standard registration plate, clean, tidy, neat. She climbed from her car, ruminating on the state of it inside and out. She looked up to see Jed Gillespie wave to her from an upstairs window. She hoped he was going to put a top on before he came downstairs.

In half a minute he was at the back door, fully dressed in joggers and white T-shirt. He smelled fresh, of generic shower gel, his hair damp and tousled, his stance friendly and face open, a direct but pleasant contrast to the other welcomes she'd had that day.

He led her through a small hallway, past a walk-in larder to the left, through the kitchen and an empty room, suitable for dining, or a study, perhaps. She followed him through into the sitting-room. He motioned for her to take a seat and said he'd make some drinks.

The comfy looking but battered burgundy settee was lower than she'd thought, and she fell back in a slouch. The room was homely but sparse. Most of the thick white paint was old, cracked and flaking, and it gave the room a shabby look. The red Chinese rug matched heavy curtains and the two two-seater settees. The open fire was burning well with a good stock of wood piled by the side. A scattering of books sat on the small coffee table next to an open laptop. As tempting as it was to take a peek, she resisted.

Kat took the coffee Jed handed her and instantly burned her top lip. Once he was seated, she said, 'So, you're leaving us?'

'You know what it's like.' He was facing her on the opposite settee, his long legs outstretched and crossed at his ankles. 'I came here to start afresh. The first thing I do is stumble over a dead body.' He paused. 'The irony is not lost, let me tell you!'

Kat couldn't help but laugh.

He smiled. 'And I have a low boredom threshold.' He reached for his cup. 'So, what's happening? I read that you've got a name for her.'

'Yes, Rosemary Fraser. She died two years ago. I'm sure you could tell that she wasn't recently deceased.'

'I'd presumed. How did she die?'

'Natural causes.'

He looked at her. 'Really? How's that possible?'

'It's possible. In fact, it's true. The impossibility is how she ended up where she did when she'd been cremated. Or apparently not.'

'So … who was cremated instead of her? Any ideas?'

'Not a clue.' She shrugged.

'What you need is a smoking gun!'

'Indeed, we do. Is there anything you can add to your statement?'

'Nothing. And I wasn't here two years ago, so…' he faltered. 'I don't know her, or anyone else around here, to be honest.'

'I know. And of course, you're free to leave anytime you like.' She looked over to his laptop. 'Are you writing anything right now?'

'No,' he said. 'It's a bit difficult at the minute. I've an aching hand.'

'That's a shame. Do you write long-hand?'

'No, it's what I call writer's block… an aching hand. I usually type, though I do use a notebook when I'm out and about for jotting ideas down. At my age you tend to forget if you don't make a note of things.' He looked at her and smiled again. 'But I've had an aching hand for a long time now. Too long.'

'I'd have thought finding a dead body would be just the thing a writer needs for inspiration.'

Jed laughed. 'I'd have thought so, too. Alas, no. But I'll have a think about your case because it intrigues me. I presume you've checked missing persons?'

'Of course,' she said, smarting a little. 'No good asking you for local gossip then, if you don't know your neighbours.'

'True. True. Though I might pick something up at the local.'

'Let me know if you do.'

'So long as it doesn't end up with me in a cell! Suspect number one.' He laughed.

'I doubt it,' she smiled taking a sip of her coffee. 'So, when do you leave?'

'I don't know. I have family in Dublin but it's a loud city, busy, chaotic, too many people. I don't know that I'm ready for returning just yet. I'm still tired. The contrast to Glendargie, well, it's just so quiet here. Or it was.' He stared off to the window. 'There's two types of tired. One that needs a place of quiet inside and the other that needs a place of peace outside. This gives me both. The place of rest that I need.'

He confused her, made her feel as if she was intruding on his peace and quiet. She knew just what he meant, could relate to the need for it. She looked down at her coffee, not sure what to say to him. She felt a connection – he was intelligent, had kind eyes, and spoke with an honesty that was all too lacking in her line of work. The Irish lilt helped. However, he was a witness. And a writer, although she wasn't sure that mattered. Did it? She needed friends and thought of Sue Kinell. She'd give her ring, see if she was up for a drink over the weekend.

When she looked up Jed was looking at her. They smiled and she knew he felt it too.

She flushed, her cheeks warm as she asked, 'So, when are you off, you didn't say?'

'No, I didn't. I don't know.' He stood up and stretched his back. He took her empty cup, his hand brushing against hers.

She didn't look at him. 'Thanks.'

'I don't know. I just feel loose end-ish. Am I needed here?'

Kat could see the cut of his T-shirt and how it fitted him across his shoulders. She busied herself searching for her keys in her bag, not daring to look up. 'I don't think so.'

'Hmm...'

Was he toying with her? 'As long as you leave a forwarding address.' She was mooching in her bag and realised the keys were in her coat pocket. 'Don't leave without saying goodbye, will you?'

When she looked up, he'd gone. She heard him clattering in the kitchen. 'I'll be off then!' she shouted.

He came back into the sitting-room, wiping his hands on a tea towel. 'I think the moment's passed.'

'Oh?' She felt the thud of her heartbeat in her ears.

'Yes, the desire. It's waned.'

'Right...' She frowned, not quite sure.

'Moving on. It was something I got into my head. I think I got spooked, finding that body ... but I have a feeling that things are going to settle down. Now we've cleared up that I'm not in trouble of course.'

Kat flushed. He was playing with her, the old blarney charm. She shoved a curl behind her ear as she slung her bag over her shoulder. 'Let's hope there's no dire consequences, then, for staying. I hope your muse returns soon.' She walked over to the front door and turned the heavy iron ring handle.

'I think she already has.' Jed leant over her, brushing his torso against her back as he reached towards the black twisted iron door handle. He gave a sharp tug.

'It's a little stiff, nothing a good yank won't sort out. Needs oiling.'

She walked around the cottage and wondered why he let her go through the charade of going through the front door instead of reminding her she'd parked around the back. It was him, the fluster, it had her off balance. This was no good, no good at all. She shrugged her shoulders, trying to cast him off. Keep away, she warned herself … and then a voice muttered … but what if I don't want to?

It was three weeks since she saw him last. She snuck through the playground as fast as she could, but he saw her. She didn't see him at first because he was sitting under the slide. He was hiding, watching, waiting for one of his little people to walk past. Watching and waiting for her.

'Hello, pretty,' he said in a loud whisper.

She tried to pretend not to hear. Her feet moved faster, her head fell down. He called at her again.

'Don't pretend you don't hear me, pretty. I've been waiting all day for you. I've brought you some Dolly Mixtures. Come on. Don't be shy, my pretty.'

She looked up and the sun made her eyes hurt, made them water a little. The sun hit her and made her cheeks red and hot and the water running down them was making her face sore.

She pretended she was playing a game so he wouldn't be cross with her. She walked around the chute, right round to the back of him, and shouted out, 'Boo!' and it worked because he laughed, and it was all alright.

'Come out of the sun and sit with me,' he said. He patted the ground next to him.

She could see the hot dust where he sat under the chute. He had made wavy patterns in it with a lolly stick. He pointed the stick at her and then at the ground. 'Come here, I've been waiting for you. Sit.'

His voice wasn't kind when he spoke, and his horsey teeth and lips pretended to smile, and she knew he didn't mean it. He grabbed her arm and pulled her close to him and she fell down with a bump, right next to him, and her foot couldn't help but kick the wavy lines in the dust. He pushed her away from him a little and then moved her closer, so they were together. He put his big leg outstretched next to her little leg, his trousers rough next to her skin. He kept hold of her hand and opened it up, stroking inside on her palm, smoothing down her fingers.

'Roundy round the garden, like a teddy bear.' He made a circle in her hand with one of his rough fingers. 'One step... two step... three step... nearly there.' He plunged her hand into his trouser pocket.

She crunched up her eyes, face sore from the sun and the water that didn't stop, and she tried not to see and tried not to think as her hand was pushed down onto him.

'Can you feel the Dolly Mixtures? No? They must be in the other pocket. Jelly snakes in this one.' He laughed.

Her eyes crunched tighter. She felt his hot breath on her cheek as he pressed his face next to hers. He pushed her hand down harder, deeper into his pocket. He moved her hand again and again and his breath became a different sound, a grunting noise each time he breathed out, and his breath smelled of bad things. She thought of dead frogs and mossy slime. She tried to think of Dolly Mixtures and nice things. And then there was the sticky and she thought of sticky toast with red, red jam, waving lines on the toast with a knife like the lines in the dust with a lolly stick.

It was done. He was finished with her. He pushed her away and he laughed. 'Thank you, my pretty.'

SHE'S NOT THERE

She stood up, her bright red face hotter than the sun and rougher than the sand. He threw a small packet of Dolly Mixtures at her. She bent to pick it up. She didn't dare not.

'One good turn deserves another,' he said. 'It's my birthday soon and I hope you've got something special for me. I like a treat on my birthday. Don't forget. Don't make me come to look for you again. You're my very special pretty thing and you're my extra special girl.' He put a finger to his lips.

She walked out of the park and dropped the sweeties into the bin and ran. She vowed never to eat Dolly Mixtures again.

Chapter 17

Kat was back at her desk. She still had to speak with Drew Fraser. The policy log was thin, outstanding actions needed results, and there were not enough forthcoming actions. There were a few more house-to-house enquiries to do to speak to Rosemary Fraser's neighbours, find out if they could add anything. She still had the crematorium operative to take a statement from when he returned from his holidays this week. She wasn't sure that any of those actions were going to take the enquiry further forward.

'Hey, Sarge! DS Dubois. There's a chappie downstairs for ye,' hollered a uniformed PC lounging into the doorway of the CID office.

Kat looked up from the papers scattered across her desk. 'Hi, Tom,' she said, recognising PC Pritchard. 'Who is it? I'm not expecting anyone.'

'Dunnae, not seen him before. Said he came by yesterday, but as you were days off, he was told to come back.'

'I don't have any messages. Can you get a name?' She shook her left hand to look at her watch. It fell loose. A present from her old colleagues. She hadn't had time to have any of the links taken out and she was now used to the way it swung round on her wrist. It was a comfort, something to fiddle with, a reminder of time and a different place. She turned the face of the watch around to check the time. 'What does he want, because I'm busy.'

'He asked for you, by your full name. He also thought you were a DI. I've never seen him before and don't recognise him. He's quite distinctive. He must be a visitor because I'd know him, if he was from around here.'

Kat looked up at Pritchard and grunted. She knew what he meant, in a police kind of way. You didn't have to know someone to know who they were, what they were, or what they got up to. A good cop knew who was on the ground, who was active, and who was who, in a criminal vs cop kind of way.

'Can you find out what he wants?' She put her head back down. When she was a DI people were more reluctant to casually interrupt. Callers made appointments and didn't just drop in. Her time was more hers and less theirs. She'd forgotten how disposable time was as a sergeant in a busy CID office.

'Thought you'd say that. I have tried, honest. He won't see anyone but you. Said he's been to at least ten stations to find you. Said it's personal.'

She scoffed. 'Personal? For who? Not me, surely?' She didn't have any sort of personal. 'What is it about him that makes him distinctive?'

Tom Pritchard looked awkward.

'In what way?' Kat was irritated, didn't need any disruptions or distractions, especially from a mystery man.

'There aren't too many six-foot, young black men with Cockney accents wearing West Ham tops walking around Perth, Sarge.'

Kat paused, didn't breathe, all noise stopped. Her heart thudded. She blinked. 'Tell him I'll be down shortly.'

SHE'S NOT THERE

Chapter 18

'Clarke! What on earth are you doing here?' Kat hugged the young man, squeezing him tight. He squeezed her too, his arms awkward but comforting. 'Surely you must have finished growing now! I can't believe you're here!' He stood before, well over six-foot. 'Why didn't you tell me you were coming?'

'Because you might not want me here?' he said. 'You might have put me off. Told me not to bother.'

'I've always got time for you. What's going on? You don't travel more than five hundred miles on a whim without letting me know you're coming!'

She looked at the boy, nay man, stood in front of her. Something must be amiss. Why else would he just turn up? She held up her hand. 'Look, hold that thought. I was going out soon anyway, let me gather my things and we'll grab some lunch. Wait here.'

She left him in the side interview room while she shot upstairs for her bag, coat, and a sheaf of paperwork from her desk. If she took the afternoon off, she could go straight to see the Fraser family in the morning. Seeing Jed the day before had given her something else to think about. He could prove useful.

She signed herself out for the rest of the day. She was annoyed with herself for not keeping in contact with Clarke as often as she should have. When had she last seen him? Or spoken to him? Months ago. She'd spoken to him when she'd moved into her cottage and told him he must visit, and they'd both laughed that he'd be the only black guy in the village. It had seemed a joke then. The stark reality was, he was right, and it didn't seem that funny. He would stand out, and everyone would know his name, and make up his story, because they wouldn't know it, but there would have to be one, because there always was.

'Right then,' she said to Clarke as they made their way to her car. 'You're staying with me. Question is, how long? And we need to do some shopping.'

After collecting Clarke's belongings from the B&B he'd been staying in, they took a detour to a supermarket on the ring road. Once they'd filled the boot with half a dozen bulging bags, Kat set off up the A9. Clarke sat in the front seat, his long legs bent, even with the seat all the way back.

'It'll take about an hour, depending on traffic,' Kat said. 'Plenty of time for you tell me what you're doing here.' She turned to look at her stepson. 'It's good to see you.' She smiled. 'I hope you've brought jumpers. It's a tad colder up here.'

The first fifteen minutes were filled with casual chit-chat. He'd first gone to Edinburgh, staying with some of his university friends. Then he'd started looking for her.

'It was difficult to track you down. Why the demotion? What happened to DI? And have you any idea how many police stations there are in Scotland?'

'You found me though.' She smiled at him. 'How did you know I'd let you in?'

'Home is the place where when you turn up, they have to let you in.'

'Home?'

'Jesting, testing ...' he shrugged. 'But no need to worry, I won't stay long.'

'You're always welcome, wherever I am. I told you that. I'm glad you're here.' She paused. 'Sorry I haven't been in touch before now.'

She genuinely felt bad about not forwarding her address. She had intended to do it but it had slipped her mind and then she'd completely forgotten.

Clarke stared out of the window and said, 'I did try calling but I didn't know if it was still your number. I thought you might have changed it when you moved so I never left a message in case it wasn't you.'

'That was you? I've had a few withheld numbers.'

'I know. I did that on purpose. In case you didn't want to speak to me. I know you usually answer no-number calls because of work so I thought you'd answer me. If you saw it was me you might ignore me, not want me in your life anymore, or think you'd call me back when you had more time but forget. I know how busy you get.'

'Oh, Clarke. I wasn't avoiding you. Never. I'm dealing with a difficult case right now and yes, I have been busy. Please don't think I'd ever ignore you. I'm happy you've found me. My bad for not keeping in touch.' The guilt squirmed up her back. 'I'm sorry. I would never drop you. Never not want you in my life.'

'It's okay.' He turned to look out of the side window. 'It's so scenic here, picturesque. I can't believe in all the years you've never brought me here.'

'Really?' Kat frowned, trying to remember.

'Not once.'

'I didn't come back that much myself. When mum died you were what, ten? We wouldn't have brought you then. Didn't you come when we went to Inverness?' Kat tried to recall the trip. 'Weren't you with us?'

'You and dad took me on holiday, yeah, but I don't remember coming to Scotland. It's stunning. Like New England with tall Scots pines and hanging mists loitering like ghosts and brooding hillsides.'

Kat laughed. 'I'm not sure New England has brooding hillsides. Or maybe they do, in Vermont, for the skiing. When did you go to New England?'

'I haven't. But this reminds me of it. The air … so fresh. You can breathe.' He continued to stare out of the window as they travelled up the busy road. 'You know, Kat, life's so fast, no time to stop and stare. You wouldn't want to inhale too much for fear of choking.'

'Still as poetic as ever.'

Neither spoke, each appreciative of the surroundings and the company.

'I like to see it through your eyes, Clarke. It is a vision of beauty, isn't it? All natural, not a facelift nor man-made landscape for miles.' Kat had never tired of it and at different times in her life had travelled the route in different emotional states, in fear and dread and in excitement and boredom. It had taken her a long time to permanently return and it was a return on her terms.

'Did you come to forget, or come to remember?'

The question hit her full in the chest. Smash. Like a shot in the chest. She hesitated, then, 'Wow.'

'Wow?'

'What a question.' How did she answer it? 'Where did you get that from?'

'I don't know. It struck me that a place like this, it's somewhere you run to hide, to escape, or in your case, to return. You've never talked about it. Hardly ever. Your accent gave away more than you ever did. I might have been too young, but if you did talk about Scotland, you know me, Kat, I don't forget much. I don't remember you ever talking about living here, what it was like, why you left, nothing. Maybe you talked to Dad about it, but never when I was there.'

She didn't know what to say.

'It's okay. None of my business, I'm just curious. I'm just surprised because I imagined where you came from was somewhere

117

like in Trainspotting, a town of derelict flats, junkies, and deadbeats mixed with some posher houses.'

Kat laughed. 'What a cliché. Those places exist, they're everywhere, not just Scotland, plenty like that in London, as you well know, but you are right, it's nothing like that here. It's just different.'

'I just can't imagine anyone living here wanting to leave.'

'Beautiful scenery doesn't pay the bills, nor does it stop real life from happening. It's just a better view, is all. I left to join the Met. Tayside police, as it was then, weren't recruiting and like most young people, I wanted change. There aren't many jobs around rural Scotland, then or now, and I wanted a career. A different life. Lots of folk move away. Some come back. Others don't.' She hoped that was enough to satisfy his questions. Stock answer she'd given every time she'd been asked why she went to London.

'But you didn't come back though, not even to visit much. And then you suddenly up and left and came back. Didn't Dad ever want to move here?'

'We never discussed it. Our life was in London. He was from London. You were there, our jobs, our home. It was never an option, and I don't suppose I would ever have come back here, if…'

Neither needed to say anything more about if.

Chapter 19

The if hung in the air, not uncomfortable, not uneasy, just there, in the face. Fact. Moving on and moving back had helped Kat to forget. She bounced it around her head. Not forget. She would never forget Bart, nor want to. It was more that the move helped her not to remember. To forget would be a terrible injustice, and she didn't want to forget, but returning to Scotland had helped her to remember other things, a different life, a life she'd chosen to leave because she did want to forget. It was a bit too complicated.

As they travelled past Dunkeld, Kat broke the silence. 'Lovely little place, Dunkeld. It has the oldest cathedral in Scotland. Big tourist spot.'

Clarke turned his head, but there was nothing to see but a barrier of trees as they drove by the small town.

'The Beatrix Potter exhibition is there, too. You'd love that.'

'I remember you reading Potter books to me. Means something different now though, doesn't it, the Potter books? That'd be an interesting comparison for an essay.'

'JK Rowling has a country house up here, hidden away. It's a rich landscape for creativity. One of the witnesses in my current case is a famous writer. I didn't know him but he's a bestseller. Jed Gillespie?'

'I'm loving it here more and more. I love his books!' Clarke scrabbled in his rucksack and pulled out his phone to bring up his kindle app.

119

'How's uni going?' Kat asked.

'Loving it.' Clarke sat awkwardly, gangly arms bent, head down, face close to his phone, biting his tongue in the same manner as when he'd been a little boy. He was so like his father, the same sense of humour and kindness and everything else that made Bart a damn good man. She missed him. She'd been doing okay, and now Clarke was here, it was like Bart sitting next to her, and she was back with the grieving pain again.

By the time they'd unpacked the shopping and Kat had filled the cupboards and the fridge, and the kettle had boiled, there was no other distraction to prevent the discussion that had hung in the air like a fat elephant waving its trunk, teasing them. It was time to talk.

Kat handed Clarke a cup of tea with two sugars and said, 'So, what really brings you here?'

Clarke sipped the tea. 'Ooh, ooh, too hot.' He waved imaginary steam and placed the cup on the table. He looked everywhere but at her.

She let it hang, like the mist in the trees, like a ghost between them. The power of silence was the best investigative technique she had. If she didn't fill it, the other person would be compelled to and, in most cases, it worked. She let the seconds tick by…tick, tick, tick…then he spoke.

'I got study leave from uni a couple of weeks ago so I went to my mother's. I didn't think it was a problem, but it was obvious it was. That I was.' He paused. 'I don't know when she was planning on telling me, but she had no option when I saw how bare the place was.' He looked pained, struggling to speak. His voice broke. 'She's moving, Kat. My mother's moving. And she's taking the girls with her.'

Kat thought he might cry. 'Oh, Clarke. You knew she wouldn't stay in the house forever. She'd never afford it. Not after…when the money stopped.'

'I know. I know. But it's not just that she's moving, it's where she's going.'

'You'll be able to visit. She must think you're settled and sorted, and you always said that once you'd gone to uni, you'd never move back again.'

'I know that … but she's going to Grandad's place. She's going to Anguilla, Kat. The other side of the world!' His tears welled, his face wretched. 'And when they've all gone, I've got nothing left. Only you. And you've already left.' He blinked too fast and the tears flowed. 'I needed to come and see you.'

She caught him as he fell, no longer the young man but the little boy he was when she first knew him. She moved them across to the two-seater settee in the little kitchen-cum-diner as he sobbed hard against her chest. And he sobbed as she moved them both, her arms still around him, to the larger settee in the lounge where she barely sat. She held him, tight, close, and she remembered him at five, tufty hair, cheeky grin, deep-deep eyes set with his dad's spark. Intelligent and loving, just like his father. She held him the way she'd held him after his cat had died, and again when his father died.

When Bart died everything changed. They were three and now their little triangular unit had lost a side and it was no longer the three of them, no longer a triangle, just two lines with nothing to join them. After Bart died, Clarke's mother didn't like him going to visit Kat, so he didn't tell her when he did, and then she became a sort of guilty secret. Kat knew it wasn't right that a fifteen-year-old boy should keep secrets from his mother and knew she wouldn't like it if she had a son who kept secrets from her, but neither did she want Clarke to stay away. He was her stepson, and they had a past, their past, a shared history, and a link to Bart. They were far too important to each other to be cut off and Kat missed him like the son she never had. She'd been his step mum for years and she'd never wanted to take his mother's place, not ever. They had their own special relationship and Kat knew that Sophie Banks didn't like it.

SHE'S NOT THERE

Kat had had ten glorious years with Bart, the gentlest man she'd ever known, the only man she'd ever let into her adult life. He was divorced with a five-year-old son when she met him. He was doing an undercover operation on her patch and they met in the canteen, both trying to be served at the same time by the overworked kitchen staff. When he laughed her heart lifted. His effect on her was instant. She was smitten.

The only problem was his ex, Sophie. She'd left Bart for a colleague of his, Ned. Bart and Ned weren't really friends, but they worked on the same team. When Sophie had twin girls, Clarke spent more time with his dad and Kat.

Kat and Bart had a good life, and in the click of her fingers, it was gone. Just like that. They had worked hard, played hard, enjoyed time just the two of them, and enjoyed time as a family when with Clarke. There was never a question of more children, they just fitted as they were.

Then Bart became ill. He had cancer in his kidneys which had spread rapidly and within three months he was dead and it was all over. Life as Kat had known it was finished.

A straight line, a numb line, a silence with nothing to fill it

Kat pushed herself at work, the only thing she knew to do to keep herself from drowning, and she was getting better at batting away grief with each case she worked on until all she had was a job that was changing, a solitary life at home, and somebody else's son who she loved dearly but wasn't allowed to spend proper time with. When she lost the difficult murder-rape case and had seen Police Orders advertising vacancies in Scotland, a home that she hadn't thought of as home for a very long time, she knew what she had to do. She left.

It was almost three years to the day of Bart's death when she drove up the A9 following the removal van.

'Why does she want to leave me?' Clarke sobbed into Kat's arms.

'She's not leaving you, Clarke. She's not. You don't need her in the same way the girls do.'

'But she is leaving me. I've lost my dad and then you, and now my mum and my sisters. Why do people always leave me?'

Kat closed her eyes. She could feel his pain as if it ran through her own body. 'She doesn't think she's leaving you, Clarke. She probably thinks she's starting again. She's doing what I've done. Going back to her roots, to her family. Her father went back to Anguilla when he retired and she's going back to be with him.'

'But Mum never lived there. She was born and brought up here. And Grandad is an old man. And she's taking the girls.'

Kat had no idea what motives Sophie had but whatever they were, she knew the move was going to have a huge effect on Clarke.

He brought a poodle with him. It was beige buttercream and had tight tiny curls. The little dog jumped up and down and up again and licked her face furiously, sloop, sloop, sloop.

She didn't like it. His doggy breath fell on her and she turned her face away. It was warm and smelly, and she could smell him, the man, too, his cigarettes and dirty things and something rotten. The complicated smells caught in the back of her throat and she couldn't, wouldn't, swallow them. She coughed and stepped back a few tiny steps, away from him and the animal. The creature jumped up again and this time he nipped her cheek with his little sharp teeth. It was a tiny gash, but poured an ocean of blood and she couldn't help but cry. Her left eye swelled in an instant and the hot tears made her cheek sore.

He kicked the animal, his black training shoe a perfect fit under its ribs, and the little dog flew in the air and landed on the other side of the slide. It screeched and so did she.

SHE'S NOT THERE

Her blood smeared across her face and the hot sun made it smart some more. He wiped her cheek with his rough arm and the red blood disappeared into his black tracksuit top. He wiped his arm over his thigh, spreading her blood across his tracksuit leg. He looked nervous, sweaty, like he didn't know what to do.

'Shut up!' he snapped at her and pushed her in the chest with two fingers. He pushed her again with the flat of his hand and she staggered back until her back was pressed against the hard metal bar of the roundabout. She stepped up onto the rim and sat down, hard, onto the wooden section that was painted red. She tried to hide her whimper as he glared at her; she saw danger and the same fear in his eyes that she knew she had in her own.

He strode over to the poodle and grabbed it by the folds of its neck. He punched it, once, direct in the face and it whimpered just like she whimpered. He dropped the animal to the ground.

'Shut up!' He glared at the dog, then at her.

She touched her face. It was still bleeding but now just a trickle. She watched him from her good eye as he dragged the dog across the dusty playground, past the slide, in front of the swings, and over to her. She bit her bottom lip and banged the heel of her new sandals against the wood panelling of the roundabout. Bang, bang, bang.

'I said stop it!' He glared at her.

She stopped the bang-banging, the biting of her lip, and the quiet whimpering she realised had escaped without her knowing.

He plonked the poodle on her lap, but it slithered off as her knees weren't properly flat. The dog fell to the ground and he snatched it up. He tried again but the dog fell down again.

'Stupid fuckin' thing!' he snarled.

He pulled the arm of the roundabout, turning it away to his left and it made a squealing sound as it moved. He jumped onto the section next to her, the green triangle. He sat down and he grabbed her clothes from the back and pulled her so that her little legs didn't touch the rim anymore.

The roundabout slowed to a stop.

'Push me,' he said. 'Push me round. Fast.'

She slid off the red wood and held onto the metal handle. She tried hard to make it move. It turned a little bit, but she was too small to make it move very much.

'Pathetic. Get back on.'

She climbed back onto the red triangle and saw her new sandals were scuffed at the toe. She'd be in trouble when she went home.

When she was seated, he plonked the dog onto her lap.

'Hold him. Don't let him go.' He pushed his face near to hers and she smelt his breath. It smelt of cold food like takeaway, a pizza, something garlicky.

'Don't let him bite you again.'

She wrapped both arms around the dog's wriggling body, both of them together, a jumble of thin arms and legs. Some of her blood smudged on its fur.

'This is Rory. I brought him for you to play with. And look what you made him do.'

He stood up off the roundabout, one foot on the rim and the other on the floor as he spun them around and around and around, and they went faster and faster and faster. She felt her tummy trip up and she tried hard not be sick when she felt it sting in the back of her throat. They went round and round and round and faster and faster and faster and she became dizzier and dizzier and dizzier. She closed her eyes. A dribble of blood fell into her mouth and she pushed it out with her tongue because both arms were still holding tight onto Rory and she didn't have a hand, or a finger to use.

The roundabout started to slow, slower, slower and slow.

Rory settled into her, nuzzling his face against hers, his tiny sharp teeth hidden away as if he now knew better. His tight curls brushed against her face, soft, bouncy, alive, but smelly. She might have liked him more if he hadn't nipped her and made her bleed. And if he wasn't smelly. She crunched up her eyes and tried to stop the stench of dog and the smell of the man's breath get up her nose and she wished for the giddiness to stop. The sun was hot on her head and the animal hot in her arms. She couldn't help it. She was sick.

He laughed and laughed and laughed and there was no end to his laughing. Her new red sandals were scratched, her red-red cheek was scratched, and his black-black clothes wore her blood. She knew the funny colour buttercream dog was in the same bad place as she was. She wobbled and closed her eyes and heard the hummingbirds by the little stream and the woodpeckers in the trees and the sun beat down on her head and everything was red and black behind her eyes.

The next morning when she woke, she saw the blood on her pillow. She had scratched her face in her sleep. Again.

Chapter 20

Kat was due to see the Fraser family and had half an hour spare, so she called at the corner shop for milk and a few other bits. She'd forgotten how much a teenage boy could eat. It wasn't just a quick sausage roll for lunch, he'd consume a whole packet of them, not that she minded. It was good to spend time with him again.

She knew she'd miss him when he left and had enjoyed having someone in the house, someone to talk to when she returned home, the fire lit, the dinner started, someone to watch trashy TV with, even though they ended up deep in conversation rather than watching anything.

Mrs Templar stood behind the till in the well-stocked post office-cum-shop. In the short time Kat had lived there, she'd learnt who the local gossips were, and Mrs Templar was one of them. It didn't take long for her to start asking Kat questions.

'You've got a visitor, hen, have you?' she said, as she picked a packet of biscuits from the basket, peering at the sticky label as if she didn't know the price.

Kat nodded, giving nothing away.

'Staying long?'

'No, not really.'

Mrs Templar tapped the buttons on the old-fashioned till. 'I haven't seen him here before. Is he one of your lot?'

'My lot?' It was easy to be offended if you chose to be, thought Kat.

'On the job.'

Kat laughed. 'No. No, he's not in the job.'

Mrs Templar leant forward, as if about to reveal a secret. Her attempt at a whisper was a loud rasp. 'Mrs Davison said she thought you'd taken him in, a waif and stray, bit of community service as it were.' She scrunched up her nose.

Kat leaned forward, and said in a not so quiet whisper, 'Nothing like that. He's a friend staying for a few days.'

'Oh!' The older woman stepped back, eyes wide, and Kat knew instantly that she thought she'd meant a boyfriend.

With a stern eye she retorted, 'No, nothing like that either! He's someone very dear to me. Family.' She wished she had it in her to feed the woman a few lines, have a bit of fun, but she knew Mrs Templar could be a good source of information, reliable or otherwise, so it was best to keep her sweet. 'I'll ask him to pop in and have a chat if you like.'

'Ooch, I'm not being nosy, hen. He doesn't have to do that.' She pushed up the back of her hair with her hand. 'Only if he's passing.'

'I daresay he'll call in for snacks when he takes a walk. He'll enjoy exploring your shop, stocked with shelves of veritable delights, the likes of which he'll never have seen where he comes from.'

Mrs Templar perked up, missing the sarcasm. 'Well, as I said, only if he's passing, dear. I'll look out for him. What did you say his name is?'

'I didn't.' She smiled. 'But it's Clarke. And you know what they say about young black men from London?'

'Oh, no. No, I don't know what they say.'

'They make great pie and mash.'

Mrs Templar's cheeks blushed. 'Oh!' She pushed up the back of her hair again. 'Do you have a bag, dear, or will you carry these?'

Kat handed over a crumpled plastic bag from her handbag.

'I suppose it's all a bit different for him up here. Fresh air, friendly faces.'

Aye, friendly faces with fake smiles, she didn't say. 'Oh, yes, he loves the fresh air. I really must be getting on now, Mrs Templar. Nice to chat.'

'Anytime, and I look forward to seeing your young man. That'll be eight pounds and six pence, please.'

Kat looked at the milk, biscuits, butter, and bread. It would have been half the price in London. Not everything was cheaper in her new life, but at least the view was better.

'Any further forward with poor Mrs Fraser? I heard she's going for cremation next week. Again.'

Kat stopped rooting in her purse. 'Who told you that?'

'Someone mentioned it in the shop yesterday. Who was it?' She put a finger to her lips and tapped. 'Now then, I was serving Clement from Archatye B&B and he was after some of that thick bacon we stock from the butcher's in Pitlochry.' She looked down at the floor and Kat had no doubt she knew exactly who it was but was enjoying prolonging her reveal.

'Ah, yes! I remember now.' She took the finger from her lip and pointed it at Kat. 'It was Michael Struan.' She hesitated. 'He was talking to someone on that fancy mobile of his about selling some land and I heard him say there were cremation arrangements being made for some time next week. I have to say, what a funny old do. How could they not know they hadn't cremated her? What, did she get up out of her box and walk off or something? Or maybe she wasn't really dead in the first place? Makes you wonder, doesn't it. How can they really know if you're dead? Now then, do you have the right change, dear? I'm a bit short on cash.'

One thing for sure, Kat knew, the dead don't walk, but Michael Struan knew more than he was saying.

Chapter 21

Kat looked at Lorna's painted chipped fingernails. She watched her picking at the sparkling pink, pushing, peeling, pick-pick-picking, as if she didn't know she was doing it. Kat looked around the room, taking in the discarded hoodies, socks, a pretty cotton skirt, vest tops, magazines, and the scatterings in the typical teenager's bedroom: make-up, soiled plates, hair-packed brushes, and an overflowing basket of unwashed clothes in the corner. Only this one had a cot in it with a sleeping toddler. And in the corner, a pile of nappies, baby blankets, a pair of high heels, and baby shoes.

She'd been surprised when the girl had invited her up to the room.

'The cooking smells are making me feel sick and Mary's doing my head in.' She flung herself onto the single bed and slouched against three pillows.

Kat looked at her. 'I came to see your mam and dad, to ask about your aunt Rosemary.'

Lorna picked at a nail without looking at it. Her eyes hung over Kat's shoulder, towards the door, as if waiting for, or willing, someone to enter. Traces of the girl she once was clung to the walls, posters with quotes that were no longer inspirational, and tickets of long-ago gigs with photos of friends pinned to a board that could have done with a dusting.

'How old are you, Lorna?'

'Old enough,' she said, still looking at the door rather than Kat. Then added, 'Eighteen.'

Kat smiled at her. 'Did you get to finish your A levels?'

'Highers. We do Highers here.'

'Yes, of course.' Kat knew that. She had her own Highers. And a couple of credible Advanced Highers, and one A level that she took at night class when she'd moved south. Not that she had any use for them. 'What did you take?'

'Five SQAs but I had to leave 'coz of the baby, no point staying on so I didn't get to do Highers.' Lorna rubbed her stomach. Her bump was neat, compact, which was probably a good thing as she was a slight girl.

'What will you do once the next baby is born?'

Lorna looked up at Kat. 'Look after it, of course. Just as I do Cam. I'm not giving it away. I'm keeping it.'

Kat hadn't meant that, but Lorna's response told her it had been discussed. It was an option, one no doubt talked about long into the night by her parents, by her, maybe others. Her response told her that like many young girls in her situation, the baby would be cared for, protected, looked after like the most treasured possession, then reality would kick in and a lifetime of responsibility would take over with two children to look after at such a young age.

'I didn't mean that. I'm sure you'll love and look after your baby very much. I meant will you go to college? What are your plans? Longer term.'

Lorna scoffed. 'College? All the way to Perth every day, with two babbies? No. I'll have to get a job, won't I? I did childcare at school, got me SVQ in it. I always wanted to be a nanny, to travel the world and work in the big houses up on the estates, and go to London, and have holidays like Lydia. We could never afford to go anywhere other than picnics in the park, or camping in Cumbria, and Skegness, once. Lydia always went to glamorous places like Goa and Marbella and Mexico. And she always had a nanny 'coz she's a Struan and

131

that's what they do, have nannies. Didn't send her to boarding school though.' She picked at her nails again.

'Her dad said the high school was good enough for her, which was good 'coz we wouldn't have been friends otherwise.'

Kat leant against the door frame and let the girl talk. It seemed like she needed to.

'Being a nanny is the only job I could think of that meant I could travel, to get away from here, 'coz I ain't clever like Lydia. Or Isla.' She looked up at Kat. 'Isla's gone to Abu Dhabi now. Somewhere like that, anyways. She's going to an international college to train to be a teacher. Isla was with him before me and that's why her parents took her away. They said he was too old for her and she shouldn't waste her time on romance. All I got was a baby an' a SVQ in looking after kids. What chance do I have now? Eh?'

Kat could feel her despair but couldn't think of what to say that didn't sound patronising, so she said it anyway. 'Don't give up your dreams, Lorna. Never give up.'

Lorna gave a half-hearted puff. 'What would you know?'

Kat didn't reply and instead she said another thing that felt patronising. 'You're young, Lorna. Life is just beginning. Don't write yourself off. When your friends are having babies, you'll be ahead of them. You'll get your life back on track.'

'D'ya have kids then?' Lorna looked at her.

She smiled at her. 'I was never that fortunate, but I have a stepson. He's at university.'

Lorna puffed again.

'It's just so bloody complicated.' She rubbed her belly.

'Isla had a fling with your baby's dad before you?'

'Yeah ... well no, not really. She was seeing him a bit but they didn't do anything. An' I didn't know when I started seeing him that she had been seeing him and he said they didn't do owt, either. I believed them but her parents didn't and then they up and left.'

Kat watched as Lorna picked at her nail varnish. She picked and Kat waited, letting the silence settle.

'I didn't know things would be so difficult,' Lorna said.

Kat became aware of the cooking smells wafting upstairs, chicken and potatoes, and the sound of the clock on the wall on the landing that ticked. Annoying. Kat waited. The clock ticked. When she was ready, Lorna spoke.

'I really thought he loved me. If he loved me, he wouldn't have gone, would he? He would have stayed and been here, and we could have been together. But he left and he didn't tell me he was going, and I don't know where he is' – she paused – 'and everyone said he was too old for me, but I loved him and when he didn't come back for me, I met someone else and now I'm pregnant. Again.'

Kat said nothing.

'And now he's not bothered either. He's left me.'

There was no more varnish on her left hand, and Lorna brushed the flakes from the bed to the floor. 'I'll have to hoover later.' She looked around the room. 'I'll have to tidy up, too. Can't bring another baby into this mess, can I?' She looked at her son in the cot as he let out little baby breaths.

'But I am bringing a baby into this mess. This mess that is my life, so what does it matter that my room is a mess. Just like me.' She lifted her hands to her face and started to sob.

Kat went over to the bed and sat next to her. She didn't touch her but sat beside her as she cried.

She hadn't managed to ask Lorna about her aunt. It hadn't seemed the appropriate time. Her parents had called to say they were caught up in traffic on the A9 so wouldn't be back for another hour or more.

As Kat drove home, she thought about what Lorna had said and it made her uneasy. Lorna really believed she was in love with the father of her first baby, an older man who was kind and gentle and made her fall in love with him. Old enough to be her father, she'd said, just, and her father was furious when he found out, which is why she'd tried to keep their relationship secret. Lorna had disclosed willingly, and Kat had no intention of pushing it. It wasn't anything relevant to her but if it put the girl on her side, then she was willing to listen. She needed an ally and the girl seemed like she needed some support. It had nothing to do with Rosemary but everything to do with the family and if Kat could help her, she would. The other thing niggling at Kat was where did Isla Garvey fit into it? Or did she? Why did the Garvey family move away? Lorna said Isla loved him before her but she couldn't see a family moving because of a boyfriend. And Lydia Struan. She was obviously a good friend of Lorna's so the Fraser and Struan family would be well known to each other. But was any of it in anyway relevant to Rosemary Fraser? Hardly likely.

And then it dawned on her. She knew where she'd seen Lorna Fraser and she had looked quite a bit different but she'd recognised the shoes.

Tottering Heels, waiting for the boyfriend in the police station who never arrived.

The things my mother should have told me... She should have told me not to trust the man with the trousers with the paint dabs, the deep pockets, and the scuffed hems.

She should have told me not to go wandering in the park on my own.

My mother should have told me to tell her everything, that I wouldn't get into trouble, that she could fix it, fix everything.

My mother should have said that I could trust her.

SHE'S NOT THERE

My mother should have told me not to hold secrets, that she wouldn't not tell me off for things that weren't my fault, and that she loved me.

She should have told me...

She should have told me all that and more.

Chapter 22

During Kat's first few weeks back in Scotland she'd relished being able to hide in plain sight. Nobody knew her name, her face, nor anything else. There were a few old acquaintances from school dotted about, but it had been many years since she'd left Kendollich and even if she was remembered from those days, she doubted anyone would recognise her. She was also sure they wouldn't have thought of her at all, long forgotten, so should someone spot her, a familiar face, they probably wouldn't even remember her name.

Kat Dubois was a whole world away from those days. However, in the present day, with Clarke by her side, she knew they both stood out and her anonymity was now trashed because eventually everyone knows your name, your face, and more about your life than you yourself remember.

'I love this place, Kat. I can't understand why you never brought me here,' said Clarke as they walked through the main street of Kendollich, a place that was too big to be a village and too small to be a town.

'I told you before, it wasn't a conscious thing. It's an eight, nine-hour drive from London and same on the train. We were too busy living our lives.'

'But you had holidays.' It was more a question than a statement.

'I suppose…but it was a different life. I had no reason to come back. I'd shut the door.'

SHE'S NOT THERE

'And thrown away the key. I never even heard you mention Glendargie, or Dunkeld, or Kendollich. Not even Perth.'

'I had no reason to.' She was starting to get annoyed at his persistence.

An unkindness of ravens had gathered on a shed roof in the tearoom garden. Kat watched them dotting about, pecking and shuffling and cawing, snatching up yesterday's stale stotties that had been thrown for them. The cackle and caw of the birds filled her with a sense of unease. Wasn't it also a conspiracy of ravens? Kat thought of the lives of the people in the town. Everyone thought they knew everything about everyone and there was a kind of acceptance of people's flaws. Everyone was broken, and Kendollich had their own kind of broken that you didn't get in a bigger place where no one knew anything, nor wanted to. You could get away with much more in a larger place. It wasn't that it didn't go on in the bigger places, it did, it was just better hidden. Hidden in plain view, like she had been until Clarke arrived. She had wanted it to last a little longer.

They walked through the town square, past the cenotaph, and up towards the cluster of shops on Lothian Street. Kat was seeing things through old eyes. She loved the way ferns grew from the crevices in the heavy stones that made up the aged man-made walls, now covered in moss, springy and tight and filled with dew, the delicate little rock flowers that found cracks to hook into and grow from, the caw of ravens rather than the coo of pigeons. She loved the brooding dark clouds and the heavy rains in winter, the way the river would rise and swell, and rush and tumble, taking no prisoners in its wake. She loved to be snowed in, no way out, and no way in, encompassed in a thick white blanket that would fold over the little town after a wild snowstorm, keeping them tucked away, tight, wrapped up and hidden, a small town put to sleep.

She also knew the sleepy little town could be a living nightmare.

'Beauty is so often skin deep, Clarke, whether it's a person or a place.'

He had a strange look on his face.

'You didn't know that?' Kat laughed out loud.

'What's funny?' Clarke looked at her, puzzled.

Kat looked at him and smiled. Such a lovely young man, so like his father. 'It's lovely to see you. I was just thinking about us being here, together, now. Me, investigating crime in this place' – she paused – 'I don't know what I was thinking, really.'

They linked arms and sauntered up the small bank and across the little bridge over the river to the old-fashioned supermarket, the butcher's shop, the post office, and the pub. Then came the undertakers.

The double fronted parlour was at the top of the High Street, the last in the row of shops. 'Graves' stood out on the frontispiece, grand and stated in silver against black woodwork, with an inlay of antique cream gloss, making the building look old-fashioned, but classy, nonetheless. Both windows were dressed in front of a light green blind. The one to the left showed a display of headstones, with a few examples of engraving styles and a little white cherub laying down with his chin resting on a hand. The other window offered buy now die later deals, a list of emergency contact details for the undertaker, and an assortment of flowers, vases, urns, with a separate display of what you could turn your loved one's ashes into.

The front door was magnificent in glossy black with a small glass window in the top quarter displaying opening and closing times. A designated car parking area lay to the side and stretched to the rear of the building. Kat guessed the turning circle was apt for two or three hearses and two or three cars. A large extension stretched behind the main shop and a set of extra wide doors hid the inner machinations. Kat presumed that's where the unmarked van would bring the bodies.

A man stood by a hearse, the doors wide open and car-washing materials on the ground beside him. He was dressed in undertaker's black and grey striped trousers, shiny black shoes, and a white shirt with its top buttons undone, his tie hanging loose. His jacket was flung onto the back seat of the vehicle. A radio played and an annoying tune with a repetitive beat was blaring out. He was stood smoking, scrolling through his phone.

Kat and Clarke entered the car park, their feet crunching on the light grey gravel. The man looked up. He could be an off-duty policeman, thought Kat. Many a retired cop turned to pallbearing, used to death and utilising otherwise often useless skills.

'Can I help you? The office is round the front,' he said, grinding his cigarette into the gravel with the heel of his shoe.

'I was after the boss,' said Kat.

'Not sure where is he. Polly's in the office. She can sort you out.' The man slipped his phone in his trouser pocket.

'Thanks.' As she left the car park, she cast her eyes over the hearse, the outbuildings, and the general set up. She took in the expanse of land at the rear, the road that led down to the school, and beyond that, a golf course. It was good stretch of open space. A cluster of houses lay further up the street but set back and off the road. Opposite the funeral home was a small health centre with a pharmacy, a baby supply shop, and a car park. Behind that stood a small not-often-manned fire station, a stand-by station operated by reserves.

Polly Abbott, as told by the name plate on her desk, was one of life's bustlers, a cheerful looking woman, well-groomed with a chignon, and plastered pink cheeks. She spoke in lowered tones, not unpleasant and certainly assured and most becoming of an undertaker's receptionist. She portrayed confidence and Kat had trust in her efficiency with the recently bereaved, whether they wanted it or even realised.

'Mr Graves will be back at two o'clock. I can ask him to call you?' Polly smiled, tilting her head with the question.

'I'll call again,' said Kat, returning the tilt unconsciously.

'He has an appointment with a family at two-thirty. Are you sure I can't help you?'

Kat looked at the clock above Polly's head. Ten minutes before he was due back. They could loiter and catch him as he returned. 'Could we wait in the relatives' room?'

'Of course, yes. Is he expecting you?'

'No, we just called on the off-chance.'

'Is it about a recent bereavement?'

'No.' Kat smiled.

'Well, then, would you like a brochure? You really can you discuss anything with me. I may be able to help?' Polly's smile grew bigger, more insistent.

The phone rang and Polly stood to answer it. She waved them into the waiting room opposite the office.

The room was painted pale blue with inoffensive prints hanging from the walls, a fresh vase of pink and cream and orange flowers on a grand marble mantelpiece, and light pipe music playing faintly. A vanilla-scented candle was set on a shelf in the alcove, way below the level where it would cause singe marks.

Clarke picked up a magazine on Highland Estate Interiors. He flicked through it and gave a low whistle. 'People live like this?'

'Yes, they do.' Kat poked her head out of the room and peered down the hallway. Polly's office door was held open with a wedge, but the waiting room had a door-closing system to ensure privacy. The door at the end of the hall was like any other inner door in a Victorian house, wood panelled and painted white, and had it been in a house, it would have hidden perhaps a scullery, a study, kitchen, bathroom, or utility. In the funeral parlour she guessed it hid the viewing rooms, the preparation rooms, the fridges, and coffin storage, and no doubt the real office, not the public one.

'Why didn't you tell her you're Old Bill?'

'That would spoil the fun.' Kat took a seat on the settee and shuffled her back into the soft cream leather.

Polly opened the door. 'Can I get you a drink? Tea, coffee?'

Clarke opted for tea, Kat water.

Once Polly had retreated, Clarke said, 'Not like you to refuse a coffee, Kat.'

'I'm always wary of accepting hospitality somewhere like this. My first post-mortem was at Poplar Mortuary. It wasn't attached to a hospital, not back then. I was naïve, knew nothing.'

'I want the gory details.'

'You don't, trust me.'

'Go on, I love your stories.'

'Stop it, flattery is not the way with me, you know that. I don't need your charm either, I'm fond enough of you without it.'

Clarke laughed. 'I've missed this, Kat. Really missed it. Missed you.'

'I know. Me too you.' She paused for a moment, enjoying their easy banter. 'The mortuary...it looked like somebody's house from the outside. It was detached and set in its own land. The assistant looked really did look like he'd come from a horror film set, world-weary and wearing one of those black oiled aprons. It was seven o'clock in the morning and I was straight off night duty. We were waiting for the pathologist and I accepted a coffee. I was handed a large mug, chipped, and not particularly clean. I'd taken a few sips before I got the first hair. I'd drunk half of it before I saw the cup had mould on the inside.' She gagged at the memory. 'I've never accepted a cup of anything else in any mortuary since, unless it comes in a glass and I can see what's in it.'

Clarke's face twisted in disgust. 'Eurgh. Enough to give you nightmares.'

'It did.'

'Why didn't you tell her why you want to see Mr Graves?'

'Because I came for a recce more than anything else. I want to see how the place operates, get a feel for it, see the layout, what goes on, who's who. Once they know who I am, attitudes will change and so will the atmosphere. I'm not saying anybody is hiding anything, but it changes how people treat you. I can sit back and observe what's going on while we wait. Probably nothing, but I like the holistic approach. It's not just what they tell you, it's how they tell you, and what you see.'

'It's that complicated?'

'Not at all and it's quite natural after all these years. Good old-fashioned policing. From this day forward, people will know who I am and I'm going to stand out so I have to make the most of the anonymity. You only get this opportunity once, because when they know who you are, it can never happen again. Simple, really.'

'I get it. I think.'

'What did you notice earlier?'

'Nothing much ...' he pondered. 'The guy out back cleaning the hearse?'

'He wasn't so much cleaning it, was he? The cleaning materials were out but he was stood smoking. While the boss is away...'

'He might have been on a break?'

'He might. But I bet he wouldn't be stood smoking by the car in full view if the boss was around. People take liberties wherever and whenever they can. Did you notice anything about him?'

'No, not really. Older than you.'

She laughed. 'Charmed! His eyes, they looked a little rheumy, his nose a bit ruddy, veiny. I reckon he's a drinker. Or has been.'

'But how can you tell that?'

'I've seen enough hardened drinkers to recognise one. I'm not talking full-blown alcoholic, I mean people who like a tipple a bit more than they perhaps should. Did you notice anything else?'

'The radio was on.'

'Yes. Anything else?'

Clarke paused. The candle flickered and spat gently as the front door of the shop opened. The little bell above the door jangled.

A shadow passed by the frosted glass. Clarke shook his head. 'I can't think.'

'And I think that's our Mr Graves,' said Kat. 'Did you clock the camera above the double doors at the back of the car park? CCTV. And the undertaker, where he was standing, was hidden from the view, I bet.'

The door opened. A tall man in undertaker trousers, white shirt, and waistcoat, and a long- tailed black jacket stepped into the room. He had large hands with clean nails, grey slicked-back hair, with a parting slightly off to the left. Kat pitched him as late fifties. She stood and held her hand out to him.

He had a firm handshake. 'I'm Doug Graves, how can I help you?'

'Hello, Mr Graves, I'm DS Dubois, from Perth CID. I'm making some enquiries into a death, or rather, a cremation, and you were the undertaker.' She took her ID from her pocket and showed it to him. 'I'd like to make an appointment to come back again with my colleague to discuss it further,' she said.

'Oh yes! Aye, I've been expecting someone along.' He sat in the chair opposite the settee, hitching his trousers up at the knee. 'Rosemary Fraser?'

'Yes. When are you free?'

'I have five minutes now if that's any good?' He leaned back in the chair and checked his watch.

'Tomorrow would be better because I need to take a statement. I was just passing with my stepson and thought I'd call in, rather than phone. Introduce myself properly, ahead of the statement.'

'I'll have to check with Polly, see what's in the diary. I know I have a few commitments but I'm sure I can squeeze you in.' He stood and indicated for them to leave the room before him.

When he asked Polly to check the diary so DS Dubois could come back for a statement, the receptionist flustered her way through the thick A4 book, suddenly nervous. She looked at Kat and said, 'You

143

should have said, officer. I could have phoned Mr Graves to return immediately, rather than keep you waiting.'

'It's fine, Polly, it was nice to sit and have a few minutes' relaxation.' Kat smiled at the woman.

'Malcolm thought you were looking for a funeral plan, I'm sorry. He said he'd seen you, thought you were relations of a deceased, come from outside the area to make arrangements, as he didn't recognise either of you.' She looked at them, one to the other. 'We didn't know you were the police.'

'No reason you would. It's fine. Malcolm's the undertaker who was outside when we arrived?'

'Yes. Och, he wasn't gossiping.' She flushed. 'Malcolm's my husband. He usually cleans the cars on Wednesdays if we don't have any services.'

'Then we may need to speak with Malcolm too, at some point.'

Polly arranged an appointment for them with Mr Graves in two days' time, the first opportunity when they were both available. As they left, Kat noticed the hearse was parked up outside the front door, spotless. Malcolm and the cleaning gear had gone.

She hadn't been to the park for over a week. It was easy to not go when she was poorly. Or pretending to be. She'd learnt how to pretend very well, so well that she wasn't sure if she was really faking or really poorly.

Tomorrow was a school day and the poorly days had run out, run away like milk that turned sour, that Ma poured away in fat clumps like the clumps of sick that got caught in the back of her throat.

Maybe Ma might come for her after school, but she didn't think so and she didn't like to ask. Da had to work and Ma had to look after granny.

SHE'S NOT THERE

The last time she'd seen him he'd said, 'I'll see you again soon, my pretty, very soon' and it was there in his voice, in the way that he said it, that gave her the shiver of fear.

She was confused. She didn't feel pretty. She knew he was lying. She knew he didn't mean it, not really, and she was glad. She didn't want to be pretty for him. She didn't want to be pretty, ever. Pretty wasn't good but that was okay because she was bad, full of bad, like the fingernails she'd bitten off. Like the ends of her hair that hung in pigtails that she chewed so much that when the strands flapped against her chin, they were prickly. Like the skin she picked off her lips when they cracked, all dry and whipped.

She knew she couldn't not go through the park on her way home and she knew that when she did, he'd be there, waiting in the bushes, waiting for her to tiptoe by, her eyes tight shut and ears pushed out from the inside so she couldn't hear, but she would still know his rustling, his low whistling, his gruff voice calling to her. If she couldn't see and couldn't hear then she might, just might, get away without him seeing her or hearing her and she could pretend she wasn't there, and he might not know she was. Maybe.

Chapter 23

Kat had the file ready for her meeting with the DI and the Chief Superintendent who had come over from Dundee especially. Statements, pathology, policy log, actions, mug of cold coffee. She looked at the office clock. Five to eleven.

She had to be at the crematorium no later than twelve thirty. Plenty of time. She called over to Guy. 'Ready?'

Guy was reading a printout that had arrived in the post a few minutes ago. 'Kat, you need to see this.'

'Hurry up, the guv's waiting. We'll walk while we talk.'

Guy took the bundle of papers from Kat and handed her the A4 sheet. It was a lab report. 'You remember when you told me to check then double check everything? Go the extra mile? Well, I thought I'd follow up on a few things, like the Frasers...'

As they climbed four sets of stairs, Kat read, squinting. She held the paper further out, then a bit closer in. 'I really must book an eye test. Still free here?'

'Yes, get in quick, they won't be for much longer.' Guy pointed to a section in the last third of the report. 'This is the important bit. I got the DNA profiles checked against each other.'

Kat read the paragraph. And read it again. 'What exactly does this mean for us?'

'I'm not entirely sure ... could be significant ... I think?'

146

'Turns it up a notch though, doesn't it?' Kat stopped on the next landing and looked at him. 'We're going have to think this through. Carefully. But first, the Chief, and not a word yet.'

'Got it!'

Kat wasn't prepared for the Chief and his point of view. There was never an endless pot of money, she knew that, never enough manpower and demands always exceeded need, but connections and systems meant there was usually someone somewhere who could help. She was learning quickly that things were different now.

Detective Chief Superintendent David Shaftoe looked the kind of boss who might squeal if his hands got dirty. She knew his type. He was a far stretch from the old-fashioned kind of senior officer she'd learnt her craft from and she'd be surprised if he had twelve years in the job. She suspected he was a fast tracker, a spokesperson, more a politician than policeman.

Once Kat had finished relaying the facts, he jumped straight in.

'You see, DS Dubois, this isn't even a murder, is it? The first coat of paint is dry on this now and we need the second layer to bring it to a close. There's some misunderstanding somewhere along the line. There has to be a straightforward explanation and I would have thought with your expertise, you'd have found it by now. We haven't time for dragging heels.'

'We are not. It doesn't help that every enquiry takes us up down the A9 like we're on elastic, and what with the road works and accidents, half our time is spent travelling. That's without going across in the other direction to Dundee. Add in waiting time for toxicology and the like, people on leave, others with court cases, and the time disappears.'

'I always get excuses and I don't want excuses. I need results. I would have thought a case like this, you'd have been finished in a week, tops. What are we looking at here? Preventing the lawful disposal of a body? What's the difficulty for a wonder-cop all the way from the Met?' He sneered at her and turned to Ken Munro. 'I would have thought, Inspector, that our hot-shot detective here would have had a case like this done and dusted without me having to blink and here I am having to take a trip specially to chivvy up an investigation that should have been across my desk, stamped, and filed by now.'

Guy spoke. 'Sir, Glendargie is a tight-knit community, one we can't go storming in and ripping apart.'

'Oh, I know Glendargie, Constable. I know it's a different world, exactly the sort of place we need to rip apart. It's like a festering boil, all fancy-pants houses, and people who like to live up the hill, thinking they're better than the rest, when really, it's a pimple on the arse of the district. Drugs, sex rings, youth crime. Get in there and find out what the hell happened and get the case closed. Someone knows. Someone always knows.'

Kat felt her face redden and the inside of her ears beat, like they did when she was angry. She swallowed down her indignation and considered her words before trusting herself.

'With respect, sir,' she hesitated. 'We have to look at the wider picture. We have to consider not just the disposal of a body. What I need to establish is not just the who. We need to find out how the remains of a body wound up beneath a tree and who put them there. And why. We know who she is, and we know when she died. We also know how she died but we need to establish what happened after that. More importantly' – she looked at Guy, then the DI, who had so far remained silent, 'we need to know whose body was in that coffin and cremated in her place.'

The DCS scoffed. 'I think you're ahead of yourself there, Sergeant. Probably nobody was in the coffin. Three bags of sharp sand, is my guess.'

'There has to have been a body. The crematorium staff would know if there wasn't. It's impossible for a body not to have been in that coffin.'

'I don't think so, officer.'

148

SHE'S NOT THERE

'I do. Do you know anything about the cremation process, sir? There's no room for mistakes like that.'

Shaftoe held up the palm of his hand. 'Enough. I've listened to what you've got. I know what you haven't. I need closure on this and soon. There's a conveyor belt of cases coming in. There's an infanticide I need to check the progress on, so I have to see the child protection team. And Harris has some leads on the distillery thefts. A quarter of a million pounds worth of whisky now stolen.' He stood, long legs and sharp suit, which he smoothed down with hands that were pale, long, and soft.

Of course. Whisky was king, any money more important than people. Kat looked at him. She didn't like men with hands that were soft. She stood too, refusing to be intimidated by any man. He wouldn't last a month in charge of a major enquiry in the Met. Big fish, small pond, full of his own importance, no doubt an expert in self-promotion, making a career out of others' hard work. She knew the type, and knew he'd take on an important role for a year, max, just to say he'd done the job and put it on his CV. But he had no background, or backbone, and no hands-on experience. He left that to 'his team' but would take the credit in a heartbeat. There'd been many like him and he wasn't a career cop, he was a career climber. Nothing more than ivy, serves no real purpose, but looks good, and gets everywhere.

Guy held up the lab report they'd received that morning and looked like he was about to say something. Kat whipped it from his hands. 'It's okay, detective. We'll get straight on it.'

She turned back to the chief. 'Right, sir, DC Lynn is on paternity leave soon, but I'll keep DI Munro informed of my progress. I'm sure I'll have it sorted and on your desk by the time he's back.' She gathered the rest of the papers that Shaftoe hadn't even looked at. 'I'll see you in the car, DC Lynn.' She nodded at her DI. 'I'm off to the crem, guv. I'll see you when I get back to the office.'

149

Kat turned to leave. As she touched the door handle, the DCS called after her, 'I close the meeting, officer. Perhaps a trip to the undertaker would be prudent?'

She turned back to him. 'Yes, sir, I'm seeing him tomorrow. All in hand. And I thought you had terminated our time. Don't you have an infanticide to deal with?' She opened the door.

'Remember, DS Dubois. Or is it Dubious? You can't kill a dead man. Or woman. It's not a murder.'

Kat felt like stomping down the stairs but didn't. Pompous git. Kill a dead man. Who the hell did he think he was? She knew more about practical policing in her little fingernail than he could ever imagine. Silver cufflinks, winkle pickers, and a cravat. A fucking cravat! Did he even have a clue?

Guy called behind her. 'Kat! Hold up. Not so fast. Shaftoe's giving old Munro a bollocking. I don't know what's up with him. The DI would have had your back, once upon a time.'

'I'm not bothered about Shaftoe. I know his type. I've got the measure of him. He hasn't a bloody clue. Sand in the coffin. As if. We do need to go back and speak with the crematorium though. First things first coffee, and crem.' She laughed. 'And then the Frasers. Need to be a bit tactical with that, I think.'

'Do you think he knows?' asked Guy.

'Who? Drew?'

'Yes, you think he knows Rosemary was his mother?'

Chapter 24

Kat pulled up into a corner of the car park at Perth Crematorium dead on twelve thirty. The stragglers from the twelve o'clock service hung around, saying their goodbyes to each other, all wearing black and sad faces.

'Are you ready for this, sarge?' asked Guy.

'Let's just sit a moment. I don't like to intrude on others' grief.'

They watched the mourners climb into their cars with tears and sorrow. When the last car had gone, they stepped into the bright and fresh air. Kat snapped the key fob to lock the car.

'What do you think it'll be like, sarge? To see a cremation in all its glory?'

'I was about to ask you the same,' Kat replied. 'I'm interested but not sure I want to be. It's different to a PM. This seems so much more … personal … somehow. A PM has a purpose for the investigation, a cremation has a purpose for the person, for their family. We need to do it though.' She sighed. 'We need to know so we can be sure there's no chance of tampering. Once we've established that, then we go back to the beginning.'

The back doors of the building opened and Mr Carr, the head honcho, beckoned them forth. 'This way, officers,' he called.

They entered the building and followed him along a plain corridor, into and through what looked like a utility room, and into a small office. Carr lowered his voice. 'We're just about to start. Ross, our technician, he's waiting for you. He'll explain everything. Anything you need to know, just ask. I hope this is of assistance.'

'How long will it take?' asked Guy.

'Ninety minutes, two hours, give or take, depending on various factors.'

Kat wondered at the various factors. She looked around here. It was clean, bright, and crisp.

No smell of death, no lingering aroma of corpses like the mortuary, just plain, bland. So far.

'Ahh, here's Ross now. Ross Thomas. He's the technician who conducted Rosemary Fraser's cremation.' Carr made the introductions. 'Do you need me any longer? I have another service to oversee but if you're still here I'll catch up with you later.'

'That's fine, Mr Carr. As we're going to be a while, I'll take a full statement from Mr Thomas today, save us coming back again. He can explain the technical stuff we discussed on our last visit and hopefully we won't have to bother you again.'

The process was mesmerising. By the end of the cremation, they knew there was no way a body could be missing from a coffin without being noticed. It just couldn't happen. And certainly, any bags of sharp sand would be detected.

Guy asked the questions throughout. 'No bags of sand instead of a body?'

'Nope. Not at all. I'd have to see a body, or I'd stop the process.'

'You couldn't get two bodies in one coffin?'

'No. Not possible. I'd see two skulls, all those limbs. It would be obvious.' Ross Thomas had a West Scotland accent that Kat struggled with. He reminded her of a friend she'd made many years ago on holiday on the Isle of Bute. They became pen-pals in the days when people wrote letters, not Internet messages. It had been the only run-free holiday she'd ever had, the summer she could forget everything and just be, without any fear or fright. She hadn't thought of that holiday for a very long time. His voice had triggered it. Triggered her. It wasn't his fault and she knew something was brewing, had been brewing, ever since she'd returned 'home'.

'And that's for the metal scraps, the hip replacements, metal plates, and such. The stuff that doesn't burn down.' Ross pointed to a large, open-topped dustbin.

From inside a tunnel, she heard Guy calling her.

'Kat? Kat? Are you all right?'

She felt someone take her arm and she was told to sit down. She was led to a chair in the corner of the small over-heated room.

'You look peaky. I'll get you some water,' said Guy.

From far away Ross Thomas said, 'Sorry, I can't leave my post but the girls in the back office can sort you out.'

Guy left the room.

Kat sat, disorientated. A peculiar feeling washed over her. She looked up to the ceiling and noticed it was in need of plastering. She saw a dusty cobweb in the corner, and the bare light bulb looked too bright, like it might burst, pop into sparticles, something she called sparks of light as a little girl. She could sense rather than smell the odour of the man in the room with her. It wasn't unpleasant, he smelled of soap, of hard work, of man, but the smells curdled her stomach.

Kat knew what was happening. She was having what she termed a displacement attack. It was her word for the thing that sometimes happened, but it hadn't happened for a very long time. Now that it had, she wondered how it hadn't occurred sooner.

She'd developed a smart technique of shutting things away, of concentrating on other things around her, transporting herself, disassociation, her mind in a different place to her body. The black boxes in her head had long ago locked those things away. When she shut off one sense, her other senses kicked in, took over, heightened her surroundings, her awareness, and kept her safe from the bad things.

SHE'S NOT THERE

Woah.

Kat felt her herself shift, her body jolt, her face flush, and she felt like she might vomit. She wished she'd had more than a couple of biscuits but there hadn't been time for lunch.

Ross Thomas plunged an empty rubbish bin between her legs just in time.

SHE WATCHED THE bee, one step, two step, three step, fly. Fly, fly away. She imagined it drizzled honey on her bare leg as it climbed. It was such a beautiful feeling, exciting and daring, and she'd hardly dared to breathe when it landed on her. She hardly dared to breathe much at all as she hid in the magnolia bushes thinking how long it would be before she could make a run for it.

She knew he'd be looking for her because she hadn't seen him for a few weeks. She could smell him. She could always smell him; turpentine, sweat, and tobacco. The last time there was a tang of Brylcreem on him. He had a new haircut and she liked him even less, if that was possible, because it made him look much younger with more fat in his face, full ruddy chubby cheeks that pushed out from under his eyes and made him look like a stuffed hamster, all pouches and pricked ears, waiting to pounce on her with his horrible horsey teeth. She imagined he spent his life pining for her, but she was nothing, nobody, and she wasn't pretty, not at all, no matter how many times he said she was.

She counted out he was seventeen, maybe eighteen. A proper man. A full-sized man. He had left the big school and kids didn't go there anymore after they were fifteen or sixteen, they went to a different place or got a job. He didn't get on the bus to Perth anymore because he had told her he had a 'prentaship as a painter with the council and he was going to paint all the houses near where she lived so he could keep his big eye on her.

154

SHE'S NOT THERE

When he said that he closed one eye and put his open eye all wide and big and dark, dark brown, right up close to her face. He said he would be painting the houses after he'd painted the swings and the roundabout and the witch's hat and the shute and the shuggy horse because that was his job now. When he finished in the park, he would be painting all the houses in her close and they would all have blue doors, so they all looked the same. But he said if that Missus at number twenty-five complained again, she'd be seeing red as well as wearing it, just like her mother would so she'd have to do what he said if she didn't want her mother wearing red.

She first thought he meant he would throw paint over them all but now she wasn't sure because she'd been thinking hard about it. She thought he might mean something else because when he put his hands around her neck and squeezed them tight and counted out ten seconds, she saw black, and then white speckled stars, and then red ones. She thought he meant he would do the same to the Missus at number twenty-five and then do the same to Ma. She couldn't let that happen and if it did then it would be her fault. She didn't want Ma to have his hands on her neck and for her to see red so she had to let him do it to her and not to Ma.

But he had to find her first.

Chapter 25

They stood on the doorstep of the Fraser house. Drew Fraser's latest excuse was that he had a sore throat. Could be Covid, he coughed down the phone.

They were all vaxxed and she said she'd take her chances. She'd taken worse. A child was crying, and someone pulled the upstairs curtains back. Then came the thud-thudding of someone running downstairs. The front door flung open.

'Yes?' The accusatory tone flew from him like a dart.

'Can we come in, please?' she asked Drew Fraser.

'It's not convenient. I said I'd call once I felt better.'

'We really need to speak with you,' she persisted.

Drew's frown deepened.

'It's about the murder enquiry of your aunt.'

'Murder?' He almost screeched. 'What do you mean, murder?' His visibly paled as he stepped back. 'She wasnae murdered!'

Alison Fraser shouted from inside the house, 'Is that the milkman, love? I owe him for the month.'

'No,' he called back. 'It's not the milkman. It's the Polis.' He stepped out of the house in his socks, no shoes, and pulled the door behind him, careful not to close it. 'What are you talking about? My aunt wasn't murdered.'

SHE'S NOT THERE

Kat spoke light as pinpricks as she looked at him, directly into the eye. 'Wasn't she? Oh.'

The child cried again. Kat folded her arms. Guy stood, hands slouched into his suit pockets, saying nothing but tapping his foot. Both of them looked at Fraser.

Finally, he relented. 'You'd better come in, but excuse the mess, it's a bigger tip than usual.' He turned and kicked the door open and strode back inside.

Lorna sat on the settee. She didn't look happy. Her thin hair hung lank, her long face sad, and black-framed glasses slid down her nose. A toddler was sitting on her lap and he was restless. His face was flushed and he looked hot, and no doubt as unwell as his grandfather.

Kat could see through the open door into the kitchen. Alison Fraser lay a tea towel over the lip of the sink. She filled the kettle. Flicked it on. Turned to face the room.

'Oh!' She hesitated and looked surprised to see them.

'Hello,' said Kat. 'Sorry to intrude. There's been a development.'

Alison shot a look to her husband. 'Right.' She picked up another tea towel and dried her hands. 'Tea? I've just put the kettle on.'

The child mewled and Lorna looked at him. Drew looked at Lorna, hands on his hips. Alison stood on the spot. The air was tangible, sharp. Nobody moved, nobody spoke. It reminded Kat of a mannequin sketch, popular a few years ago, when people would act scenes for charity.

The second hand of the clock tick-tocked.

The sound of the kettle boiling bubbled in the background.

The breathing of the toddler sounded like a rattle.

Drew broke the silence. 'So, what now?'

Lorna stood and said, 'I'll take Cam upstairs.'

157

Kat smiled at her as she left the room. Once she'd gone, she turned to Drew. 'I don't know why you've been avoiding me, I thought you'd be coming to me asking for answers.'

He splayed his hands and shrugged.

'Shall we sit down?' Kat asked.

Drew and Alison looked at each other. Drew nodded.

When everyone was seated, Kat began. 'We've confirmed with the doctor that he signed Rosemary's death certificate as lung carcinoma. The crematorium has confirmed they carried out her service and cremation …or believed they had …but there's gaps.'

'What do you mean? Gaps?' asked Alison.

'Well, obviously a body doesn't appear like that. It doesn't disappear from a coffin.'

Alison put her hand on her husband's arm. 'Drew and I knew there'd be an enquiry. I can't begin to imagine…it's just…well, so bizarre.' She turned to Kat. 'Do you have any idea what happened? What it's all about?'

Kat appreciated Alison was taking charge, controlling the situation, trying to lessen the mood and be calm in the hope her husband might take her cue. Kat looked at the large canvas of the two girls, Lorna, and Mary, and back at Drew. Kat noticed his lower jaw had a slight malocclusion, a little protuberance that showed when he held his mouth in certain positions. Just like Rosemary. Mary had the same and looked much like her father whereas Lorna resembled her mother more. Those little traits, the genetic peculiarities, they were the clues if you chose to look for them.

Drew piped up with a challenge. 'I want to know how this terrible, awful thing happened. What are you doing about it?'

Kat turned to him. 'We're doing everything we can at the moment. We'll get to the bottom of it, trust me.'

Drew nodded. 'I'm sure you will. Dead people don't walk out of coffins.'

'The coroner needs to release Rosemary's remains for burial, or cremation, whatever you prefer. It can be done once they're satisfied there's nothing to prevent a proper disposal. We have no objections. In the meantime, the investigation is continuing.'

The front door burst open. 'S'only me! I cadged a lift off of Hamish's dad's tractor,' shouted Mary. 'I've just got owned by the headmaster! Proper showed me up he did. My skirt's torn and ripped to pieces and dirty, so I've come home to get changed. Will you give me a lift back, Dad?' Her voice sung with the innocence of a fourteen-year-old. She stopped short when she saw Kat and Guy. 'Oh!'

'Hello, Mary.' Kat smiled at her.

Mary looked from her father, to Kat. 'What's going on?'

'Just talking about your aunt,' said Kat.

Alison said, 'Go upstairs and get changed, love. Tell me about it later. Dad will take you back soon.'

As Mary left the room, Kat asked, 'I see there's bulldozers up near where Rosemary was found. Do you know what's going on up there?'

Drew shrugged. 'I don't know. It's Struan's land. I've heard he's selling it off.'

'I heard that too,' said Kat. 'And I also heard that you've already arranged a cremation for next week?' She caught a glance pass between Alison and Drew.

'No, we haven't. Not yet. We've asked about it, eager to do right by her, but like you said, we have to wait for permission first, don't we?'

'What will you do with her ashes?' Kat asked, looking at him.

Before Drew could answer Mary poked her head around the door and said, 'Putting them under the tree, ain't we, Dad?'

He looked at his daughter. 'We haven't thought about it.'

'Where did you scatter them last time?' enquired Kat, light, as if the question was irrelevant, an aside, a sudden thought.

Drew turned to her, and hesitated before saying, 'We didn't.'

Alison rescued him. 'We never quite got round to collecting her. We kept meaning to but what with the roadworks …and the weather …and making a special trip to Perth to collect her, it was something we kept meaning to get around to, and we've had so much going on … so Mr Graves suggested they were scattered in the remembrance garden at the crematorium. So that's what we agreed. Isn't it, Drew?'

Kat wasn't taken in. Alison's ready rambling, the forgetting, the remembrance garden … Rosemary meant more to them than that. They didn't get them because they knew they weren't Rosemary's ashes. She was sure of it. So, whose ashes were they? And why?

'We haven't decided where to scatter her … down by the river maybe, a bit here and there … but I'm not sure on the permissions you need to scatter ashes. I don't want to break any regulations or anything.'

'The tree where she was found, was that a significant place for your aunt?' asked Kat.

Drew Fraser shrugged at the same time as his daughter said, 'Yeah.'

Alison pointed to Mary and waved her finger for her to go upstairs. 'Go and get changed.'

Drew Fraser's statement regarding his aunt's death and funeral was short and straight to the point, he didn't vacillate like most people when relaying a tale. He answered questions and offered nothing else.

As they walked to their cars parked up in the lorry park, Kat turned to Guy. 'Didn't make it easy, did he?'

Guy kicked dry leaves along the footpath.

'There's something. It's a bit like digging into sand. The more you dig, the more the hole fills up.'

Drew had told them his aunt had been diagnosed with a number of cancers and she knew she was dying. She refused to go into the hospice or a nursing home and Drew and Alison and their girls looked after her in her own home until the day she died. Drew and

Alison had been with her, along with a community nurse, when she died. She'd told the family what arrangements she wanted a long while before she passed, and was quite specific on it, Drew said. Graves the Undertakers had come to the house and taken her body away. Her cremation was booked at Perth a short while later and it was as well attended as expected for someone in their mid 70s who had little family and a scattering of friendships. She didn't leave much in the way of inheritance and as her only relative, Drew was the beneficiary. They received about thirty thousand pounds and it wasn't that important to him, as he'd rather have his aunt than her money because she'd been like a mother to him. That was all the information he could – or would – give.

'Why I don't get is why is he so narky? Did you notice, he never asked us anything? Why not? Why isn't he questioning it more?' Kat mooted to Guy.

'I dunno. I take it you didn't want to tell him about the DNA just yet?'

'Absolutely not! Not at this stage. Let's leave that a little longer. I've a feeling we can use it to our advantage. When the time comes.'

'He's an odd one for sure. Want me to confirm what happened to the ashes that weren't Rosemary Fraser's?'

'Yes, check if they were actually scatted at the crem.'

'Can you get DNA from ashes do you think?' asked Guy.

'I was thinking something similar. Tell you what I do know, though.'

'Go on?'

'I think Mary Fraser knows more than her family would like her to.'

'Good luck with that, Sarge. You'll have to get past her mother and father first.'

'Don't you think it's telling when she said about putting the ashes beneath the tree? She was put there on purpose, I know it,' said

Kat. It started to spit with rain. She looked up to the grey sky. 'Guy, give me a good old straightforward murder. I know where I'm at with them. How are you getting on with the missing persons enquiries?'

'It's a bit difficult when I don't know what I'm looking for. There's people missing from years ago and those more recently disappeared, but what, or rather who, am I looking for?' He shrugged. 'You don't suppose she became a burden, do you? And they finished her off themselves?'

'No, we've covered that,' said Kat. 'Why, if they had finished her off, go to the lengths of burying her in the ground? She's better off cremated.'

'And we've ruled out Ross Thomas as being involved? Not telling us fibs?'

'As far as we can, I think he's legit. Nothing to suggest otherwise. Yet.'

They stood by their cars for a moment, musing on the possibilities for the umpteenth time.

'Just a thought, Kat, did we check with Graves about the other funerals around the date of Rosemary's? Was there a burial around the same time?'

She looked at him. 'I didn't check. Lax of me. And I like your thinking … I think. There could be a coffin buried with no body in it, with whoever's body it should be, swapped with hers?'

'Yes, but then why go to those lengths? Why not give her a burial in the first instance? Why cremate her?'

'Exactly. Rosemary knew she was dying and I presume she made her wishes known. But we need to check. This is a head wreck. I need to think about it more, get it straight in my head.' Kat looked at her watch. 'It's half past two, pointless me driving back to the nick now, only to drive back up in a couple of hours. I'm going to do some more enquiries up here. Will you let the boss know I'll be in early in the morning?'

162

'I would, but he's got another of his mysterious appointments this afternoon.'

Munro was distracted. Whatever he had going on, he was keeping to himself, but at least it was keeping him off her back. She wondered if Clarke was up for a walk. There was a tree she needed to have a conversation with.

HE LOOKED AT her with piercing eyes that hurt. She didn't know whether to nod, to cry, to shake her head, or do something else altogether. What she really wanted to do was to run.

Run, run, away, far, far away.

'I said, can you see what it is yet?'

She squinted her eyes at him, but really wanted to close them.

He laughed and said, 'That's right, come in for a closer look. Can you see what it is?'

She didn't want to see what it was. Her face burnt and her eyes watered. Her head went around and around, and she felt like she might fall over.

'Can you see it wriggling? It wants to say hello. Come here and say hello.' He pulled her arm so that her feet stuttered closer to him.

She was so close that she could feel his breath on her face and taste his breath on her tongue. When he laughed it felt like a gust of wind that might blow her over. He took her hand into his bear paw and plunged it into his half-zipped jacket. 'There! Have a feel.'

Her hand touched something furry, something moving, wriggling. She pulled her hand back and he pushed it further into his jacket. 'Say hello! Be a good girl. Do what I say.'

SHE'S NOT THERE

She felt something rough lick her fingers and she squeaked. It was a bit tickly and a little prickly, like soft sandpaper that her Da used to score the woodwork with before he painted it, but not as rough. It didn't feel scratchy. It felt soft and warm and a little bit wet. She opened her eyes and looked into a tiny pair of blinking blue eyes that made her think she was looking into her own. She squeaked again, this time not afraid or frightened or scared. This time with a teeny bit of delight.

'Can you see what it is yet?'

She could. She could see clearly what it was, and she wanted to hold the furry bundle into her, to squeeze it tight into her chest, to take it away from inside his jacket and hold it to make it safe. She wanted to look after it.

'You can take it home if you like.'

'I can't.'

'I've told you before. Stop saying "I can't". You sound like a baby. You can. And you will. You will do what I say. See?'

She nodded. She would take it home but maybe not show anyone. They might not like it. They might not let her keep it and then it would have to go away. Maybe she could say she found it? All by itself in the park? In the bushes?

He pulled the kitten from his jacket and thrust the mewling animal at her. She grabbed it, her arms, and elbows, and hands, and fingers juggling the poor little kitty-cat. She felt his fur touch her lips and she sniffed him. The little kitty wriggled in her arms and she gently managed to wriggle him into the crook of her left elbow, like she did with her dolly. She tickled him under his chin and on his chest in between his top paws and soon the kitten was purring like a tractor engine.

'See?' he snapped. 'See?'

She wasn't sure what it was she was supposed to see but she nodded anyway. He liked it when she nodded. When she saw.

'See what I bring for you? The gifts I give you. Sweeties, kitties, nice little presents for my nice little girl.'

He stroked her hair with a finger. She couldn't help it when she turned her head, and she knew straight away that he wouldn't like that she did that. He took his hand away and stared at her and she looked down.

'I've told you. Be grateful for what you receive. Haven't I told you that?'

She nodded and kept tickling the kitten on his chest in between his paws.

'Now you take kitty-cat home, and you tell your ma that you found him, and you want to keep him.'

She nodded.

'Got that, precious?' She nodded again, concentrating on kitty-cat. 'And you can come back tomorrow and tell me how he's doing. What shall we call him?'

'Smoky. Smoky Joe,' she blurted out. She had her own name for him, and she didn't want to share it, she'd keep that to herself. Kitty-cat had light brown kitten fur and blue eyes just like her and he reminded her of the colour of trees and logs that they chopped up for putting on the fire.

'Smoky Joe,' she said again.

He smiled. 'I like it.' He nodded and she knew he was happy with her. 'Smoky Joe he is. And you promise to look after him?'

'Yes, yes, I will. I promise.' It was the most genuine promise she'd ever given him. Smoky Joe was someone like her, something that needed protecting, something that didn't need to be with him. He pulled her closer by her jumper, crushing Smoky Joe between them.

'And if you don't look after him, you know what will happen?'

She looked at him, at his face and into his eyes, and it made her feel cold.

He stepped back and kept looking at her as he ran a finger across his neck and whispered, 'Clitch.'

SHE'S NOT THERE

Chapter 26

The mountains had a bleached look, covered in snow that hadn't yet melted. The rains had passed, rolled on, along with the thunder, and the low sun bounced off the snow,

Clarke loved exploring and was intrigued with the Fortingall Yew tree, the oldest tree in the United Kingdom, at around nine thousand years old, and loved the folklore that Pontius Pilate had been born in the shade of the tree and was said to have played there as a child. Kat was well versed in the myth but loved to see it through his eyes. The tree was changing sex from male to female because of environmental stress and Clarke liked that.

'Totally fascinating, Kat,' he gushed. 'Like the environment is in synch with society. Not that gender is a stress issue but I love that acknowledgment. Not that it's so good for the double-gendered fish though.'

They were halfway up the hillside to the other tree, the Fraser tree, as Kat had dubbed it, when a gunshot echoed through the air. Then another.

Clarke grabbed Kat's arm and she could see his fear. She laughed. 'Don't worry. It's only a farmer, or gamekeeper.'

'Doing what? Shooting rabbits?'

'Maybe. Too early for pheasants. A rogue dog chasing sheep maybe, or shooting deer, could be anything.'

'It's odd after spending my entire life in the city.'

167

'You need to come back in summer for the Highland Games. So much fun!'

Kat was fourteen again, staying at Brenda's house, sneaking a few plastic bottles of warm cider into the Dunkeld Games on the final night. She still insisted it was the helter-skelter that caused her to puke.

'Do they really throw the haggis?'

'Oh, aye, and toss the caber! Highland dancing, sheep dog trials, the best-looking coo, tug-o-war, the lot. The hazy days of Scottish summers and ceilidhs and pipe bands.'

Clarke took hold of her arm and raised it above his. He moved under the arch and said, 'You'll have to teach me the Gay Gordon.'

'My ceilidh days are over, but you'll have no trouble finding a lady friend to teach you.' She wasn't sure if he'd prefer a man friend but would wait for him to disclose, should he wish. She'd never ask but had long wondered, as had his dad, if Clarke was gay.

'Kat!' He lightly pummelled her in the back.

The sun was warm, the air fresh, little clouds of midges gathered here and there. This tree, the Fraser tree, was significant, Kat was sure of it. She stood under one side, under its branches, Clarke next to her. She looked down onto the small town, the Tay winding in curves and drops, the riverbank lush and flush, a conglomeration of activity taking place. Canoeists and kayakers criss-crossed the rapids at two training points. There were a couple of spots where overgrowth interfered with the water line and a small landslide had altered the flow with a violent struggle of rocks, rubble, and soil. A few of the larger riverside cottages and grand houses had exclusive gardens that led down to the river at its widest point. Privately-owned rowing boats were moored here and there, bobbing about, tethered with no escape. The Tay held an appreciation of beauty, far from the working river of the Thames, which was thick black and tarry and full of city grime.

Clarke interrupted her thoughts and said, 'Try giving it a hug, Kat. It might talk to you.'

'I don't know what it would say but I'm intrigued.'

'Maybe your lady came here to look down onto the people living their lives, on her life. It is a magnificent view. Peaceful.'

She watched the town going about the day, the cars manoeuvring along the tracks and roads, people going about their affairs, schoolchildren leaving for the day, builders constructing new houses, sheep and the cows dotting the fields, chewing the cud…their world going about its business.

Kat looked back at the tree and fingered the gnarls and twists and turns of the hard, solid bark. Maybe that's just what it was, a quiet spot, or a place for romance, a getaway with a picnic, or a bottle of wine, maybe both. Kat knew Rosemary did have a love affair because she had a child, but with who? Maybe they met here? Perhaps it was significant to her, to them? Maybe she wanted to be buried in this spot but knew she'd never get permission. What if the family had substituted her body with an animal? A deer? A cow? A calf? There were plenty of animals around to cull to replace her. Though maybe a cow would be too heavy and too big to go into a coffin. She'd have to check how possible that theory was with the undertaker and the crematorium. But why not scatter those ashes here like they're going to do this time? It's nothing to scatter ashes of an animal. Was it a significant point?

'Boo!'

Kat elicited a scream as she spun round.

An arm reached out and touched her shoulder.

Clarke grabbed hold of her arm to steady her as Jed Gillespie held on to her shoulder. 'Kat! I'm so sorry. I didn't mean to scare you. I was out for a walk and saw you and thought I'd say hello.'

Her heart pounded like it would burst. She turned and leant back against the tree, rested her hands on her knees, and took deep breaths. 'For god's sake, yes, you did … give me a shock. I didn't see you.'

'That was sort of the point of the 'boo'. I'm really sorry, Kat.'

She composed herself. 'It's okay. I was just thinking, lost in thought.'

'I could tell. I should have just called out. Sorry.' He did look sorry.

'Do you work together?' asked Clarke.

'My sorry this time, I'll introduce you,' said Kat. 'Clarke, this is Jed Gillespie, Jed, this is my stepson, Clarke.' She could tell Clarke was excited to meet him. His eyes lit up and she knew he was itching to talk to him. 'Clarke's a big fan, Jed.'

Jed shook Clarke's hand, said he was pleased to meet him.

'I'd love a chat sometime if you don't mind? I'm studying literature at uni and I love meeting authors. Especially those I love reading.'

'Of course! We can grab a coffee … or a pint, though not sure I qualify for the literature stakes,' Jed laughed. 'Let's sort something out before you go back.' He turned to Kat. 'How are you getting on with the case?'

'We're not, not really,' said Kat. Not that she wanted to give him much information despite there not being much to say.

'I've been thinking, the dead don't walk …'

'Funny that, exactly what my boss said,' said Kat.

Jed either didn't pick it up or chose to ignore her sarcasm. 'If you wanted to get rid of a body, what would you do? You'd bury it, but there's no need to bury her. From what I know, it was a perfectly legitimate death … but what better way to disguise a murder? Cremation would destroy all the evidence.'

'I know that,' said Kat, wondering where he was going with it. She'd been thinking along the same lines herself since leaving Guy in the car park.

'A body in a coffin is just that, a body in a coffin, so the cremator wouldn't know if it was the right person or not.'

Kat nudged him with her elbow. 'I'd already worked that out.'

'They have to be linked, Kat.'

'Possibly. Probably. It's the who and the why I'm struggling with.'

'Only someone close to her would put her here.'

'I know … and I think I know who it was … but honestly, the rest of it eludes me.' She looked at Jed.

'If I was writing this, I could imagine.'

An idea was developing. 'I'm sure. Could you meet me on Saturday? I have a proposition for you.'

Chapter 27

The River Tay had broken its banks, another indication of the bizarre weather for the time of year. Jed stood at the door of the local tavern, the Open Reach, watching as farmers tried to herd sheep and drowning cows who refused to budge.

The sheep tottered off together as a flock, wool bouncing on their backs as they trip-trapped over the makeshift bridge the workmen had erected when they'd fixed the road a week ago. Cows were stubborn, hefty, unmoveable. It would make good TV, mused Jed as he stood grinning, watching them trying to move the impossible, then realised it would maybe feel like mocking so stopped grinning when he saw one of the older farmers slip down on the mud.

He felt a sharp pain and raised an arm to the right of his chest. He fell forward into his open hand and suspected he'd broken a rib from the fall he'd had the previous night. His trips were becoming more frequent, a symptom of his condition, but he was reluctant to use a stick. He had to learn to live with it, and living with it was exactly what he was doing.

Jed watched as the two farmers, the older man and a younger lad, tried to shift a Friesian up the bank. He'd kill for a cigarette. It wouldn't take the pain away, but it might ease it a bit. He knew from oh so many experiences that a rib would take four to six weeks to heal. He looked at his watch. Five minutes to one. Kat had said just after the hour. He kicked a few stones, dislodged some dust that had gathered in the corner where the door stanchions met the stone wall, and when he was bored of flicking the dirt, he crouched down to sit on the stone wall. He leant forward to ease the pain and his mind wandered to Kat. Was this meeting just about the case? Would he be so willing to meet up with her if she was male? Yeah, probably, he dismissed. He was a sucker for the intrigue.

The chatter and clatter of a stag party interrupted his thoughts and he looked up to see a gaggle of guys walking from the rear of the hostel, making their way across the road, down to the river. Typical stags, rutting to be the best, T-shirts with logos emblazoned with names and statuses Jed couldn't be bothered to read. In groups of two and three they carried kayaks and canoes and paddles, some wore wet skins, a couple had shorts and T-shirt, and one wore luminescent lemon underpants. The obvious stag.

The rapids were running fast and this stretch of water was infamous, used for practice by trainee Olympians. None were out today but perhaps they knew something the stags didn't. Jed envied their jollity and freedom, but he'd been on enough stag dos to know the stories behind the faces. He watched as they chattered, joshed, and pratted about, probably half soaked already, or at least hungover.

As the group disappeared down the bank out of view, Kat's car slowed and turned into the driveaway leading to the car park at the rear of the pub. Jed looked up and smiled at her as she gave a small wave as she passed him. True to her word, she'd arrived on time. It had perturbed him somewhat when she'd asked to meet as she had something to ask him. He had a pang of paranoia. What did she want? What did she know? Or think she knew?

He heard the car crunch to a stop. A loud yell echoed from the river and he turned to see the cow being manhandled up the bank. It gave an exuberant howl, akin to a dinosaur. Jed watched as the animal slid back, taking the old man with it. It landed atop the fella, and his screams were drowned out by the lowing of the dinosaur cow. The stags stood rooted to the spot. Jed sprang into action.

173

SHE'S NOT THERE

It was the third time she'd seen him as part of the investigation. There were still lots of questions looking for answers and it probably wasn't the way she'd have done it in the city, but why not meet him for a pub lunch in the quaint hostel-cum-bar near the River Tay? It was a casual meeting, just a catching-up, that was all, not a proper interview or even an information-gathering exercise, just a brief chat, that sort of thing. Of course, she would justify it if anyone asked, though she was confident nobody would. She wasn't drinking and she wasn't technically on duty, and it was the only time they could both make it. So why was she looking for reasons? For excuses? For obstacles?

Kat entered through the rear door. She looked around the bar but couldn't see him. He'd been sitting outside when she drove up. Maybe he was in the toilet? She ordered a tonic water, ice and lemon. She took a sip and waited. A few locals held up the bar. She didn't know any of them. She took a seat on the sofa by the unlit fire and placed her drink on the low table. She picked up a magazine about home design and flicked through it, wishing she had the money to be creative in the style she liked but couldn't afford. She took another sip of tonic and wondered where he'd gone. She glanced at the menu, typical pub grub. The place had a good reputation for food. Her breakfast seemed a long time ago. She swapped the magazine for the menu and was perusing the back page when a bustle of people burst through the front door. Jed was holding up the rear and he waved at Kat, an arm high above the small crowd. She saw him lower his arm and clutch at his chest as he wound his way past the group to the sofa.

He stood tall above her. 'There's been an accident down by the river. A pregnant cow has fallen on top of the farmer and it looks like he might have a broken back.'

'Oh my!' Kat stood up. 'What can I do?'

He waved her back down. 'It's all in hand. There's a stag party staying, as luck would have it, a group of doctors from Inverness.

They were on their way down to the river when it happened. The ambulance has been called and the farmer's grandson is with him. Nothing for us to do.'

'Crikey,' said Kat, amazed, but also not, at the differing events of the country to the city, things she'd long forgotten. Or hadn't experienced. 'Hope he's all right. I didn't see anything.'

'It happened as you were parking up. It's getting a habit, me being anywhere, everywhere, at the wrong time. I've been thinking this might be the wrong place for me after all. Can I get you a drink?'

Kat shook her head. 'I'm fine, thanks, I've just got this one. Though I'm tempted to swap it for a gin.'

Jed waited at the busy bar. Most of the stags had returned, their foray into the rapids curtailed for the afternoon. Hilarity and laughter bounced around the group. Someone hollered that it was turning into a busman's holiday.

Kat mused what a pleasure it was to be in a bar that didn't have sticky carpets and salubrious clientele, but laughed to herself at the irony that trouble always found a way in. Appearances were deceptive. The surroundings might look better but there was always something going on if you cared to look for it.

By the time Jed arrived back with his drink, blue flashing lights had stopped outside. He sat next to Kat, rather than opposite her, and took his first sip of ale. 'Controlled chaos out there.'

She sipped her tonic and watched him taking a gulp of his drink.

'Sorry you're thinking of leaving,' she said. 'Again.'

'Oh, I haven't decided really. I love the area, the cottage, the seclusion, and I wasn't sure my time here was done quite yet but the last thing I need is to get involved in a murder inquiry, and now a health and safety investigation.' He looked glum. 'I was hoping for some peace and quiet.'

'I never said it was murder. We only have a body so far. No one is particularly interested in the why or wherefores. People wander off and just die, apparently.'

'Really?' He looked surprised.

'Something like that, yes.' Kat didn't want to give too much away, not that she had much to say, yet.

Neither spoke for a couple of minutes.

'I don't know, where do I go? I briefly mentioned it to the owner of the cottage, and he thinks it's because of the dilapidation but I'm not a demanding tenant. I've put up with a lot worse and knew what it was like when I moved in. Lots of work to be done but that suits me.'

'Then don't go. Why would you?' She looked at him. 'Unless…unless you're skipping town because you have something to hide?'

He looked straight back at her, his eyes crinkling up at the sides as he laughed. 'What, any more than anyone else? We all hide secrets. Thought you knew that?'

She did know that but didn't fancy telling him. She finished her drink and reached for the one Jed had bought her. She took a sip.

'You put a gin in it?'

'I did. Thought you said you wanted one.'

'I said I was tempted, but it was a wish rather than a want. I'm driving.'

'You can always leave your car and get the bus. You said it was your day off.'

It was tempting, a nice idea. She hadn't done anything like that for a long time. Not since Bart. Grief, there it was again, unbidden. Clarke turning up was like Bart was there, yesterday, sitting beside her, larger than life itself. And she liked it. But it made today a bit awkward. She remembered Clarke was leaving to go to Edinburgh to see some friends the next day and she wanted to see him before he went, spend his last night together, to reassure him, remind him she was there for him, any time, all the time.

Kat pushed the glass towards Jed. It might be nice, on another day, to sit and have a few drinks with a smart, good-looking man, but today wasn't it. 'Sorry. I can't. I have to be at work in the morning and I need my car. Too complicated.' She thought she saw disappointment, or was that wishful thinking? 'I'm sure you'll find another companion this afternoon. Those doctors look set in for a session.'

She motioned across the room as a spurt of laughter erupted. 'I wasn't thinking of a session, just a few drinks, a spot of lunch, an easy lazy afternoon.' He looked at her. 'With good company.'

His eyes weren't brown at all, but dark grey-green with a fleck of a colour she couldn't distinguish. Her heart sped up and she felt it pulsing in her jugular, and in the suprasternal notch, and she raised her hand to her neck as though to stop it. His gaze unnerved her. She felt fluttery. He made her back prickle when he looked at her. It unnerved her. Was he aware of the effect he had? Did he have that effect on every woman? Was he a charmer or was it something just between them?

She looked away. Whatever it was, there was no room for it. Plus, he was a transient visitor, soon on the move. She wasn't looking for anything extra and she certainly didn't want a complication like him.

'What was it you wanted to ask me?' he asked, almost in a whisper, intimate.

'What do you mean?' She sounded defensive and surprised herself at her response.

'You asked if we could meet up. So here I am.' He splayed his hands in offering. 'At your beck and call.'

'Oh!' She laughed. Yes. She had asked to meet him and now felt confused, temporarily forgetting why. 'I just wondered if you could do me a favour, is all. Nothing official, just a request, if you're up for it?'

'Anything,' he said, looking her in the eye. 'What do you want me to do for you?'

There it was again. That flutter. She closed her eyes. Counted to three. 'I just wondered if, when you're out and about, in the community, like here in the pub, in town, at the library, that sort of thing…'

'Oh, I get it. I understand. You mean be your eyes and ears? Be your grass?' He looked at her, a little quirk in his eye.

'No, not a grass, nothing like that. Just, you know, be vigilant. People relax, talk freely, gossip in a way that they don't and won't if I ask the questions. You're an outsider, a bit like me, so you'll notice more what people are saying and what they're not, and you'll pick up things that other folk, local people, take for granted. You're an intelligent man, you write about people's lives and how they live them.' She smiled. 'You know how people work. The difference is, I'm a cop. And you make it up.'

'Flattery gets you everywhere, DS Dubois. When do you want me to start?'

She laughed, shaking her head. 'Nothing official. Just a helping hand. And an ear.'

'Of course, Sarge. Now are we eating or just sitting here not drinking?'

'What are you having? On me,' she said. 'Then I really do need to go.'

'The meat pies are great, home-made on site. I'll have whatever pie is on special today please. Now that you are my Boss.' He grinned. 'No chips, just the pie. Please.'

Kat ordered his steak pie and a prawn and lemon mayonnaise granary sandwich for herself, another craft ale, and a tonic with ice. She was glad she wasn't drinking. She might say or do something she might later wish she hadn't.

Chapter 28

The road to Glendargie was long. Guy looked for the overtake, but with three HGVs, a coach load of schoolkids, and a caravan in front of them, it was impossible. He slouched back to a sensible distance, and Kat knew it would be another thirty or so minutes before they reached the town. She looked out of the window and smudged the glass with her sleeve where it was daubed with the fingerprints of children. Guy's car was littered with children's books, a dolly with no clothes, a stuffed goldfish with an eye missing, and a box of tissues shoved into a plastic box, designed for a family on the move. She wondered how she'd cope when he was on paternity leave.

'You don't think she was playing dead, do you, sarge?' asked Guy. 'You know, faking it?'

'Why would she do that? For what benefit? I doubt the GP would sign her off.'

'Suicide? You know, a mercy killing, end-of-life days sort of thing?'

Kat dismissed him. 'We keep coming back to this. No. It's tight with end-of-life-plans, directly because of Harold Shipman. I just don't know how it would be possible today.'

'Not worth a GP's career, is it? Why dump her? We know cremation would get rid of any evidence. It doesn't make sense.'

'That's precisely why we keep going around in circles.'

By the time they arrived at the undertakers it was nearly two o'clock. Doug Graves took them into his office and explained he might have to leave as he was waiting on a call to pick up a deceased from Glen Lyon.

'An expected death, Miss, an elderly chap, passed away at lunchtime.'

Miss. Kat hadn't been called Miss since her days at Hendon Police College. Was it sexist? Did it matter? She was sure Mr Graves was being polite, if a tad old-fashioned, and wondered when polite had become so controversial.

It was a sparse office with a bright light but no outside window. A couple of pictures hung on the wall, one of Wade's Bridge on a sunny day, a fly fisherman casting his line. The other was a snowy Schiehallion. Piles of files were stacked top of each other, each one of them a death.

'Do you bring them all back here, the bodies?' asked Guy.

'Those that don't need a post-mortem. Or those that have had one and are ready for the coffin. We store them in refrigeration units out the back.'

'How many can you hold?'

'We have room for six, but we never usually have more than four or five at most. Winter is the worst time but even then, we've only ever had six once. That was January 1996. It was a bad winter.' He leant forward on his desk, leaning on his elbows. 'I presume you want to have a look, to see where we keep everything, make sure we are watertight.'

Kat answered, 'Once we've taken the statement, yes please. Do you have the records for Rosemary Fraser?'

Graves had everything they asked for and supplied his records readily. Rosemary Fraser had made a funeral plan a couple of years before she died and had contacted the undertaker upon her terminal diagnosis to ensure her wishes were recorded. Her nephew, Drew Fraser, would be the liaison upon her death. She was to be cremated in Perth and wanted only the cheapest coffin, no frills. Family flowers only. An announcement in the Perth Advertiser for one day, no more.

One hearse only, for Drew and his family. The service was to be taken by a regular celebrant from Perth. Although not a religious ceremony, she'd requested 'The Lord is my Shepherd' followed by 'Amazing Grace' on the pipes, which she'd said was to be her only extravagance. A wake was to be held in a local pub of the family's choosing and she'd given five hundred pounds to cover the catering and first drink. She hadn't expected many to attend and in the event of a full house, Drew would take care of it.

'It was standard, simple, no fanfare or exceptional circumstance. We collected the body from her house. The GP and the Frasers were there. Dr Keeys, one of the GPs here in the local surgery, signed the certificate and the cremation order was issued a couple of days later. Drew Fraser registered her death at Perth registry office.'

'Was it an open coffin?' asked Kat.

'No. We dressed her in the outfit that was provided by the family and the coffin was closed. I dressed her myself, with Malcolm.'

'Was she embalmed?' Kat knew she wasn't because that had been confirmed in the post-mortem but she still wanted to check.

'No, we don't tend to these days and no need if it's a cremation, unless the family request it especially, but it's usually reserved for burials.'

'Was there any question of a burial for her?'

'No, not at all. She didn't want the expense and was adamant she was to be cremated.'

That boxed that question off, thought Kat. 'How many other funerals did you have around the same time?'

'Thought you might ask that,' he said. He reached for a ledger. 'I can confirm there were three other deaths in March last year. All cremations. No burials.'

And that boxed that question off, too.

'If we show you the clothes she was found in, could you say if they were the ones you dressed her in?'

'Perhaps, I think so. We prepare a lot of people and I don't recall off the top of my head, but I might remember if I saw them.'

Kat took the file of photos from her briefcase and showed Graves the prints of the packaged clothes in exhibit bags.

He shrugged. 'They certainly look like something Miss Fraser would wear. They're the sort of thing she wore for church, or a Town Hall occasion. I can't say for definite but am happy to say likely. Drew Fraser would know, or his wife. They brought them in, to my recollection.'

His phone rang. It was Polly informing him that he was to collect Mr Anderson. 'Please excuse me if we're done? Can I leave you with Malcolm to show you the back rooms?'

It was bigger on the inside than the outside made it look. Malcolm showed them the interior of the fridges, except for the one marked Edward Ruislip. 'Funeral next Monday,' he said as explanation. The coffin had been delivered and they were waiting for the family to decide if it was to be screwed down or if they wanted a viewing, and the deceased wasn't prepared yet, hence him still being in the fridge.

Kat could smell the stale alcohol on Malcolm.

'So, if there was no viewing, he'd be in the coffin now?' asked Guy.

'Potentially, yes. We only have three of the fridges running unless we have an influx. The bodies go into the coffin as soon as they're ready. If there's no viewing the lid is screwed down, name plaque fixed, and then it's left on the stand ready to be transferred to the hearse on the day.'

'And if there's a viewing?' asked Kat.

'Then we prepare the body as requested, dressed, or covered up to the face if not clothed, make-up applied, hair tidied up, whatever we need to do to make them presentable.'

'Do they all have make-up?' she asked.

'Some do, others not. If someone's taken a fall for example, and hit their head or face, we do our best to cover any marks. It also depends on the state of the body. Sometimes Mr Graves advises the family not to view, if there's decomposition or any other reason against it.'

'Do you remember Rosemary Fraser?'

'I don't, to be honest. I remember her passing, her name, but I don't remember anything specific. I think I missed that service. I wasn't at work that day and I don't remember them all. We have a number of guys who work as pallbearers as and when we need them, on standby.'

'Do you drive the hearses, Malcolm?'

He reddened. 'No … well, I do in the yard when I'm cleaning them. Private land.'

'No licence?'

He looked at her. 'No … but I imagine you know that.'

She didn't but had immediately presumed as much from his response. She'd put a dollar on him being disqualified for drink-driving. She made a mental note to check it out.

Guy showed him the same photographs Kat had shown Graves.

He shook his head. 'I dunnae. They nearly all have clothes like that. Sunday best, an' all that.'

Kat asked him, 'You said the bodies may be covered up. What do you use for that?'

'Coffins are lined but if we don't have any clothes or if they need to be covered, we use sheets.'

Kat asked to see one and Malcolm took them to a store cupboard where white linen sheets were piled up, pristine, folded, and wrapped in plastic.

'Can I have one?'

'Oh, I dunnae, I guess so, I'll need to ask Mr Graves,' he said.

'I tell you what, I'll take one and you can tell Mr Graves to bill me.' She reached over and picked the top one. It was heavier than she'd expected. 'There's one in every coffin, is there?'

'No...' Malcolm hesitated. 'I'm not sure you can take that.'

'Where are they purchased?'

'Dunnae...' He shrugged. 'My wife does the ordering. She'll know.'

'I will, thanks.' Kat pulled back the thin plastic layer. She was sure it was the same sheet that Rosemary's body was wrapped in.

Chapter 29

On the way back from Graves they called at the Fraser's. Mary lounged against the doorframe, tapping her foot on the stone step. 'They're not in. They're at parents' evening.'

Did these girls ever see their mum and dad? Kat tried to keep the exasperation out of her voice. 'When will they be home?'

'Dunnae. Might go for a pint afterwards, they usually do. To either drown their sorrows that they produced a stupid child or congratulate themselves on a bright one. Depending on which offspring they're talking about.' Mary rolled her eyes. 'Me ... or the golden child, though she's not so golden now.'

'Let them know we've called, please? I need to talk to your dad again. Something important.'

Mary frowned. 'What's that then? I can tell him.'

'I need to speak to him in person. Tell him it's something I think he'll want to know.' Before Mary could say anything else, Kat said, 'Thanks, Mary. Hope you get a good report.'

As she turned to leave, she said, 'How is your sister?'

Mary hesitated as if not sure what to say. Ten seconds, twenty, then, 'She's okay.'

'Is Cam's dad helping out?'

Mary blushed. 'Him? He's dead in the water. We don't speak about him.' She stood holding onto the door as if hesitating whether to close it or not.

'Just ask your dad to give me a call.'

Mary nodded and shut the door.

Kat and Guy turned and walked down the path, onto the crescent. The nosy neighbour from number five dropped her net curtain as they passed.

'Drew Fraser will be on the phone, if not tonight, first thing in the morning,' said Guy. 'You going to tell him? About Rosemary being his mother?'

They approached Kat's car. 'No reason not to. Unless there's a good reason not to tell him, we really should.'

'Can you imagine being brought up by a woman believing she's your mother, when in reality, she's your aunt and your aunt is really your mother? A bit of a head-wreck.'

'Look at Eric Clapton. His mother was really his grandmother and he found out when he was ten, or something. And a fella I used to work with, he found out just before he joined the police when he asked for his birth certificate. It's a common story that spans the ages.'

'It's a bit messed up.'

'I've been thinking about it. As Drew and Rosemary share the same surname, Fraser, it must be her brother and his wife that took him in. He'd have had a different surname if his supposed mother and Rosemary were sisters.'

'Maybe ...'

'His parents were both Frasers. They were killed in a car crash over twenty years ago. I was researching him on the internet and it flashed up, an old newspaper article. Then I realised I remembered it.'

Guy looked at her. 'You know Drew Fraser?'

'No. I don't. I didn't. But do I remember the accident. It was just before I moved to London. Big crash on the A9, a coach full of schoolchildren, couple of HGVs, and a few cars. It was horrific. There were quite a few fatalities, two of them Andrew and Stella Fraser. As I read the article, I realised it was them, his parents.'

'Awful.' Guy shook his head.

186

'Families. You forgive them everything but forget nothing. Rivalries, secrets, nasty arguments, they make the world turn. In business and friendships, you can shut people out, but not so much in a family. They are still there, needling our sides. We manage to find a way to forgive but nothing is as it appears, not really, not ever.'

'You study philosophy?' Guy laughed.

'Psychology, not philosophy. And no, no studying, just people observation. Every case uncovers the unspoken, the unknown, or the unbelievable. People's lives, they're full of it.'

'What else did you turn up in your research? Anything?'

'It was very interesting.' She turned to him as she unlocked the vehicle. 'Our resident crime writer, he's a lot better known than I gave him credit for.'

'I did tell you. Have you read anything of his yet?'

'No, but I ordered his first and his last, just for research, of course. He's an ex-serviceman, though I did get that impression.'

'Yeah, special ops, I heard.'

'Didn't say that on his blurb. Something else I found out that might be interesting though … he has a dead girlfriend, which we knew, but what I didn't know is, her family blame him.

Chapter 30

The rain was lashing down for the third day in a row. The daylight hours were only a few shades brighter than the night and although not quite in a valley, the clouds hung low with no prospect of scattering. The dull, morose mood permeated every street and every inch of the air. Low lighting glowed dull behind windows and the roads were deserted for all but essential traffic. It was like day had become night and night was a black veil. No stars peppered the sky and rains kept the frosts away, and everyone knew, once the rain had stopped, the snow would likely follow, spring or no spring.

Kat had a long weekend on leave and was ready for it. She had intended to take a trip south to tie up a few loose ends, but with treacherous weather the A9 was blocked both north and south and the A1 had roadworks at Newcastle and Grantham. Kat reckoned it would take twelve hours, if she was lucky, and then some. She'd make the journey next time she had more than two days off. It was a trip she'd have to make at some point, but was glad to defer, for now. There was plenty to get on with at home and now Clark had gone, she had a few days off with only herself to please.

She bundled herself up with a hoodie, winter jacket, scarf, gloves, and boots. It was the end of April, three o'clock in the afternoon, and chill to the bone. Dawn had hardly broken and dusk was setting in. As she walked along the footpath beside the Tay, she spotted a small rowing boat bobbing by the bank on the far side of the river. A man and a boy were trying to tether it to a post and not having much luck. Lightning lit up the sky with a stark flash. She watched father and son, teacher and pupil, as they slid towards the water again.

She became aware of footsteps behind her and slowed her pace down, moving over to her left to let them pass.

The steps behind her slowed.

She shrugged her shoulders as if to shake them off, but the person still didn't overtake.

She was about to turn when a hand touched her shoulder. She yelped. She spun round.

'Hello!' A voice said.

'You!'

'Fancy an afternoon rendezvous?'

'What the hell are you doing creeping up on me like that!' she stuttered, a tad louder than she intended. 'That's the second time you've done that to me. You better not be stalking me!'

She gulped deep breaths, cold air hitting her lungs like sharp daggers of ice. Her heart pounded in her ears and her chest. Again. Rex, Jed's dog, leapt at her leg, trying to smudge his wet nose into her hand. She was wearing gloves and glad of them as he was covered in mud and sludge and whatever else he'd found to dig his nose into. She patted him down, looking at Jed, trying to work out whether she should stay cross, or not. 'You gave me a shock.'

'I'm sorry, I kept behind for a moment rather than jump out in case I gave you a fright. I guess I did that anyway.'

The rumble of thunder was close, the air tense. Lightning lit them up as it flashed, twice. Fat drops of rain started to fall, both hot and cold.

'Fancy a drink? Get out of the storm?' Jed suggested, smiling at her.

'I'm supposed to be clearing the air.' She looked up at him, tall, gruff, and bundled up in his waterproofs with rain running down his face like it didn't bother him, like he was made for it. She saw in his smile and his face that his eyes were willing her to say yes.

A friend. And a witness. That is all he was though, and he was a friend … with a dead girlfriend. She looked up at him. And I have a dead husband. He is a friend in a place where we are both strangers. Sort of. She looked at him. 'Why not.'

'If we take the path when it turns to the right it leads up to The Thistle.'

She smiled. 'I know.'

So, how's it going?' he asked, handing her a pint of cider.

She led them to a table. She felt small beside him. 'What, the enquiry? Or life in general?'

'I meant the enquiry but hey, life, if you like.'

'Tough, to be honest. I'm not used to the lack of urgency, or the slower pace. Or the apparent disinterest…though that's probably the wrong word…' She paused to take a sip of the enticing orangey drink as the bubbles floated and popped at the rim. 'It's just different. The way they do things. I'm used to rush, to buzz, a much faster pace, as well as my own way of doing things. Here it's a bit of a geographical oddity. Thirty miles at least from anywhere or anything that carries importance in terms of resources or assistance and what took me a day now takes me a week or more. Don't get me wrong, I'm not being critical, I do love living here, but the way things work, it's alien to me. Frustrating.'

'My default position, the frustrated resident alien.' He took a long slow drink of his ale.

'Do you move around a lot?'

He placed his glass on the table as he considered her question. 'A fair bit, I suppose. More so in recent years.'

'No family?'

'Nope. No wife, if that's what you mean.' He looked at her as he drank some more.

'I didn't. I presumed you weren't married, living alone, no wedding ring. Or not a wife you're with, at least.'

'My family are all in Ireland. I left at sixteen. I go back sometimes to see my ma, sisters, my brother, their families, but no, never had a wife.'

'Children?'

'No children, either. Never fitted with my lifestyle. And never had the right woman for long enough.'

He took another drink. Kat looked at her glass next to his. He'd drunk half a pint in the two minutes they'd sat down. He was either thirsty, a heavy drinker … or anxious.

Chapter 31

The next morning as Kat was looking for a packet of paracetamol, she felt her phone vibrate in her pocket. She slammed the kitchen drawer and answered her mobile to the withheld number.

'Hi, Kat! Bob Harris. When ya back in the office? Only I've got to go out and we're a DS short and there's a body in the bin.' He laughed. 'Quite literally.'

'It's my weekend off, Bob.'

'I appreciate that but we need someone in the office. Now, today.'

'But I've got plans.'

'And I've had a breakthrough.'

Her heart stuttered. 'What is it?'

He must have heard her urgency, because he laughed. 'No, sorry, Kat, not your case, but mine. You know that team of thieves robbing the distilleries?'

'Yes, your big job…' she said, deflated.

'One of the suspects, Corrie Blakely, his head's been found in a wheelie bin. Though he's not the body in the bin, the one in the cells I need you to deal with.' He guffawed, finding himself funny, all the more irritating Kat. 'A fairy tale come true! I have to get across to Blairgowrie and meet up with the CSI's over there.'

A head in a wheelie bin? She leaned over the sink. 'What's the one in the cells?'

'An alleged rape last night. Lassie claims she was assaulted leaving Loft Nightclub. He grabbed her, dragged her off the street, and raped her by the cinema. She stopped uniform patrol and pointed him out walking up Crieff Road. The paperwork's on my desk. More up your street, eh, Kat?'

Why did blokes think women wanted to, or had to, deal with all the sex offences? All a victim wanted was a competent officer who they could trust. The days of 'women's work' were supposed to be long gone but there were some that still believed it. 'Does the guv'nor know?'

'Aye, lass, he's the one that telt me to call ya in.'

Marvellous. 'Okay, I'll be there as soon as I can,' she said.

'Righto, I'm leaving Perth now. Don't want the press getting wind of this head yet. Imagine they'll have a field day, gives a different connotation to bag-heid, aye?' said Bob Harris, finding himself very funny again as he chuckled.

'They'll be setting up a murder team then. Who's dealing with it?'

'Some bloke from Glasgow is coming over. Dunnae his name. He said they couldn't spare any bodies as they were all out with that occult case over Dundee, so I'm guessing a selection of 'tecs from the stations where the robberies were reported.'

'Right,' said Kat, knowing very well that if Bob Harris was seconded, she'd have even less time on the Fraser case and more on the running of the CID office, especially with Munro absent as much as he was. If the criminal fraternity knew how few officers there were, there'd be a lot more of them.

Traffic was backing up again and it was stop-start-stall. Every so often her brakes slipped, and she had to press hard to slow down so she didn't slam into the back of the van in front of her. She made a mental note to ask Sue Kinell if she could recommend anyone when she saw her later that night. They'd planned a night at Sue's local but whether she'd get there, she was beginning to doubt. She slid through the gears to slow the engine down. She'd prefer a good night in, after last night. She'd stayed out far too long and drunk far too much but Jed had turned out to be really great company and one drink had led to another and another and … and it had been a long time since she'd enjoyed herself as much.

She thought of Jill, her colleague on the street offences squad in the West End, one of the best friends she'd ever had. Then she found Bart, and neither of them had seemed to need anyone else, and so her friendship with Jill had drifted. She wondered what she was up to now and made another mental note to find out. She missed having friends.

Three hours later, Kat felt like banging her head on her desk. She'd dealt with the 'rape', which had turned out to be an assault by a guy who was chancing his luck, but nothing more serious than that, thankfully. The poor girl was in a dreadful emotional state but luckily for both victim and suspect, CCTV had shown exactly what had happened. The lad had left the nightclub and stopped to help her when he'd seen her on the pavement, crying. He was consoling her and trying to get her to walk. He bought her a bottle of water from a vendor outside the club, and they were hugging. He tried to kiss her, and she pushed him off. They continued walking and outside the cinema they embraced again until she pushed him off again. She was shouting at him, screaming in his face, so he pushed her away and walked off. She fell over, grazing a knee, and uniform officers had discovered her sitting by the roadside crying. She was now being offered support from the various services and the indications were that he was remorseful, and horrified, when he'd watched the footage. It was now in the hands of the procurator fiscal to consider any charges.

If only the Fraser case was as straightforward. Munro had called into the office and she gave him an update.

'I'm telling you, Kat, I know you want to put the screws on Drew Fraser, but a good brief will work his way out of the door and we'll have lost what little we have. We don't have enough. Not yet.' Ken Munro looked pale, tired in his eyes, and not well. 'If there's one thing, one bit of advice I'd give you, Kat, is don't be in any rush. Slowly, slowly, catchy monkey. Bide your time. Wait a little. It might be right under your nose but you're in such a rush. Slow down.'

'Shaftoe is the one putting the pressure on, guv, you know he is. If we made it official with Fraser then he might give something away. Someone knows something and I'd put money on it being him.'

'I'll handle Shaftoe. He's a blow-hard who wants results. He's a career man. As for Fraser, just wait. Have you told him about his mother yet?'

'No, not yet. I'm dealing with it, but what if another body turns up tomorrow? I have to leave this one? I know it's not your decision. I know you've got things going on and none of that is any of my business, but I came here to do a job and in my transfer interview, they praised my expertise. I'll do you a good job but I need another hand. Guy will be off soon, so I'll be a person down. SFIU have rubbed their hands and given us dust, and not offered any help. What about someone from Gartcosh, the serious crime units, or Tulliallan, the training school? Surely they must have a detective somewhere with some sort of experience who could help me out?'

Ken Munro sighed. 'I know where you're coming from but trust me, everyone is thin on the ground.'

'I get you, boss. I know. Frustrating though. When are you off?'

'Tomorrow. For three days. I'll make a phone call before I leave today.'

Kat sat down and looked at her DI. 'Are you all right, Ken? Really?'

Munro looked at her, his eyes sunken. He'd aged in the short time she'd worked for him. It was telling. His stance had stooped, his gait had changed, he walked unsteadily and his eyes looked dull, like he'd lost a spark. She knew something was going on with him.

'I hope so, Kat.' He looked down at the files on his desk and she knew that was all she was going to get. She didn't hold out much hope for the phone call, except that sometimes, once in a while, miracles did happen. She needed one.

Chapter 32

Jed called Kat and asked if she fancied a grand night out.

She laughed and asked, 'What's a grand night out in your book?'

'Depends what I'm writing about.'

'I didn't mean, in your books. I meant, what do you mean by it?'

'I know what you meant.'

'Well then, unless you're taking me to the Michelin-star restaurant by Stochry I don't know where there is around here to have a grand night out.'

'I tried there, Kat, but the waiting list is six months long.'

'Yeah, I bet you did.'

He laughed. 'Okay, you got me. I just had a little tidbit for you, bit of info, and wondered if you fancied trying the new Italian in town?'

'Can't you tell me over the phone?'

'I could...but why waste the opportunity?'

She arranged to meet him the following night at 8 p.m.

Kat failed to see why he couldn't have just told her what he had to say over the phone. It didn't really add much other than an interesting link. She knew why he hadn't and although she knew she'd been played, she'd been game. She hoped it wasn't one that would become too complicated. She wasn't sure of the rules.

Jed told her he'd been in the Open Reach, the pub where they had met and which had rapidly become his local. It also transpired that it was the place both Drew Fraser and Michael Struan frequented. Both were more often seen at the back end of the week. This wasn't surprising news to Kat. It was the local for many of the Glendargie community, and Kendollich, Strathtay, and surrounding areas.

'If I was writing a book,' he said, 'I would link people together.'

'Of course.'

'And there's no such thing as coincidence.'

'I'm aware.'

'Are you playing with me, detective?' His eyes smiled at her.

'I'm listening…'

'I work out where people fit.' He moved the salt and pepper, napkin, and knife and fork, as if working out a plan.

'Go on.'

'Okay, your undertaker.' He picked up the salt cellar. 'The one who cleans the cars.'

'What about him?'

'Malcolm?'

'He's the only one I know, though there are others. It takes six pallbearers to carry a coffin.'

'Yes, well anyway, one of them, I presume Malcolm, the one you mentioned to me last Saturday, he was in the pub Monday evening having a drink with …' he moved the pepper pot to the side of the salt … 'Michael Struan.'

'Interesting.' She'd forgotten she'd told Jed about her trip to the undertakers. Drunk lips and all that. 'How do you know it was him?'

'He was wearing his undertakers' outfit and a black puffer jacket with 'Graves' embroidered on it.'

'Okay …'

'I don't know what they were saying but they had their heads together.'

'That's it?' She looked at him.

'Like I said, no such thing as coincidence.' He shrugged.

'But…but people around here know each other. Went to school together.'

'Not your undertaker, he's English, I can tell by his accent.'

'Well, there's every chance there's a connection with everyone involved in this case. Two men having a pint in a pub is hardly a break.' She was disappointed. 'Or was this a ruse for you to get me to come for dinner with you?'

'Would you mind if it was? After all, you did recruit me, so technically, you should be paying.' He sat back, one shoulder leaning away.

'You asked me, but I'll pay my way, don't worry about that.'

'I'm not.' Jed rearranged the tableware and Kat watched him, long fingers, hard hands, strong. He wiped condensation from his glass and ran a finger around the rim. He took a small sip of white wine. The mood changed.

'I'm not simple, Kat. I'm a liability.'

'What do you mean? A liability?'

His forehead creased, the line across the top of his nose deep set.

Genetic trait, or lifelines, mused Kat.

'I feel like wherever I go, trouble follows.'

'We both make a living dealing with people. Their past, their present, often their future too, only difference is, they are real for me and invented for you.' She drank her wine. It was fresh, fruity, chilled. She felt herself easing into this … this date … if that's what it was. The wine was helping. Romance, love, companionship, friendship, none of it had entered her head. She'd never thought that she might meet someone and neither did she wish to. She hardly knew anything about Jed but equally, she felt as if she got him. He was different, and she liked that.

Jed drained his glass, topped hers up, and poured the rest of the bottle into his. 'We both live in alternative realities.'

'That's one way of looking at it. But that doesn't mean we don't have our own. Everyone has their own reality that doesn't align with anyone else's.'

'Tell me yours,' he asked, sitting back in his chair, looking at her.

She took another drink. They were going to need another bottle. She waved at the waiter. The restaurant was quiet. Only two other couples, each a decent distance away and concerned with their own conversations. The waiter was at the reception, busy tallying up receipts, engrossed in his work. Other staff were out of sight, in the kitchen, maybe having a break. Music filtered through a hidden speaker, inoffensive in the background. Kat hesitated. She couldn't look at Jed directly. Whenever she did, she couldn't look him in the eye for long for fear of the intensity she found there.

He was sitting, waiting, silent, using one of her own techniques.

She copied him and ran a finger around and around the rim of the glass, and when she realised she was copying, she stopped. A sign of flattery, of engagement, of being in synch. She took another sip of wine and felt herself hold back. 'I'm not one for talking about myself. I prefer to be the one asking the questions.'

'I've gathered. A lady after my own philosophy, I fear.' He took another drink. 'We could play chess all night if you wish, hopscotching across each other, cherry-picking the bits we feel we can reveal, but why bother with the games? I get it. I do. My life is patchwork. If I wrote it, some wouldn't believe and others wouldn't be that interested. Truth is often stranger than fiction, and I've no hidden secrets, just a life, in all the ways we live it.' He hesitated. 'I've always been a private person.' He paused again. 'But I don't mind discussing it with you.'

He leant forward and she felt his eyes toying with her.

His mouth did a little grin, teasing her as he said, 'Maybe you bring out the confessor in people.'

She still couldn't reach his eyes. He was right. There wasn't one person she knew who hadn't suffered, and their suffering came in different forms. She raised her head and flicked her eyes a glance at his and looked away again, lest they linger.

'We can all have sadness, be sad,' she said.

He leant further towards her, lowering his voice to match hers. 'I'm not sad. Not anymore. My glass is half full today.'

She pointed at the glass and gave a little laugh. 'I'd say it needs filling up.'

'We need bigger glasses.'

'I don't need glasses, not yet.' She played with a curl of hair and tucked it behind her ear.

'Beer goggles, then,' he said.

They laughed.

She looked down at the table set for two, white fresh linen, a white lupin in a sheer thin glass vase set to one side, silver-sparkle cutlery doing its job.

'Hopeful. That's the word I was looking for,' he said.

'Maybe you're not the sad optimist, maybe you're pragmatic. Is that better?'

'You're getting there,' he teased.

She felt the energy tangible around them like a warm veil. She shifted in her chair. 'Shall we order?'

Chapter 33

Kat was tired and irritable as she negotiated the ring road. 'At least with London traffic you're unlikely to miss your turn off,' she grumbled to Guy. The three nights out in a row were taking their toll. It was unlike her to socialise on a school night but she'd figured as Monday and Tuesday were later start shifts, she'd be reckless, though the extent of her recklessness would make her look boring to many of her colleagues. It was hardly rock and roll, three nights out in a row, though she was tired.

'You should have let me drive, Sarge.'

'What's the point of that?' she snapped. A wasp zinged as it repeatedly flew against the inside of the window, desperate to escape. She slid the window down and it hovered on the edge of the glass, teetering, as if deciding whether to brave the sixty mile an hour rush or hop back into the warmth of the car. 'Wasps? Isn't it a bit early for wasps? And if you drive me everywhere, I'll never find my way around again, will I?'

'It hasn't changed that much since you've been gone, has it?'

'You're joking, right?' She floored the accelerator to shoot past a slow-moving biker with a helmet plastered in dead insects. 'You must have been a primary one boy when I left Scotland. You wouldn't believe the road developments since then.'

'That's one positive, Sarge. Be careful, you'll have me smiling next.'

'Sorry. I don't mean to be grumpy. I hate not knowing where I'm going. I had a sleepless night last night thinking about the case. My current theory is, what if there was a murder and the bodies swapped? I'm sure that's what's happened but we have no evidence. We don't have a victim. The only crime is preventing the lawful disposal of a body, with no suspect or suspects.' The wasp decided on the warmth and Kat tutted as she raised the window. 'There's so many whats and whys. How much further is it to this damn lab?'

They were at Gartcosh, for less than half an hour, a quick in and out. Kat said she'd drop Guy off and drive up to Glendargie to continue with the house-to-house enquiries.

'Why couldn't they have phoned with the information? All this way for that!' grumbled Guy.

'I said I'd go because I wanted to drop the sheet off from Graves for comparison, see if it was the same, and I also wanted to see where the lab was, so I know how to get there the next time. It's my fault.'

'I could have told you, it's not worth it. My mate Shaun could have told us over the phone.'

'Well, it was worth it, but not earth shattering, I give you that.'

'What I don't understand is, if they have blood from the bedsheet, and a profile from it, and they know it isn't Rose Fraser's, why don't they know whose it is?'

'That's too technical for me, Guy. But it does leave us with the question of not only whose blood it is, but what is it doing there? Was it from the person who buried her, or someone else?'

'Someone else like who?'

'Whoever was in that coffin instead of her.'

'Could be old blood, not connected at all. Just happened to be on the sheet that was used to wrap her in. People have nosebleeds, cut themselves, all sort of reasons why blood could be on it.'

'Now you sound like Shaftoe and his bags of sharp sand. Don't go all doubting Thomas on me too.' Kat was back on the ring road and heading north. 'I must get these brakes looked at.'

'You tell me that now,' said Guy, bracing himself in mock panic.

'I take your point about the blood, but if we accept there was a body swap at some stage, and we do think that's the most likely scenario, don't we? The blood could easily come from the other body. And if it was murder, we might expect a bit of blood. So … what we need is a victim. At the moment we don't even have a missing person.'

'Wouldn't they be able to match it to someone if they were already in the system? Like they do with prints?'

'You'd think so but it's a different budget and different team, so it has to be worth the cost. They'd rather check against one name than millions. It always comes down to money, in the end, so let's find them a name.'

'And we do that how?'

'We start off with what we know. And who. Call your mate from the lab and get him to run the following names through the system – Michael Struan, Drew Fraser … and on the off chance, Malcolm Abbott.'

Chapter 34

Red geraniums sat in a pot on the windowsill, reminding Kat of her childhood. When she closed her eyes, she conjured the dusty red and thick green scents, thick, cloying, strong. The furry petals took her back to a time when life held a bucketful of dreams, promises ... and heartbreak.

The front door opened before she knocked.

'Were you going to rap, my dear?' The old lady looked at Kat, her cottage-bread-bun hairdo loosely twined, gently nodding along with her head.

'I was,' said Kat. 'I was distracted for a moment by your lovely geraniums.'

'Pot them and they flourish. That's what my ma said, and I've always done the same.'

'I make her right.'

'Me too, hen. What can I do for you?'

'I'm DS Dubois from Perth police office. I'm conducting enquiries about Rosemary Fraser. Did you know her?'

'Aye, I do. Ma pal, Rosie.' Her head bobbed and the grey-white bun precariously wobbled as she held onto the doorframe. 'I'm a bit unsteady, hen, so please, come in. I've a pot of tea brewing. Almost as though I was expecting you.'

'That would be lovely, thank you. Here's my warrant card to prove I am who I say I am. You mustn't let people into your home if you don't know them.'

'Oh, I know ya, hen. You're Mari Wallace's daughter.' She hesitated then turned to walk down the short dim hall. 'I remember when you went off down sooth to join the polis.'

Woah. The dim light from the hall hit Kat, her head swayed, and she reached out for the doorframe. She hadn't used Wallace in a while. She took some deep breaths. Mrs Fletcher had a good memory. Kat didn't recall her as she looked at her retreating shape warily but it had been inevitable someone would recognise her sooner or later. She had to do this. She stepped into the house. Closed the door behind her. She had to keep it together, professional, no deviance from the task in hand.

Kat followed Mrs Fletcher into the front room, the one kept for best and guests and Christmas. Antimacassars lay across the back of her pale green tweed armchair and settee. A small table with thin wooden legs, Ercol design, stood in the middle of the room. An old-fashioned sideboard housed a lace runner and china tea set painted with red roses, matching cups and saucers and tea plates all edged in gold. The room had not a speck of dust or cobweb but held the smell of an age ago. Landscapes were trapped in frames hung on the walls, no portraits or pretty pictures of children, or grandchildren.

Mrs Fletcher wore a wedding band that had thinned over time. Her hands were gnarled with arthritis, but she held the large bulbous teapot firm. It was covered with a knitted tea cosy, pink and white, and brimming with golden honey tea. Kat's hand shook a tiny bit as she took the china cup from Mrs Fletcher.

'Help yourself to a biscuit, hen.' She pushed across a plate of shortbread from the tray she'd brought in. 'Not home-made these days, alas. I haven't the stamina for standing long and it's cheap enough to buy, for the amount I need.'

'Thank you,' said Kat, picking up a sugar covered petticoat tail.

It was long since she'd had authentic shortbread, nothing like the packs from the train station or given out at conferences, a packet of two bland fingers, mass market. Kat looked across to the far wall, next to the window. The tiny whimsey animals were a collection she remembered from childhood but couldn't recall from where. Tea packets? Cereal? Somewhere else? She remembered playing with them, but they weren't in her ma's house when she cleared it out. Perhaps her mother had given them to a charity shop?

Kat was flummoxed, though pleased it was Mrs Fletcher that recognised her rather than someone from high school. She didn't wish to revisit all that. Not yet. At some point she knew she might have to, but not now.

'Please, call me Iona. You came to ask me about Rosemary?'

Kat held the cup and saucer tight in her lap. She didn't trust her hands not to shake. 'I did, yes. As a neighbour, I'm taking a guess you knew her well?'

'I did.' Iona Fletcher nodded, the bun waving, strands escaping across her face. She swept them away over her brow. 'A great lady, indeed. Very kind.'

'You were close friends?'

'In our time, we were, yes. And then again in the latter years.'

'What can you tell me about her?'

'What can I tell you? Well, where to begin...' She looked off to the right, paused for a minute, then, 'I think what she did was a marvellous thing. Such a caring woman. And so good with children. Just a shame she couldn't keep her own.'

Kat frowned. 'I'm not with you, what do you mean?'

'The children, they flocked to her like a magnet, like sheep to Little Bo-Peep.'

'What children?'

'She would help out with the neighbours' children, looking after them, holidays, evenings, weekends, always helping out she was. And then with her own, her family.'

'I see,' said Kat, not really seeing but imagining her as some sort of Mary Poppins. 'What do you mean, she did a marvellous thing?'

'She'd do anything to protect her own, she would, and anyone else's come to that. She was a very loving woman. Shame Struan didn't do the right thing by her, the auld bastard.'

Kat was taken aback with the expletive, but also a tad impressed. 'What's Struan got to do with it?'

'Everything. And don't believe otherwise.' She looked at Kat and shook her head, hair threatening to fall. 'These new townspeople, they have no idea what he's really like. Landowner, yes, but he forced people out if he took against them, no sympathy with folk who might have needed a helping hand. They didn't need a boot oot the door. He wasn't a good man, trust me. I don't know why Rosie wasted her time on him.'

'I didn't know Miss Fraser was involved with the Struan's. I've met with Michael, his son, but I had the understanding that he was a good landlord.'

'Aye, Mike, his son, he is. I don't mean him. I mean the old man. He was always catastrophising and making life hard for Rosie. He'd never leave his wife, but why would he when her family would make his life difficult? Rosie put up with a lot as their housekeeper. Even when Mrs Struan passed on, he wouldn't have Rose live in. She would have made him, or anyone else, a lovely wife.' She looked over her cup at Kat as she sipped her tea. 'And a wonderful mother, had she been allowed to.'

'Are you saying Miss Fletcher had a child?' Kat wasn't sure who knew what but knew someone always knew something – or thought they did.

'She had a son, yes.' She paused. 'But she had to give him away.'

'Why?'

'He made her do it.'

208

'Who did? Who made Rosemary give her son away?'

'Struan, of course. His father.'

Kat looked at her as this piece of information sank in. She placed her cup and saucer on the table. 'Who did she give her baby to, Mrs Fletcher?'

'Don't you know? I guess you don't.' She put her cup down. 'She gave her son to her brother, Andrew Fraser. His wife miscarried many times and Rosie, well she couldn't face giving him up for adoption, so she gave him to her brother and his wife.'

'In 1978?'

'That would be about right, yes.'

Kat calculated it in her head. Rosemary's son had not only been given to her brother, but he'd also been named after him. He couldn't be named after his real father because he already had a son called Michael. Struan, junior. And that made them brothers. Half-brothers. She wondered if either of them knew or had ever suspected.

'Was it a secret, Mrs Fletcher? Or did everyone know?'

'Well, it wasn't really common knowledge, hen.' She lowered her voice, even though there was nobody else to overhear. 'I don't even know if the boy himself knows. I think the plan was to tell him, when he was old enough, but when is that? When is old enough? And then of course, it was too late, far too late, when they died. Rosie took him in and became the mother to him she'd always wanted to be and I could be wrong, but I don't think she had the heart to tell him, after the grief they both suffered. What purpose did it serve to tell him then? He might never have forgiven her and she couldn't bear to lose him.'

'Did Struan know?'

'Of course, aye he did! He paid for her to go off and have the baby, somewhere far away. But she only went as far as Edinburgh. Far enough. Struan had his own son, Michael, and his wife was also pregnant at the same time. That hurt Rosemary. Especially when it was another boy. She brought her baby back and gave him to her brother. When she found out Struan had another son, Rosie disappeared for nearly a year. When she returned, life had moved on. Her baby had been accepted by everyone as Stella's and nothing had changed. Except for Rosie.' The coiled bun shook precariously. 'You know, my dear, an awful lot goes on around here that folk don't know, doesn't it?'

Kat felt the woman's eyes on her, little black beads seeing straight through into her soul. 'I…umm…err…' she stuttered. She knew exactly what Iona Fletcher meant. She'd warmed to this old lady, even if she did unnerve her.

'I think I'm the only one who Rosemary told about her son but it's not my business to discuss it like gossip. Live and let live, I say.' She looked at Kat. 'I don't tell secrets. They're not mine to tell. I'm only telling you because you're the law and you need to know this. It's a funny old do, and I need to tell you her story because there's no one else that can. You do understand that don't you?'

Kat felt her face flush. She understood. She gave a little nod, accepting what she was being told. She finished her cup of tea. She wasn't a tea drinker, didn't usually like it. Milk always tasted greasy in tea and it wasn't sitting very well inside her stomach.

'It's different now she's dead though, isn't it? It does baffle me how she ended up on Struan's land, by her tree.'

Chapter 35

Kat called round to Jed's. She hadn't known she was going nor had she intended to. The conversation with Iona Fletcher had shaken her. It had been an unexpected turn of events, not least because she'd recognised Kat. She needed time to digest it all.

Jed opened the door on her second knock. He ran a hand through hair that looked like it hadn't been washed in days. Rough stubble told an equally damning tale.

Kat hadn't seen him like this before. 'I just called on the off chance,' she said. 'Sorry, is it inconvenient?'

Jed stepped aside. 'Never, please, come in. Sorry for the attire.' He swept his hand over his jogging bottoms and grubby sweatshirt. 'I've sort of lost track of time. It happens when I'm writing. Did you try to ring? I'm not sure if my phone is alive or dead. I forget to keep it charged it sometimes.'

'No, I didn't call, sorry, I should have…but then, you wouldn't have answered anyway if it's switched off.' She stepped into the cottage and noticed a bundle of coffee stained A4 papers on the settee. The open fire was down to the embers and Jed's laptop stood on the small table over by the far window, near the staircase. He'd improved the sitting room since the last time she'd been there. Rex came bounding over and started jumping up at her, licking her hands, until she petted him down.

She nodded at the papers. 'How are you getting on?'

211

'Getting there,' he said, shutting the door and pulling a drape behind it. 'I still haven't fixed the handle, though.'

Kat thought of the house where she'd grown up. Her nan always had a curtain behind the front door to keep the draught out. It was thick and red, crushed velvet, but more likely velour. She used to hide behind it playing hide and seek, waiting to be discovered, reading a book until someone noticed she was missing.

Jed clattered lumps of coal and logs onto the ashes. 'I'm not sure I'll be able to resurrect this fire. As for the plot I'm working on, it stinks like a net of red herrings.'

'Not unlike mine, then. That's why I'm here.'

'Tell me more. But first, coffee? Or would you prefer something stronger?' Jed waved for her to sit down as he went to the kitchen.

She ignored his wave and followed him. He filled the kettle and pulled out a couple of mugs from the top cupboard, a spoon from the sink, and milk from the larder hidden behind a door. 'I don't have a fridge yet but the milk's fine. It's cold in there.'

'My nan had a larder. It was more like a cold store. It was huge and really cold. I used to hide in it. My nan and her sister used to cower inside in thunderstorms. They didn't have electricity when I was little, and had candles dotted all over the place. I remember my Grandad had coloured pipe cleaners in jam jars on the windowsill.' Bang. The memory was there as if it was now, present today, in front of her. She hadn't thought of that for such a long time.

'Sounds like a nice memory.' Jed spooned instant coffee into the mugs.

'Yes.' She needed to change the conversation. Was it talking with Mrs Fletcher? Being in this cottage? The memories were coming fast now. 'So, do you have your plot sorted?'

'No, not really. Seat of the pants, that's me. Did she live around here then? Your nan?'

'I'm not in the habit of telling suspects my life story, Mr Gillespie,' she joked.

He leant back against the sink, both hands resting on the rim behind him. 'Oh, I'm a suspect, now am I?' He looked affronted. 'And here was I thinking I'm assisting in enquiries. Do you think I did it in the larder with the candlestick? Or would it be the revolver?'

'My money's on poison,' laughed Kat.

Jed adopted a fake accent and a pulled face. 'It wouldn't be poison, my dear, that's a weapon that belongs to the fairer sex.' He said sex like it was shexsh. 'My choice would be a dagger. Straight in. Straight out. Clean cut.'

Kat pulled an exaggerated face. 'Mr Gillespie, a dagger is a sexual weapon, one often used by men as an extension of the penis. And please, less of the Sean Connery.' She laughed.

'In that case, I'd use something kinkier, maybe wrap the body in cling film, suffocation…' He paused. 'Bloody hell, Kat, that's it! You've done it! Thank you.' He walked over to her and placed a hand either side of her face and plonked a kiss on her forehead.

Kat took two steps back. 'Hey, steady on.'

'Oops, sorry. I didn't mean…you know…to be inappropriate.' Jed ran a hand through his hair as he moved away from her. 'I'm sorry.'

'The kettle's boiling if you're still making that coffee.' Kat flushed. She liked the banter and wasn't sure if it was him, or her, who'd been the more inappropriate of the two. The first rule of policing was never to mix business with pleasure. Here she was, top of the class hypocrite.

Time seemed to pass so slowly as Jed made the coffee, his back to her. She wondered what he was thinking.

She went through to the sitting-room and sat down in the armchair by the fire which was now burning bright and heating up not only the room, but also her. She felt her face zing. She blamed the cold but knew she was lying to herself. She unzipped her jacket and pulled it open. Perhaps the roll neck was too much. She slid her jacket off and let it slip to the floor. Rex made straight for it, rubbing his snout in the armpit.

Jed pushed a mug into her hands and pulled Rex away. He slung her jacket over the back of the settee.

She couldn't read his body language but then noticed the smile dancing on his lips as he lowered himself onto the settee next to his papers.

'Bit warm in here now,' he said, and sipped his coffee. 'So, what can I do for you? I presume you called round for more than coffee and my company?'

'Err, yes…' she stuttered. Why had she called? Why really? 'I was just wondering…well, I thought…' She had a mental block. What had brought her here?

'You thought I might like to come crime-hunting with you?' he teased, eyes on her, waiting.

'Not quite,' she said. She stalled as she took a gulp of coffee and nearly choked. It was far too hot. She was used to coffee that was tepid as she rarely managed to drink to it while it was hot. 'I just wondered if you'd heard anything else down at the Open Reach?'

'Oh, I see. Jed the informant.' He smiled.

'Well, you are my ear on the ground. As you're often down there I'm interested in what the current gossip is. If you've seen, or heard, anything else of note?' She placed the cup on the fire hearth, out of reach of kicking-over distance. 'Just your usual people-watching skills. Overhearing and the like.'

'Like a wise monkey. Hear no, see no, speak no, but take it all in, aye?' He cocked an eye. 'You know what they say about monkeys? Give them enough rope and then hang 'em.'

'Old wives' tales. And that's only the French ones. The spies.'

He laughed.

'Not unlike your red herrings.' She arched her back into the chair. 'I don't know, Jed, another wee bit of local gossip would be good right now.'

What she really wanted to know was if anyone else recognised her. She'd been shaken by the gamekeeper and now Mrs Fletcher. Her name – Kat Dubois – would mean nothing to anyone, she was sure of that, but her face could tell all, if they looked close enough.

'I'll pop down tomorrow night, see what I can find out. Payment in kind, is it? Or is this one on the books?'

'I'm sure we can come to a mutual agreement, Mr Gillespie.' She noticed his jaw clench.

This was fun … and also a little bit scary.

Although she'd wanted to pay her share the night at the restaurant, he'd insisted on paying the full bill. They'd had three bottles of wine between them. She'd pre-ordered a taxi to pick her up at 10.30 p.m. to ensure there was no get out clause and he hadn't pushed. He'd pecked her on the cheek before holding her just a little too tightly in a hug that nearly toppled them both over onto the pavement. They'd said goodbye and left it at that, each knowing they'd see one another again without having to make any formal arrangements.

'Fancy going to see a tree?' she said, standing up.

'Erm, not really.' He ran a hand over his clothing. 'Hardly tramping weather.'

'Did I say you looked like a tramp?'

'You didn't have to.'

She laughed. 'I need to go there, now. See what she saw.'

'She saw nothing. She was dead.'

'I mean before she died. Why there? I want to see it again, try to look at it through her eyes.'

'The dead don't see.'

'Yeah, I know. They don't speak either, or walk, but they do give clues. Are you coming, ready or not?'

He jumped up, took a pose, knees bent, hands positioned like a karate chop and did a daft, 'doh, doh, dododo, doh doh.'

'What the hell is that?' She laughed.

'Whadya mean? It's my best Mission Impossible!'

'Pass my coat, I've pulled a muscle, laughing so much.'

He stood, hands on hips, and cocked an eye at her. 'I'm no mussel, I'm the best cockle around here!'

'Winkle, mate. It's winkle. We used to go winkle picking on the beach on the Isle of Bute when I was a kid.'

'Winkle pickers! Ha. They make me limp.'

'Oh, do behave. Get yourself sorted if you want to come along. It'll be too dark soon.'

'Aye, aye, cap'n.' He gave her a salute and took the stairs two at a time.

She heard him moving around in the room above. She didn't mean to be nosy, told herself she wasn't that interested, but couldn't help herself when she looked at the papers he'd been working on. Like someone in earshot who can't help but hear, she saw and couldn't help but read. The A4 sheets were typed, scrawled with pencil crossings out and additions, but the page that stood out was the one with only two words.

For Cassie.

Chapter 36

Jed had set himself a word limit of two thousand five hundred words. He was ready and eager but before he could think about the first line of the day, the fresh crab he'd had for lunch repeated on him. He felt a chill and hoped it wasn't the start of poisoning. He shouldn't have joked about poison with Kat.

He went upstairs to close the bedroom window. He liked fresh air and to sleep in a cool room with heavy blankets rather than a duvet, but the open window was blowing a hooley. He hoped it was the draught rather than an upset stomach that caused his chills. As he clamped the old metal arm shut, he noticed the mountains towards Schiehallion. They were still covered in snow and looked magnificent. He noticed the hanging posy of dog roses that lolled by the front gate. If this was his own cottage, he'd be putting solar panels in the roof. Maybe Struan would let him put an offer on the place as he was selling off land, always a sign of a landowner short of cash when they did that. With the investigation going on he might be open to a bargain.

Jed admired the view a little longer, straightened his back, stretched his chest, grabbed a hoodie and went downstairs to his waiting laptop. Ninety minutes later he'd written twelve hundred words. Not bad, but not two and a half thousand, yet. He leant back in his chair and spotted a robin sitting on the windowsill, cocking his head at him.

'What do you want, old fella?' he asked the bird. 'Who are you here for, eh?' Jed had seen the robin on many days now. Every day since the first day that Kat Dubois had first visited. 'Did she send you to spy on me?'

The bird cocked its head again as if pondering the question and responded with bird chatter, then flew off. Jed would see him again, he was sure.

Twelve thousand words in three days hadn't yet made Jed email his agent, but it had sent him to the local DIY store to buy free-range eggshell emulsion, a couple of paintbrushes and some soft rollers. He'd also picked up a new handle for the inside of his front door, cringing with embarrassment remembering Kat's visit. Was it her? Was she his new start?

Jed finished painting the three rooms upstairs, bedroom, box room, and bathroom, now all white and clean. He stood, stripped to the waist, admiring his work, eager to start typing again.

It was Saturday morning and a shoot had been arranged on the Struan Estate. More reason for Jed to stay indoors. He could quite easily become vegetarian but wasn't quite there yet. He'd tried before, twice with a girlfriend, and the last time, a medical experiment. It was a bacon sandwich that had got him on all three failures. He had a few thick slices of prime back bacon lounging on a shelf in the cold store that needed eating. A sniff would tell him if they were still good enough. He could do with a decent meal. There were also half a dozen free-range eggs, fresh from the local shop and a couple of dried-up mushrooms, too. He also had a handful of cherry tomatoes, which he much preferred to tinned. Tins were for beans and he had plenty of them, too. Shame he'd had the last of the bread the night before, a couple of stale slices toasted for a snack before bed because he'd been so engrossed in writing that he'd forgotten to eat anything all day.

He was halfway through his brunch when he heard a vehicle pull up. The engine ran a few seconds then switched off. He heard car door slams, more than one. The gravel crunched with footsteps. He didn't do visitors. The signpost to the medieval church with the painted ceiling often misled people up his path so whoever it was he hoped they'd be lost tourists wanting directions rather than guests, not that he had any idea who could be paying him a visit.

On the second knock, Jed put his knife and fork down and took a slurp of tea. On the third, his head fell back, and he closed his eyes. Leave me alone!

The door rattled and he heard low voices. He picked up a tea towel and wiped a small drip of egg yolk from his bare chest. He stood and gritted his teeth. He strode to the kitchen and the back door. On the next rap he yanked it open.

'Jed! Good to see you, my man!'

Jed's blood pressure dropped, his heart rate rose. His eyes flickered from one man to the other. What the fuck?

Chapter 37

Two hours whizzed by and Kat couldn't believe she'd been sitting there so long. She'd started with googling Jed Gillespie and found out what she wanted to know, or what she thought she did. He'd been in a relationship with a woman who had died, which she'd already ascertained. He'd had to give evidence at the inquest and the article reported that Cassie had severe mental health issues. There had been domestic violence, but not perpetrated by Jed as far as Kat could see. Since the date of the inquest, Jed had fallen off the general radar – until he turned up in Glendargie and was now firmly on her radar.

After reading with more than a little interest she idly clicked onto an Ancestry research site.

An hour later, she'd discovered that Rosemary Fraser had given birth to Drew in Edinburgh. No father was shown. She also found out that Michael Struan, senior, had been married to a woman of equal family means and status and they had two sons. Michael, born two years before Drew. The other son, Cameron, was born three months after Drew Fraser. She wondered if any of them had suspected they were brothers.

Michael was keeping a low profile, keeping himself busy and out of the investigation in every way. His connection with the undertaker may or may not be a red herring and she'd never heard of Cameron, so maybe he was worth speaking to.

She needed a further discussion with Drew and there was someone else she wanted to see. There was no time like the present because Bob Harris was on the lookout for someone to take a statement for him and the last thing she wanted was to get involved in the whisky job.

Kat parked up at the Motor Grill, debating whether to pop in for a quick cuppa before knocking on the Fraser door. She grimaced as she bent into the car to pick up her bag from the front passenger footwell. She needed a cup of coffee and a couple of paracetamols for the twinges in her knee which she knew needed to get sorted out but she didn't have time. There was always something that was more pressing. She hadn't felt right since her encounter with Mrs Fletcher. She fancied comfort food, a bowl of soup, tomato, tinned, with bread and butter, because she'd skipped lunch in favour of going to see Marion Struan.

It hadn't taken long to find out that it was Mrs Struan the ex that had phoned the incident room and provided Rosemary Fraser's name. Neither had it taken long to discover where she lived.

Kendollich had lot of grand old buildings that had been converted into apartments, labelled as such to sound more upmarket than flats. Strathallan Terrace had lost the grandeur and glamour of the 1800s when it was the home of a Laird, though today it was far from like the tenement buildings that lined the streets of larger Scottish towns.

Marion Struan lived in the largest ground floor apartment, situated on the west corner. Her patio doors stretched half the width of the enormous communal garden. The place was clean, simple, and decorated with cream and gold furnishings. Few possessions littered the surfaces. Marion certainly wasn't drunk when Kat knocked on her door, but rheumy eyes and shaky hands were the giveaway. She was a slight woman, stylish though dated, and fully made up as if she was about to go out. She invited Kat in readily.

'Tea? Coffee? Something stronger, officer? The afternoon has begun after all.' Marion's voice tinkled as she gave a little laugh.

'I'm fine, thanks.' Kat saw a bottle of Aberfeldy whisky sitting next to the kettle. She wondered how Haggis was getting on. She didn't feel one iota of guilt for sneaking out of the office. 'I won't keep you long, Mrs Struan.'

'It's about my phone call, is it? Thought you'd come eventually.' She stood by a low side table and played with some fresh flowers that didn't need rearranging. 'Take a seat, please ... if I can't get you a drink.' She indicated to the plush double settees facing each other.

Kat felt the bounce of the cushion as she sat, certain it wasn't used to being sat on. 'You phoned in the name for the face we reconstructed. I'll need a statement. How you know, sorry, knew, Rosemary Fraser, that sort of thing.'

Marion sat on her hands. 'I wasn't going to call. I didn't mean to. I was sure someone else would ... but I'm afraid to say that it all just got the better of me. I'm not proud of my actions.'

Kat looked at her, confused. 'What actions?'

'I shouldn't have done it.'

'I'm not with you ...'

'I recognised her straight away of course, when her face popped up on the news. I was having a drink with some friends in The Trossachs, that lovely little bar behind the High Street, you know.'

Kat knew of it, a micro-style pub that looked inviting and cosy but cramped if it had more than a dozen people in it. It wasn't the sort of place she'd go to when it was busy, and it always looked busy. 'I know it, yes.'

'When I came home, I phoned Michael. Given that she was found on our estate, on our land ... sorry, his land ... I just ... I wanted to speak with him. I'm embarrassed to say I'd had a few glasses of wine and as usual our conversation soon deteriorated into an argument.'

'I'm sorry to hear that, Mrs Struan. Not amicable then? Your split?'

She shook her head. 'Not really. He told me to keep my mouth shut, not to go blabbing about things I knew nothing about.'

'Did he know it was Rosemary?'

'Oh, I don't know, he's not a pleasant man, Kat. Can I call you Kat? I've had years of living with a very narcissistic man, but … I can't help it. I still have feelings for him. Hate, love, love, hate, both. He has no time for me now and every time we talk, it always ends up in a row.'

Kat nodded. She could imagine. The more he ignored her or treated her badly, the more she'd turn to the drink and pine for him. She'd seen it many times, with friends and in her work. 'I'm sorry to hear that.'

Marion sat down opposite her, sitting with a hand beneath each thigh as she leant forward. 'But to answer your question, yes, he would know it was Rosemary. Of course he would. He said he hadn't time for television and hadn't seen it on the news. I don't know what he knew or didn't but of course he knew Rosemary. She'd worked at the big house for years when he was a boy.' Marion leant back. 'Whether he knew she was buried there or not, I don't know, but when he told me to say nothing and to shut up … I don't remember all the conversation … the more I was determined to do the opposite. If he'd spoken to me like a decent person, talked to me properly … I only phoned for a chat, to gossip I suppose … had he not got angry with me, I probably wouldn't have phoned it in.'

Why would Struan not want his ex-wife to ID the body. Was he just narked because she'd phoned him drunk? Because he had no time for her? Or was it something more? When he told me to say nothing and to shut up – was that exactly what he said or Marion's interpretation? Each word was important. Was he telling her to say nothing to him or nothing to the police?

'If I hadn't phoned, someone would have. Others may have for all I know, so I can't be blamed for anything can I? Everyone around here knew her, so I figured it made no difference in the end, if it was me or someone else.' Marion looked sheepish. 'I'm more embarrassed than anything, Kat. I won't have to go to court, will I? I'm really not good with public speaking.'

As Marion rubbed the side of head, Kat noticed her hand shaking even more than before and knew the minute she left her apartment, the woman would be reaching for a drink.

Kat sat by the front windows of the motor grill. She clocked Mary Fraser sitting in a corner booth with a gaggle of girls, all of them wearing school uniform. Mary caught her eye. She saw the girl blush as she turned to speak to her friends. Kat looked away and smeared the condensation around the window to look outside.

Raindrops glinted in headlights as an HGV slowed to turn into the lorry park. She heard girly whispers and remembered the time when she'd sat there doing similar, remembering fourteen all too well and neither would she have wanted to be recognised by a police officer. Police at your door always meant something was wrong, bad news, never good, someone either a victim, or a witness, or a suspect, rarely anything positive. Police meant distress for someone in some way or another. She thought back years ago, when she was much younger, and remembered the knock on her own door all too well.

By the time she'd pulled herself back to the now, both her coffee and soup had cooled and the girls had gone. She didn't feel like it was the right time now. She didn't want to be knocking on anyone's door, disturbing their peace. Not tonight. Drew Fraser could wait. She knew where she wanted to go.

Half an hour later she knocked on the front door of Sue Kinnell.

'Kat! Come on in. What took you so long? And where's the wine?'

Had she known she'd have received such a welcome, she might have called sooner. 'It was just on the off chance, Sue. I fancied seeing a friendly face.'

'Get your coat off, I was only catching up on the soaps. Coffee? Or something stronger.'

'I'll have what you're having,' she smiled.

Sue's place was compact, neat, new build two up two down with three toilets, one in the hall, one in the upstairs bathroom and an en-suite. 'Far too many for a single person,' she laughed as she handed Kat a glass of clear fizz. Rhubarb gin. Better than parma violet but still as potent. And she would always prefer tonic to lemonade but as she'd turned up empty handed, she didn't feel she could argue.

The evening was just what she needed – to relax, to chat, to switch off, even though she knew she'd have a hangover from hell the next day.

She tumbled out of Sue's spare bedroom at 8am the next morning, red eyed and in need of a shower. They'd put the police force right, or as right as they could with plenty of references to TJF – the acronym for The Job's Fucked. They'd discussed the problem of single living and multipack buying, and then created their own tick list of their perfect man.

It always came back to him. Bart. It was always Bart.

Chapter 38

The brilliance of the paint shining in the evening sun was like nothing else existed, only him in an empty room. The whole world was white, devoid of anything other than four walls, two windows, one back, one front, and a grey slate floor. After grazing the paintbrush along the wall for the last time, he could do no more, no matter many more coats he gave the stone walls. It was fresh, looked fresh, smelled fresh, and the taste on his tongue told him it didn't get any fresher, or brighter, nor cleaner than it was in this moment. If the room could speak it would tell him to stop, right there, right now. He'd been at it since dawn, and every corner, nook, and cranny was filled with thick masonry paint, white globs stuffed into crevices that cobwebs usually coveted, his brush shoved into crumbling cornerstones now covered with crisp white. It was done. He was done.

Kat would be impressed. Kat. She was busy. She was never not busy, but he liked it when busy included him. He'd left a voicemail and called once more since. She'd know he'd tried, and it was up to her now to call him back. She hadn't.

He'd kept himself busy writing, or trying to. Sleeping, or trying to. Then he tried painting, a job that needed doing but he had been putting off since moving in. He needed to be busy and a creative mind did things to a man while waiting for a call. He'd spent enough time waiting on calls, of having to drop everything to run, and keep on running, when all around him were running the opposite direction.

Not unlike policing, or any other public servant. These days he much preferred writing, despite not doing much of it in the last three years. Not since that last call, the one he hadn't anticipated, the one he'd missed, the one that changed his life forever.

The bare glare of the room was inviting him to fill it but was it worth the investment? Would there ever be anyone else to share the space with? Would he share a table with another again? Would there be dinner parties? He'd stopped responding to invitations and eventually they'd stopped coming. He'd gone from an after-dinner speaker to a one-man comedy stand up with only himself to laugh at.

He told himself to construct something, to invite people and they would come, of course they would. She would. She will.

He left the room and found himself in the kitchen. He fell against the sink as he lost his balance. He twisted the tap and freezing water spluttered and coughed. He filled the kettle and looked across the fields towards the Munros, proud and full of stealth. His eyes were drawn to the tree in the distance. It looked black against the sky, in direct contrast to the white new world he'd created. Black on white. Nothing was ever black or just white.

When the guys had turned up, he'd feigned being pleased to see them. He wasn't ready. He'd told himself that for the last three years. He didn't want to remember, he only wanted to forget. When he'd given his brother, Max, his address, he never thought he'd turn up, least of all with Grant. He'd last seen Cassie's brother, Grant, at her funeral and now he said he wanted … needed … answers and Jed couldn't hide anymore. It was time, whether he wanted it to be or not.

They'd spent three hours talking.

Grant knew his sister, Cassie, had mental health problems and she'd lived on anti-depressants and anxiety medications since being a teenager. An abusive marriage had left her fractured, damaged beyond repair.

Jed had met her at a literary festival. He'd been at the top of his game ten years ago and loved his life, ex-SAS turned writer, and although he hadn't expected to make any money, he'd been surprised when he could give up security work to write full-time. He'd done sixteen years in the military, mostly on dangerous assignments, at the beck and call of various governments, and after almost being blown up for the third time, he left it behind for a specialist post protecting celebrities and the mega rich. He'd travelled the world, eaten some of the best restaurants, courted many women, but there was always something missing. In his downtime, waiting around in lonely hotel rooms, he turned to writing. His debut was a hit and had caught him by surprise. By the time he'd penned five books, and had a contract for another three, he was in demand at writing events and festivals and found he could step away from his day job. He was more than ready to leave the glamour and glitz.

Then he met Cassie.

Cassie had mistaken him for another writer, and he knew she felt foolish for her faux pas so after his panel talk, she'd bought him a drink to say sorry.

He'd laughed, found it funny, and they started chatting. Her friend had wandered off, not so star struck by the man who wrote fast-action thrillers, in favour of a lady who wrote cosy crime. Jed bought Cassie a drink in return and by the end of the night, he'd asked for her number.

After six months she asked him to move in. He kept his own place and although he could spend most weekends traipsing the country attending various writing festivals, he didn't. When he was actively writing he liked his own space so would return to his house for days, sometimes weeks, keeping his head down and returning to Cassie when he was done.

'What you have to realise, Grant, is that I knew a different Cassie to you. You were siblings, she was much older, but we were partners. I don't mean to patronise you, but I lived with a Cassie that was not the one you knew.'

'What do you mean?'

Jed heard the defensiveness in his voice. 'When she was on form, she was brilliant, she was lovely, lively, fun, sparky, independent, kind.' He hesitated. 'I couldn't love her more. They were great times but truthfully, when she wasn't on form ... well, it was terrible.'

'Terrible, how?'

'She was erratic, unpredictable. Her behaviours were bizarre, not right, and she was jealous when I went away. She could have come with me, but more often she refused. She also started drinking excessively.'

Grant stared at him, eyes like gravel.

'She also became abusive, and I don't mean just with words.'

'I don't believe you.'

'I'm telling you the truth, Grant. You came here looking for answers and I'm giving you them. I can't sugar coat it. She had demons. She was beautiful, when she was Cassie again, gorgeous, funny, all of that, but when the real Cassie disappeared, she was less and less the woman I first met.' Jed remembered the love and the hate, wrapped up in one person, pushing him away only to drag him back in again, push-me pull-you, and although she pleaded, she would change, acted like she meant it, he had to manage it. 'I urged her to seek help, to speak to her GP, to get counselling.'

'So you're saying it was her fault?'

'I'm not saying that. She needed help. The right help. The night she attacked me in a drunken rage so that was it, I had to call time. I didn't want to, I loved her, but she had to get help.' Jed swallowed, remembering her crying, begging, vowing to stop drinking, promising to change, tears and snot and saliva smeared across her face. He shook his head to clear the vision.

SHE'S NOT THERE

When he first suggested she stopped drinking, she laughed and said he was the biggest alcoholic she'd known. He did like a drink, drank with the best of them, and yes, on occasion he drank more than he should, but he wasn't an alcoholic. He knew alcoholics, and that wasn't him. He wasn't sure she was either because she could do without it for days at a time, but it was what it did to her when she did drink, and she drank often. She lost control of what bounced around her head once the chemicals had taken over and without proper intervention, he knew he had to walk away.

He promised that if she sought help, he'd be there for her, wouldn't abandon her, but made it clear he didn't want to be in a relationship with her. There was nobody else, he didn't want anyone else, and desperately wanted her to succeed. He wanted the Cassie he knew was in there somewhere to come back, for her sake, but her demons were too big for him to fight, and they were hers, not his.

Jed tried to explain this to Grant, who listened but didn't believe, and wouldn't have it that his sister was as he portrayed. Jed showed him the scar on his leg where she'd stabbed him. 'I couldn't let it escalate. For either of us. She needed help.'

Grant looked at him, nodded, and said, 'Yeah, she did. And what did you do to her?'

He had Cassie's eyes, striking blue, and the same different shades of blond in his hair, only much shorter and coarser.

Jed sighed. 'Nothing, Grant. Only love her. Very much.' He leant forward in the armchair, his elbows on his knees, and his hands open. 'It wasn't enough. I wasn't enough.'

'Why abandon her? Why not help her?'

'I tried. I did what I could, found support groups, help lines, even offered to pay for her to go to a private facility, but she wouldn't. And I couldn't force her.'

'The best your money could buy, eh?' Grant sneered.

'Your sister had some very deep-rooted problems.'

'So why did you not do more?'

'Do not think there's not a day goes by when I don't wish I'd handled it better. Do you not think I've blamed myself?'

'I don't know what you think,' Grant looked at him with disdain. 'All I know is, you left my sister when she needed you most.'

Jed looked Max, his own brother, sitting on the settee next to Grant. Max shrugged.

Grant said, 'You didn't care. You moved away and kept moving. I couldn't keep track of you.'

'I did care. I do care.'

'Then tell me again, how you let my sister kill herself.'

Jed put his head in his hands. 'Okay, I'll tell you, again. I'll tell you as many times as it takes to try to explain. I wish it was different.'

'Your sister often threatened to kill herself and I tried to help. I even saw my own GP for advice. He gave me the number for the crisis team … but she didn't want it. I even put in her phone contacts for her, should she change her mind.'

'She was stubborn, I'll give you that.'

Jed saw the smidgeon of a smile on Grant's face and felt a prick of confidence as he inhaled, preparing himself for the next part, the part he had tried hard not to think about.

'I was in Coventry when it happened, teaching on a creative writing weekend. Before I left, we'd discussed Cassie going to a clinic in Oxford and she told me she was going to seriously consider it. I last spoke to her on the Friday night and said I'd call the next day. On the Saturday I had a full day teaching and didn't have time to ring before the evening event. After dinner I returned to my room and found a number of missed calls from Cassie. That in itself wasn't unusual.' Jed shrugged as he remembered. He constantly had to delete her messages as they took up so much space. She'd mumble and ramble and sometimes fall asleep with the phone still connected so the voicemail would exceed the memory. 'She'd left a voicemail, and I could tell she was drunk. She said she was better off dead, that I could take my five grand rehab and shove it, who did I think I was, buying her way into a mental hospital, trying to get her sectioned, that sort of stuff. Her last words were 'you'll regret it'.'

Jed looked down, legs jiggling, hands clenched together, remembering the words clearly as they echoed in his head. He couldn't look at Grant.

After a silence that seemed to stretch, he continued. 'I tried to call her. Of course, I regretted not making time earlier. When I did ring it was near midnight and her phone was off. On Sunday morning, she was dead.' Jed regretted not acting on her voicemail, but she'd threatened suicide plenty of times before and was always remorseful when sober. If he'd left that night, he'd have been too drunk to drive and he wouldn't have made it in time to save her anyway. 'The amount she'd had to drink, with the pills she'd taken, together they depressed her respiratory system. It was too much.'

Jed genuinely believed she'd never meant to, that it was yet another cry for help. She wanted the pain to go away, the whirling dervish to stop. That was what she wanted to kill, not herself. 'My biggest regret is that I never contacted her family to tell them how bad she was.'

'We thought she was happy. We thought she was safe. With you.'

Jed felt the accusation and took it. He didn't say what he thought, what he felt, that they knew she suffered but nobody had thought to tell Jed this was her, her life, a pattern of behaviour since being a teenager. He didn't blame them, and it would serve no purpose to say this to Grant. During the inquest Jed had discovered Cassie had been diagnosed with bipolar and other mental health issues and he wished he'd known because he may have been able to deal with things differently. For a long time, he blamed himself and did what he thought was the best thing he could – run. But he always saw her face. Her dead face. Her lifeless face drained of love, of living. He saw her laying there, in her coffin, eyes closed, dead. Flash. Flash. Flash. Unbidden, she'd come to him in the shower, in his dreams, when he was walking down the street. She came to him everywhere. And so, he kept running. And still she came.

Jed was exhausted when Grant and Max finally left. Grant had cried, claimed nobody had explained anything to him about Cassie and he felt he couldn't ask. They had the same father, but different mothers, and their dad wouldn't speak of Cassie, didn't tell him anything.

'I tried to find you, Jed, but I couldn't and each time I thought I had, you'd moved again.'

'You found me now, though.'

'I remembered meeting Max at a family thing so went to find him instead and persuaded him to bring me to you.'

Jed commiserated because nobody had spoken to him about Cassie either, not when they were together, nor afterwards. They cut him off.

'It had to be done, man,' said Max when Grant was upstairs in the bathroom. 'For him, and for you. You still blaming yourself?'

'Not so much.'

'Good. It wasn't your fault. Anyone else would have left long before you did.'

'Maybe.'

'You had counselling?'

'No, just living my life. Sorting out my head. And before you say, I know I told Cassie to get counselling, and yes, I know you'll say so should I, and it's probably the way to go, but I'm okay. Really.'

'You going to stay here?'

'Maybe…' smiled Jed.

Max grinned at him. 'Ahh, I see. You've met someone?'

'Maybe…' He hesitated. 'I don't know. It's not like that.' He looked down at his feet, shuffled them like an awkward teenager.

'But you've got an interest?'

'Mmm, maybe…' he looked up at his brother. 'I'm writing again, though.'

'Good. You look brighter. Any good? Or your usual trash?'

'Piss off,' he laughed.

'Great to see you, bro. Don't be a stranger, eh?'

'Right. No. I mean, I won't.' He picked up the empty cups. 'The lad needed to hear it. There's a lot for him to think about and you're right, I owed it to him. If you'd have called to say you were coming, I'd have been out.'

'You did a good thing today. The way you told him, you didn't criticise her, you said it as it was. I hope that means you can see it like that, too.'

Jed heard but didn't answer as he took the cups to the kitchen.

Chapter 39

When Bob Harris had asked to see her, she presumed it was to take over some of his cases. As she'd suspected, he'd been seconded onto the whisky job full time and to be fair to him, he had done a chunk of the investigation, collating information and intelligence work. No coincidence that he was fond of the amber nectar, either.

He said he might have a lead on the Fraser case.

'This head in the bin…' he said, as she approached his desk. 'Might be something in it for you.'

'Yeah? How so?' She had no idea how it might be connected. 'Go on?'

'Cameron Struan.'

'Ah, him! I only knew he existed yesterday.'

'Really? I could have filled you in on him. You caught up with him yet?'

'No. Don't know where he is. Tell me all.'

'He runs with the Dundee lot we think are responsible for the distillery robberies. He hasn't been seen for the last wee while. It's been suggested it might be his head in the bin.'

'I thought it was Corrie someone or other?'

'So did we but he turned up in the clink in Durham doing a five stretch for aggravated burglary. Took the rap for the gang leader, by the sounds of it. Anyway, the head could be Struan. It's too decomposed for an ID. The pathologist can't date it yet, it's such a mess. Palmerston reckons whoever did it might have tried to burn the head. It was second homers that came up for the week that found it in their brown bin. No idea how long it's been there.'

'So…' She hesitated. wrapped her finger around her chin. 'When will you have a formal ID?'

'Not sure. Your Dr Grey is looking at it for us. She was full of you when I saw her yesterday. We've got plenty of Cam Struan's DNA in our files so he'll be checked first. I'll give you the heads up when we anything back.' Harris chuckled. 'Heads up, hahaha.'

Kat tutted and sat at her computer. She typed in Cameron Struan. The intelligence files were lengthy. He first came to notice in the mid-2000s for petty crime, involved in drugs and pushing them out to the kids in the skatepark in Perth. He got a three-year stretch, did fifteen months. He'd been nicked a few times for minor scuffles in London, Glasgow, and Dundee. A robbery at a post office resulted in another stint in Perth Prison, and she noticed a number of domestic incident reports. They mainly involved Cameron turning up at the door drunk and harassing his ex, often on social media and too often in person. He had a list of known associates pages long. Kat wasn't familiar with any of the names yet. She clicked on a few and they all had similar histories – thefts, drugs, robberies, violence. Same offences, just different names and faces, a regular pack of cards.

She searched his ex-partner, Hannah Robertson. Nothing other than the reported DV incidents. Kat wondered if she was still living at the same address. Block 2, Flat 6 Inchcape Lane.

Kat checked the street index for the third time but there was definitely no trace of the new estate, or Inchcape Lane. It would have to be old-fashioned leg work. She knew it was a long shot but might be worth it. She had no idea where Cameron Struan fit into things, if he did, but as Jed had reminded her last week, there's no such thing as coincidence.

Eventually, when she was fairly sure was at the right address, Kat knocked on a door. After a few more raps she heard movement from inside. A petite blonde woman answered.

'Copper, right?' she said, looking Kat up and down.

'Miss Robertson?'

'What's it about?'

'You're not in any bother. I'd like to speak with you please. About Cameron Struan.'

'He isn't here. I told the last copper that knocked the same and he didn't believe me either.'

'I don't think he is here. I'm not here for him. It's you I'd like to speak with.'

'For why?'

'I know you had trouble with him, Hannah, when he was harassing you and all the social media stuff. I'd just like a word if that's okay?' Kat saw the suspicion in her eyes lift a little.

'I haven't seen him for a long time. He hasn't bothered me for ages.' She opened the door a bit further and Kat saw into the hallway. A side table with a vase of budding lilies on the right and a voile curtain hanging at a window at the far end.

'You'd better come in but be quiet, yeah? My son's asleep.'

As she entered the hall, they passed a bedroom with the door ajar. Kat saw a child sleeping in a cot.

'I didn't know you had a son.'

'Why would you? You don't know me.' Hannah frowned. 'Do you? You from the social?'

'No. Nothing like that. I promise. I read the domestic reports and thought you might know where Cameron is. I have information for him, something that he should know. An address would be good.'

'I have no idea. Have they sent you to get me to talk? 'Cos yous can't find him?'

'No, I didn't know anyone else was looking for him,' Kat said, not quite a lie. She hadn't known, not until this morning.

'Well I'd like to know where he is myself 'coz there's things I need to tell him too.' She nodded to the bedroom. 'So, if you find him, he needs to get his scabby arse back around here.'

'How old is your boy?' asked Kat.

'Two and a bit. Cameron doesn't know about Harry, 'cos last time I saw him I didn't know I was pregnant.'

'Harry's Cameron's son?'

'Course! I ain't no slag. I've heard nothing from him, or about him, since that last time when I phoned yous. Not seen him since. And none of his pals are giving anything away either. I'm dead angry with him. He should be here for his son. I want nowt to do wiv him himself, but a boy needs a dad.'

She wasn't as young as Kat first thought she looked. Thirty, maybe. She hadn't remembered seeing her age on the DV report. 'Well, when I find him, I'll make sure he knows.'

'He's always flitting off. I thought he'd was banged up, but you wouldn't be here if he was in the nick would ya? He could be deid for all I know.' She laughed then looked at Kat. 'Is he?'

'Not that I know,' said Kat, beginning to wonder.

'I knew he must be shacked up with someone when he stopped bothering with me. He had a bit of skirt up north. He's always gone from one lass to another. When I found out I was expecting I thought someone must have told him which is why he didn't come back but I dunnae ken, I've heard nowt off him and neither has anyone else that I know of.'

'Whereabouts up north was this other lass?'

'Somewhere up near his old man's place. He must be getting ready to croak, unless... is that why you're looking for him? His old man deid?'

Kat saw her face change. 'No, not his old man.'

'Who then? My son is heir to the throne an' that. I have a right to know.' She lightly snorted.

Kat didn't reply.

'I heard he had a young lass up on his dad's estate. He'd been banging her mother years ago when they were kids and he thought it was bloody hilarious he was now banging the daughter. When I asked him, he didn't even deny it, the git. He just said, "You don't begrudge me a jump, do ya?" Bastard. He only ever comes back to me when the others kick him oot, when he's got nowhere else to go. He always comes back to me, eventually…and I always let him in. So, who's croaked?'

'I didn't say anyone had. Who is she, this skirt? You got a name?'

'Dunnae, I don't go no further than Perth. The one he was knocking off before, the older one, she's called Ally or somat, I think that's her, but he's had plenty o' women and she was long afore he met me. Mind you, his bit o'skirt, they're getting younger and younger, so maybe you wannae check the dirty get out.'

'I will, thanks. When I find him, I'll tell him to get in touch.'

'Me too, love, me too. For Harry's sake.'

By the time she'd returned to the office, Bob Harris was waiting for her. He handed her a cup of weak coffee and said, 'All bets are off. It ain't Cameron Struan.'

'What do mean? You sounded fairly convinced to me.'

'I was. Shame on me. I was halfway oot the door when I got a call from the team from the witchcraft case. It's one of theirs. The rest of the body turned up in a right mess in a student house. They'd tattooed his body and tried to burn it before chopping his head off, and a couple of toes, few fingers, an eye out … and they daubed him in symbols.' Harris shook his head. 'Ugh, anyway, body's a match so nothing to do with either mine, or yours.'

Another wild goose chase. She'd hoped that it was Struan's head in the bin and the rest of his body in the coffin. She tapped her pen against the desk as she tried to join the dots, dots that had now gone off on a tangent. She need time to think because the connections were starting to look complicated, but she was sure they were joined together somehow.

Her phone vibrated in her trouser pocket. It was Jed. She'd phone him back, didn't have time right now, and slipped the phone into her bag, still on silent.

Cameron Struan hadn't been seen or heard of for the last two years or so. He wasn't on the missing list because nobody had reported him missing but neither could he be located. Intelligence records made him look fairly itinerant, a number of old addresses, pages of associates, and jobs, all manual and menial, nothing becoming of a Laird, or his son. He probably had a trust fund to keep him going and wandering off the grid didn't seem unusual for him.

She needed to speak to Drew Fraser. It was time to tell him the truth. She couldn't delay it any longer. It was a shame Guy was at his wife's final antenatal appointment. Kat decided to do it on her way home and whilst there she'd take the opportunity to ask him about Cameron. No such thing as a coincidence. He'd been with a woman called Ally and now her daughter. Alison Fraser's daughter, who had a son called Cam. Ally must be Alison Fraser. Cameron Struan, Lorna's older boyfriend, the father of Lorna's baby. It fit together too well not to be. The older man who had promised to stay around but then done a flit. It shone a different perspective on Drew Fraser, first his wife and then his daughter. He'd have an axe to grind. A first-class motive.

For the first time, Kat felt confident she knew who was in Rosemary's coffin. But could she prove it?

Chapter 40

KAT WAS ON her way to Fortingall Crescent when Jed called again. She told him she was on hands-free but he said it was too important to discuss whilst she was driving.

'Give me a clue? I'm on my way to the Frasers'. There's been an interesting development.'

'In that case, you might want to call to see me before you go.'

'Can't you tell me now? Time's getting on.'

'Not when you're driving, no. Might be something, maybe nothing, but I'd rather see you before speaking with Drew Fraser.'

Ten minutes later she pulled into Jed's driveway. He was stood at the back door waiting for her.

'What's the panic?' she asked, walking past him through the kitchen and into the sitting-room. 'Wow! Someone's been busy! Looks fabulous. So bright!'

'Yeah. Finally got around to it. Still got some touching-in bits to do. Have a seat. You might want something stronger than coffee.'

'Intriguing!' She sat down, pulled her coat open but kept it on, her eyes on him.

He sat down opposite her. 'I was in the Open Reach last night, minding my own business, as instructed,' he grinned.

'Good lad, go on.'

'Thanks! Patronising much.'

She smiled. 'Get on with it.'

'Well, I couldn't help hearing, not actively listening at that point, but noticing, just as you asked...' He paused.

'Get on with it!' She wound her hand around to hurry him up.

'Put it this way, Kat. I may be looking for alternative accommodation in the near future. Just as I was starting to settle down, too.'

'Struan?'

'Yup. And Fraser.'

'Surprise, surprise. Not.'

'Really?' He cocked his head.

'Really, but you first. Go on.'

He relayed he'd been sitting in the corner booth, the one tight in the corner, hidden behind a partition and the Courier. He'd spotted Struan talking to a man he didn't know. He really wasn't listening but couldn't help but overhear, especially when one of them said 'that bloody writer'. He was hardly famous, or that interesting, and there must be other writers hiding in middle Perthshire, and he was paranoid, of course he was but nevertheless, he knew he was the object of their discussion. He couldn't hear everything that was said, but surely, he hadn't pissed that many people off yet.

The men were arguing. The barman handed them a couple of pints and said, 'They ye are, Mick. Eight punds to you.'

'Fuck's sake, Trev. Put it on me tab.'

As Trevor went across to the fire to pile on more logs, Michael bent his head and said to the other man, 'Stick to the script. Why would anyone question? They know nothing, trust me.'

The smaller man said, 'I don't like it.'

'Cameron could never be relied on. Always disappearing, months at a time. Years, if he's in the nick. The only tracks on him were the ones in his arms. I know ye ken this, Drew.'

'Aye, but he always turns up agin.' Drew downed his pint in three gulps. 'You said she'd be gone. Forever. Would have been okay if that bloody writer hadn't turned up. Or you hadn't decided to sell that land.'

Michael shrugged. 'Could have took her right up top where nobody goes. Could have dug deeper. That's your fault, not mine. If you hadn't insisted on doing it where we did, she'd have been gone forever.'

'Don't go blaming me,' Drew said, gripping the bar. 'Look, I have to go.'

'Ally not happy?'

'I'm not happy!'

'One for the road?' Michael beckoned the landlord from the front door where he was having a smoke.

'No. Don't want to be nicked for drink drive o'top of this.'

'Who ever got done for drink drive round here? Apart from Mally Abbott and we all ken why that was.' He laughed.

Jed continued listening while the men bantered between themselves. The door opened and a bloke wearing undertaker's trousers walked in.

'Malcolm,' hollered Michael. ''Aven't seen you for long while. Come and have a drink wi ya pals. Trev, whatever the man's having. Put it on m'tab.'

'Nae thanks, whenever I drink wi' you two, it's dangerous. I lost two days and a week's pay last time. I'll stick to myself.'

The barman shouted over, 'Hey, Malcolm, don't want any trouble. I only said I'd lift ya ban if ya behaved yesel. Three pints tops. Nae more until you can control ya temper.'

'Fuck's sake, Trevor. Can't a man have a pint in peace? I get enough nagging indoors. I'm having one pint an' I'll be off. Not the sort of company I like to keep in here, anyways.'

Michael insisted on buying the man's drink.

Jed watched them, hidden in his cubicle, busting for a pee but not daring to move. He hoped the barman didn't come over or ask if he wanted another drink. He'd have to wait until Struan left. The other two didn't know him, but Struan certainly did.

Then Trevor blew his cover.

As he tidied up the bar and placed down fresh coasters, he said, 'Did I hear you talking about that writer whose moved in? The locals love him.' He nodded towards the corner cubicle. 'He's sitting over there if you wanna chat, dead friendly chap he is. Hey, Jed?'

All three punters turned to look in his direction as he tried to hide himself further down the seat, thinking fast on his feet. He'd have to blag it. He folded up the paper and stood up, stretching to his full six foot two. 'Nice to see you again,' he acknowledged Struan. 'Just dropping off there, head in the paper, full of Witches Fang, and heat of the fire.' He looked at his watch and stifled a yawn that he hoped looked authentic. 'I'll catch you guys another time. Must dash!' and took his leave by the back door.

'Sorry, Kat, I have no idea if they knew I'd heard anything or not. I didn't stay around to find out.'

'And you didn't think to tell me this earlier?'

'I've been calling you all day!'

Kat smarted. He had but she'd been too busy joining the dots. 'Hmm. I'll need a different plan. Can't go to Fraser now without him being suspicious. And I am suspicious. I need a strategy, and quick.'

'I wrote it up earlier when I couldn't get hold of you.' He handed her a piece of A4, written in neat tidy letters, different to what she expected of him.

'Brilliant! It's coming together. I can't go into it all now but I've just found out that there's another Struan brother –'

'Cameron, per chance?'

'Aye, Cameron. But there's a third, too.'

244

'Really?'

'Yes, really … but I need to work it out clearly, how it fits together, how they fit together.' She stood up and started pacing, rubbing her chin.

'Are you going to tell me who?'

'What?' She looked at Jed. 'Oh, yes. Bet you can't guess?'

'I know him? Who?'

'Can't you guess?'

'No, I don't know anyone. Who?'

'Drew Fraser.'

Jed looked puzzled. 'What? You're making me dizzy. Sit down a minute. How is he a Struan? They didn't look very brotherly. Though why I said that, the brothers I know …'

'Because I don't think they know. Rosemary Fraser worked at the big house as a housekeeper and had a baby with old man Struan. He wouldn't acknowledge his son so she gave him to her brother and his wife to bring up. I don't know if Drew knew she was his mother or not, I doubt it, but it means that all three – Michael, Drew, and Cameron, they're brothers.'

Jed gave a low whistle. 'So they buried Rosemary together? Why? Where does Cameron fit into it?'

'I think I know but …' Something was niggling her. Something that if she was right, could blow the family apart. 'I have to go. I'll call you.'

And she was gone.

SHE'S NOT THERE

Chapter 41

Instead of going to see the Frasers she phoned their house and Mary answered. She asked to speak to her father and Mary passed the phone to him without asking who was calling.

When Kat asked him to come and see her at the station, he put her off with one excuse after another. Once he realised it was either that or a knock at dawn to bring him in, they finally agreed on Friday morning at 10am. She had thirty-six hours to piece it together, to work on a strategy. He had thirty-six hours to work on his own.

She was increasingly confident that it had been Cameron Struan in the coffin instead of Rosemary Fraser. They'd never be able to prove murder without a body ... but there had been cases convicted on circumstantial evidence. Motive? Sibling rivalry was a good enough reason, but did they know they were siblings? She doubted it. There wasn't enough evidence to arrest, not yet, but Fraser didn't know that and she was confident something would give.

Drew Fraser stood with his wife in the foyer of Perth police station. He looked like he hadn't slept and his hands were shaking.

'Can I come in with him, Sergeant?' Alison asked, grabbing her husband's hand, gripping it tight.

'There's only a few questions. He's not under arrest and he can leave at any time,' smiled Kat.

'Then I can be there too?' Alison asked.

Kat shook her head. 'No, sorry.'

'There's nothing you can't say in front of me,' she said.

Drew couldn't meet her eyes. 'Do I need a solicitor?'

Kat looked at him. He wasn't the rough-tough logger he'd been in his own house. 'Do you think you need a solicitor?' Naughty, she knew. She should offer him the opportunity of a solicitor but was this really anything more than gathering evidence?

He hesitated, did the goldfish impression, opening and closing his mouth.

'It's my fault, Sergeant. It's because of me. That's where this all started,' Alison said.

'Do you need a solicitor?' Kat wasn't expecting this. Was she going to get a confession?

The doors opened and a family burst through to the front desk, a gaggle of children with a frazzled dad, chatter-chatter of excitable kids.

'We'll go through to the witness room and talk more there.' She led them through the side door to the room designated for witnesses, victims, the place where statements were taken and bad news broken. Perhaps she should do that first and if she was going to break the news of his parentage to Drew it could be handy to have his wife there. Judging by the state of him Kat wasn't sure how he'd take it.

Kat still wasn't sure what the truth was. Drew and Alison Fraser had both declined solicitors, even after she'd given them their proper rights. Michael Struan had brought a hot-shot solicitor from Rafferty & Nath but it was Michael Struan who had called the shots in his interview.

Kat questioned them all with Guy Lynn. He should have started his paternity leave but had stayed on for the interviews, with crossed fingers, hoping his wife didn't go into labour over the weekend.

Michael Struan and Drew Fraser had different versions of events.

Struan described how he and Drew had left the outhouses on the estate in one of the jeeps. 'It was a vast starry night, bright stars that lit up the sky on what was to be a fateful and treacherous task.'

'Right.' Kat wasn't taken in as she watched Michael Struan feign emotional pain. 'So then what?'

'The engine made a terrible screeching noise, like squealing chalk, as it slid-skipped down the hill. The fan belt was slipping,' he said, looking at Kat, mansplaining.

'Carry on.' She knew he was stalling. She'd had experienced enough patronising masculinity to last a lifetime.

'It was supposed to be fixed but the garage hand went off to a music festival and spent three days high. I'd sack him if he wasn't so damn good on the job.'

Kat had heard about Dougie Porter, the mechanic, from Sue when she was trying to sort her own car problems. Sue had told her that he was good at his job and for the jobs on the fly, and a worthy asset to the town as the main garage charged a fortune. Her assessment was if only Dougie could keep his women away from each other, he'd have a lot less hassle and a lot more fun.

'I know of Porter.' There was no harm in letting him know that. She kept her gaze on Struan, arms folded while she waited.

'The slipping engine brought out the hounds and I had to swerve to avoid running over one of my dogs. I wound the window and shouted at it. It was cold and I laughed at Drew shivering like a little boy.' He paused. 'Well, we had a mission, and cold weather or not, it had to be done.' He shrugged.

'What exactly was that mission, Mr Struan?' asked Kat, keeping her eyes locked with his.

'The vehicle bounced down the track though I tried to avoid the pot-holes. We had a conversation about filling it in. I asked him, did he have any idea how much that would cost? People have no clue about this stuff and I have more pressing things to spend money on than a bumpy road. It costs a fortune to keep the estate running, despite what folk think. I'm doing more and more myself to keep costs down. My father has dementia and his carers cost me a bloody fortune. If he hangs on much longer, there'll be nothing left.'

Kat knew he was waffling as diversion but let him ramble on.

'The jeep bounced and slid, bounced and slid, down onto the main drag. I flicked on full beam. The accelerator and exhaust rattled as we drove down the lane to the main road and the Open Reach.' He stopped.

Kat waited. Looked at him. Waited more.

'I told Drew it had to be tonight. I mean … that night.'

Chapter 42

The next interview was almost identical.

They both described how they'd plied the undertaker, Malcolm, with a pint and a chaser, another pint and chaser, and so many more that the poor man couldn't stand. He was easy prey. Every Tuesday and Thursday, the nights he wasn't on-call, he was in the Open Reach. Everyone knew he was a heavy drinker. The plan was to get him pissed, throw him in the back of the truck, drop him home, take his keys, and he'd be none the wiser. They'd done dummy runs, offering him a lift and dropping him home a few nights over the preceding weeks so nobody would question it as odd. One of the nights they'd taken his keys and dropped them just inside his front door so he'd find them the next morning and believe he'd dropped them on his way into the house. Set a pattern.

Once they'd finished with them the night they needed them, Struan threw the keys in the river. Malcolm would believe he'd lost them, as he had previously, and be none the wiser.

The next stage of their stories matched.

'Be careful, Michael, you might bruise her,' whispered Drew, despite no one being there to hear him.

Michael grunted as he manipulated the body from the coffin. 'Who cares? What does it matter? This bloody smell! Worse than a decaying cow.'

'Don't compare her to a cow! I bloody hate you sometimes, Michael.'

Drew thought he was going to vomit when he caught a glimpse of the lividity marks on his aunt's body. As they turned her, something cracked.

Drew hid his gag behind his hand.

It took a few pulls and tugs to lift her completely from the coffin.

Michael snapped, 'Get it done and get this lid screwed back down.'

'Graves won't be able to tell, will he?' said Drew.

'Why would he? What time's the funeral?'

'Eleven.'

'Let's hope Malcolm sleeps off his hangover in time. Look the state of you, you'll need to sort yourself out by morning.' Michael checked his watch.

'We leave here nine thirty to get to the crem. It doesn't give them long to notice anything amiss. Malcolm will look like shit tomorrow.'

'You look like shit now.'

'I feel bad.' He struggled to hold back tears.

'What fa? Killing my brother? Or switching his body with your aunt? Or getting the undertaker pissed and nicking his keys? Which one? Or is it all of them?' Michael spat. 'Don't be a fucking pussy now.'

'I ... I dunno...'

'No time for that. What other choice is there?'

'But it was an accident.'

'But it was an accident,' mocked Michael. 'It might well have been a bloody accident, but who do you think will believe ya? Anyway, late now.' He tapped his temple with his forefinger. 'Think. You want to do thirty years in the jailhouse?'

'I'm living with it … this … for the rest of my days. I dinnae want any of this to happen.'

'Don't start panicking now. And trust me, she's not the only dead body buried up in these hills.'

'No?'

'Never mind that. This way there's no court case, no daughters or wife or anyone else giving evidence. No raking over the past. We both know what I mean.'

'But if we're caught …'

'We won't get caught. Now shut the fuck up and give me a hand.'

'If your fucking brother could o' kept it in his pants… away from our girls …'

'Help me get him into this coffin,' grunted Michael, bending down.

As they lifted the body wrapped in sheeting, the top one slid away, revealing a head.

Drew Fraser came face to face with Cameron Struan.

Chapter 43

Kat now had some answers that had been evading her. Both Drew Fraser and Michael Struan had confirmed it was Cameron Struan in the coffin. She had no way of proving or disproving that part of the story, as CCTV only held the three weeks data, but the lab would match his blood to that found on the sheet and she was confident the Procurator Fiscal would be able to prove prevention of, or unlawful disposal of, a body. That still left the question of how it all came about and why.

When Kat interviewed Alison, she asked her if she'd known Cameron Struan. She confirmed that eighteen years ago she'd had a 'thing', something little more than a fling, with him. He was attractive, free-spirited, funny, and dangerous. He was a chancer, a heartbreaker, and she fell for his charm. She described him as cheeky, witty, and when she was with him, he made her feel like they were the only two people who existed in the world, and he was intoxicating. Like everything dangerous, he'd left her with a lasting hangover. They had three wild summer months and then he was gone, enticed away by a woman he called a raven-haired beauty from Blair Atholl.

Then she asked her, 'Is Lorna his daughter?'

Alison stared at her. 'How did you know?' She paled. 'Is it common knowledge?'

'No, I just joined the dots.'

'But how?'

'Loose lips. He'd told someone that he was seeing the daughter of a woman he used to be with years ago. Men brag. People brag. I can see that Mary's like her dad, she has the same jaw, but Lorna is more like you. It was a possibility and one I thought was right.'

Alison started to cry. 'We've kept it to ourselves all this time. We tried to hide it from her. Lorna doesn't know.'

Guy left to get tissues and tea. When Alison had calmed down, stopped sobbing and hugged her cuppa, she said she wanted to tell them the truth.

By the time Alison realised she was pregnant she was already seeing Drew Fraser, steady, easy-going Drew, who she knew from school, had fancied like mad, but hadn't seen around much until she bumped into him at the Highland Games. His parents had both been killed by then and he was living with his Aunt Rosemary.

Lorna was born and Drew knew that she wasn't his but took her on as his own, happy to do so. They'd put his name on her birth certificate, and no one but Alison and Drew knew any different. No one but them knew that Cameron Struan was Lorna's biological father. There was no need to tell him as he was hardly a positive role model and he wouldn't have cared. He was into harder drugs and peddling to the kids in the skate park in Perth and looking at jail time. He was off their scene and not a consideration.

Three years later they had Mary Rose, naming her after Rosemary. Their family was complete. Skip forward sixteen years, and Lorna confessed to being in love and being pregnant.

'You can't imagine. Our world was knocked on its axis when she told us. It was bad enough being pregnant, we could cope with that. It wasn't what we wanted for her, but we'd help. She'd left it too late to do anything about it but that wasn't the biggest issue as we'd never have pushed her into not having the baby. It was when she said who the father was. I was physically sick. Drew was beyond livid. But we couldn't tell her. We've never told her. I couldn't begin to explain why to her why it was so wrong. And she'd never get over it. Never.'

'The father, Cameron Struan,' stated Kat.

'Yes. She'd kept him secret. He'd told her that him and her dad had bad history and it wouldn't be a good idea to tell us about them seeing each other, about their relationship.' She scoffed. 'Relationship. It turns my stomach. He didn't tell her about me and him. She'd have said something for sure if she knew that. Of course, he had no clue who she was, that she was his daughter. She also looks a lot like me at the same age so I could see her appeal to him. He'd have got a kick out of it. It disgusts me.'

'So where do Isla Garvey and Lydia Struan fit in?' asked Guy.

'He'd met the girls at the Highland games. Bloody games. Should be banned, they've a lot to answer for! Cameron had a one-night stand with Isla Garvey and her mum found out. Next thing, the family moved away. Think they were moving anyway but Pam Garvey couldn't stand him and didn't want him anywhere near her daughter. He'd courted her before but I don't think she slept with him. She had a reputation as tight but, hey, I don't know. You know teenagers. We were all teenagers together. He went through women like he went through a pack of cigarettes. One after the other, after the other. Chain-smoking women.'

'And Lydia?'

'He didn't know she was his niece. Not at first. He hadn't seen her for years. The last time, she was a little girl, dark hair and a bit dumpy. When he met them, the girls were attractive teenagers, young girls, old enough but not shrewd enough to keep away from a charmer like him. She started seeing him at the same time as Lorna and the girls fell out, but I didn't know it was over him, not then.'

'He had a sexual relationship with his niece?' asked Guy.

'I can't confirm that but I suspect so. At some point she must have said who she was, or where she lived, or something that made him realise. I don't know how far it went with them. I know that when Michael found Cameron was back, he was livid. He sent Lydia away travelling, and then Covid hit, and she's not been back since.'

Kat's head was spinning. No wonder Michael Struan was complicit in getting rid of his brother's body. But which one had murdered him? Or was it both?

'You can imagine how we felt. Not only was Lorna pregnant by a man old enough to be her father, he was her father. And we couldn't tell her. I just couldn't. That poor boy… she named him after Cameron and the only thing we can take from it is that Cameron didn't know Lorna was his daughter. I am certain he wouldn't have gone anywhere near her if he did. I really do. Nor Lydia. I don't,' she paused, corrected herself, 'didn't … have any good to say about him but I'd give him that. He wouldn't have got involved had he known she was his.' She looked at Kat. 'We're going to have to tell her, aren't we?'

'I think so, yes.'

'If we hadn't have kept him secret in the first place, none of this would have happened.'

'How did he die, Alison?' asked Kat.

Alison shook her head. 'I can't … that's for Drew, not me.'

257

Chapter 44

Drew Fraser sat in the second interview room. Kat and Guy looked at him as he picked at his fingernails. He had declined a solicitor.

'Has she told you?' he said without looking up.

Kat looked at the face of a broken man. Lorna was seventeen and although nothing illegal in a relationship with a man much older than her, there was the moral aspect, and then the incest situation that neither she nor Cameron were aware of.

Drew pleaded, 'You can imagine how I felt?'

Kat imagined very well, though neither confirmed nor denied it. Her job was to gather the facts. His emotion, his motive, that was for mitigation, for the court room, not for her. Whilst she might understand his motive for murder, she was neither judge nor jury.

'You felt murderous?' she asked.

'No! That's the thing, I didn't. I didn't want to murder him. Why would I murder him to ruin my life? It wasn't like that. Really.'

Guy jumped in. 'Who killed him?'

Drew put his head in his hands.

The silence lingered. Guy looked at Kat. She looked at Drew Fraser

'I did,' he whispered.

'You murdered him?'

'Yes. No...'

Silence.

Eventually Drew said, 'Yes.'

'You killed Cameron Struan,' asked Kat.

'I did.'

'After discovering your daughter was pregnant with his child, the man who years earlier had seduced your wife?' she continued.

Drew shook his head. 'She wasn't my wife, not then. Not when she was pregnant. We weren't even together then.'

'Alison said.'

'It's true. He'd already disappeared off the scene before she found out.'

'He then seduced your daughter,' stated Kat.

'His daughter. He seduced his daughter. How did that happen? I didn't even know until she was pregnant who she'd been seeing. It was too late to stop anything by then.'

'You killed your daughter's father?'

'Yes.' He sobbed.

'How did that happen?'

Drew looked at her, shook his head. 'I never meant to kill him. I went to confront him. To tell him Lorna was his girl, not mine. She was supposed to be meeting him but I went instead. She was in a mess, crying and that, and didn't want me to go to see him. We didn't tell her the truth, that he was her father. She screamed and kicked off at me but we eventually persuaded her to stay with Alison. I went to meet him by the outhouses. They're being demolished to clear the land for housing. Struan's selling a lot of his land off.' He paused, shuffled in his chair.

Filler, avoidance, but Kat let him talk.

'Anyway, he was there, waiting for her. For Lorna. He mocked me, laughed at me and called me a small man. I told him it took a real man to bring up another man's daughter. He didn't get it, not at first, and I had to spell it out to him. I told him Lorna was his. He didn't believe me, thought I was lying to stop them being together. I told him the dates and asked him to work it out. He got it, he realised I was

259

telling the truth. I saw it dawn on him, the incest thing, and that their baby wouldn't be his child but would also be his grandchild. He got angry ... so fucking angry ... he was raging. He went for me, got me in a headlock and said he should have been told. Fair enough, he had a point ... definitely had a point. He said he'd never have touched her had he known. I believed him. I said so.'

Kat saw the look in his eyes and knew he was telling the truth. His truth.

'Didn't matter though 'cos Cameron got angry, he flared up. I saw it cross his face. He said it was all my fault, that I'd let it happen and if I had told Lorna the truth about him being her dad, it would never have happened because even if he hadn't known, she would have ... and ... and it's true. He was right. It's my fault.' His head was down and he was picking at his cuticles again.

Kat waited.

Drew sniffed loudly, tears, mucus, pain. 'He got a few punches in. I was never great at boxing.' He paused, shifted in his seat. 'I managed to give him a jab, a hook that caught him in the midriff, and he staggered back a bit and he released his hold on me. I caught him square on his jaw. He fell backwards and ...' he coughed and cleared his throat. He looked up at Kat.

His eyes brimmed with tears as he closed them.

Kat waited.

'The old tractors,' he coughed the crack out of his voice. 'The tractors ... the ones they don't use anymore ... he fell back ... it was just one punch ... he fell onto the bale spike. It went straight through his neck.'

They took a break. Drew was in no state to continue. Kat asked him again if he wanted a brief but he shook his head as he took the cup of tea from Guy.

'No. I accept responsibility. I don't want them telling me to say 'no comment'. I need to get it out.'

SHE'S NOT THERE

Kat looked at him. Drew had a classic motive for murder and there had been plenty of time for him to concoct a story. This story was one of accidental death, careless, reckless, and not the first time it had ever happened. He could claim self-defence, and they were fighting. It usually happened on a night out gone wrong, all it took was one punch and they fell, hitting their head, hard impact, smacking down onto a kerbstone or hard surface. One punch was enough. Dead. Classic manslaughter.

They resumed the interview.

'Mr Fraser,' challenged Kat. 'What I don't understand is why you didn't phone the police? Or at the very least an ambulance.'

'He was dying. I didn't know what to do. I panicked. I could hear his throat … he was gurgling, spitting up blood, his eyes … oh god … I … I …just froze … and then Michael was there.'

'What happened then?'

'This is the part where it becomes muddy. I don't know.'

'What do you mean, you don't know? You must know what you did next.'

Drew closed his eyes. 'We got him off the tractor. He was still warm … blood everywhere. His eyes were dead. He was definitely dead.' He cried, snuffling snot and tears.

Kat waited.

'Michael didn't give a stuff. It was his brother and he just kept saying how he wasn't going to be missed, what a waster he was, a druggie an' tha. Said he'd always brought shame on the family, and … and I don't remember, really, but then I was telling my aunt, Rose. She always knew what to do in a crisis.'

'And what did she say?'

'She said she'd think of something.'

'And did she?'

'Two nights later she called me to go and see her.'

'And?'

'She had a plan but said it would only work if we kept to it and kept calm. I don't know what Michael was planning on doing. Bury him right up the top of the Munro, maybe. That would have been the best thing.' He drained his tea, shuffled his feet a bit. 'Rose knew she was dying and said if she did anything else for that family, it would be this. She told me that when the time came, to swap her body for his in the coffin.'

'She thought of that?'

'She did. She said she didn't know how but we would have to work it out. She wanted me to bury her and told me where. She kept saying it was better than burying him because if he was found there would be too many questions and the police would think murder straight off whereas with her, she'd never be found and her death would be natural causes anyway so it was the best thing and Michael laughed when I told him and said why not, said he was game and … well, it was just time waiting for her to die.' He rubbed his forehead.

'What did you do with Cameron's body whilst you were waiting?'

'Michael kept him in the big freezer, the one they keep the animal carcasses in. We'd wrapped him in a sheet from the big house and we just waited.'

He told her the same story that Michael Struan told. 'We didn't want to compromise Malcolm any further than we had to. He was easy. And he got himself barred from the pub not long after that. He's that sort of drunk, see, troublesome. We couldn't risk anyone else being involved, except I told Alison. She didn't get involved in any of it though. None of it.'

'Did the girls know?'

'No.' He looked at Kat. 'Definitely not.' He paused. 'But I'm going to have to tell them now though, aren't I?'

She looked at him, raised her eyes and said, 'Best they hear it from you.'

He nodded.

'What about your clothes?'

'What clothes?'

'The ones you were wearing when you killed Cameron?'

'I didn't mean to kill him. I told you that.'

'And the clothes you were wearing when you switched the bodies over?'

'I burnt them in the garden. Mine and Michael's. We had a...a bonfire. The wind whipped up and took the flames and caught the shed. We lost the roof.'

Kat remembered the shed from her first visit to the Fraser home. They'd never repaired it.

'What about Michael's wife?'

'What about her? I don't think she knew. She does her thing, he does his.'

'What about his daughter?'

'Lydia? What about her? She was friends with our Lorna, but we haven't seen her for a long time.'

'Did Rosemary know about Alison and Cameron? About him being her father?'

'Yes, she knew. I'd told her years ago that I wasn't Lorna's dad. When I told her who was, she said something about the apple not falling far from the tree.'

'Did she know about Lorna and the baby?'

'Yes, I told her. She said, 'that poor boy' and told me to look after him, that it wasn't his fault. We know it wasn't the bairn's fault and me and Alison, we said we would help Lorna.'

Kat pulled up an evidence bag containing the locket that had been found with Rosemary. She ripped open the bag and handed the necklace to him. 'Open it.'

He looked at her and said, 'She used to always wear it. We buried her in it. I never looked inside though. Didn't know it could open.' He found the tiny indent on the underside of the locket and slid a fingernail into it. He flicked it open and looked at the photos, black

263

and white, old, faded. One of Rosemary and the other of a man that looked vaguely familiar. 'Rose, yes. I don't know who the man is though.'

'Really?' She was surprised he didn't know who it was.

'I knew she had an unrequited love when she was younger, but never knew who it was. Someone who left her is all she ever said. She used to meet him under the tree, which is why she wanted to be buried there.' He shrugged. 'Sorry, can't help you, I don't know who it is.' He passed the locket to Kat.

She held her hand up and said, 'Take another look.'

He frowned as he looked again. He held the locket closer and examined the photos.

'Can you see who it is?'

'No. Should I?'

'The man, he's Michael Struan. Senior.'

'Really? Is it?' He scrutinised it, squinting. 'Mmm. Maybe. I can just make it out now you've said, but he didn't look like that the last time I saw him, though that was a few years ago.' He looked at the photo again, then back at Kat. 'You're telling me he's her mystery man?'

'Yes.'

'I can't believe it. Auld bastard. Awful man. Used to hit us kids with a stick if he caught you on his land.'

'They had a long affair, over many years.'

'Did they?' He looked incredulous. 'She never once said.'

'They had a baby.'

'Did they?' he repeated.

'Yes.'

'Rose never had any children. She never said. Did it live?'

'Yes. He did.'

'She never kept it? Did she have it adopted?' He looked at the photos again. 'She loved children, would have been a marvellous mother. How do you know this?'

'It's true. I've seen the records, Drew. No doubt.'

'I'm sort of struggling to believe this.' He shook his head. 'What happened to him?'

This was going to be one of the hardest things she'd done, almost as bad as delivering a death message, certainly on a par with it, because once he realised the full implications there would be no going back.

He looked at her, frowning, trying to work it out. 'Not ... not Cameron?'

She shook her head. Looked him straight in the eye. She was anticipating his shock, his pain, the realisation. Kat felt her own emotion build so straightened her back to pull herself together. It was obvious that he was oblivious.

'I'm sorry, Drew. He's you.'

Chapter 45

He was charming to Ma when Da brought him to the house. I knew it might be easy for somebody who didn't know what he was like, to like him. He laughed and was funny and pretended to be kind, but I never laughed, and I never liked him. Neither did I like the prickly beard he'd grown over the summer. I hated him, more hate than any hate I knew. I hated everything about him, the way he made me dig deep into his trouser pockets for snakes, how he'd make funny noises as he forced me to rummage for sweeties.

After the dolly mixture day, there never were any more sweeties. He'd started another little game, of pulling coins out of his nostrils, but I knew they'd had been tucked behind his fingers all the time. I didn't want his coins, I didn't want his money, and he couldn't buy me.

I managed to forget about him when he wasn't there, put him in a box in my head and lock it. He didn't exist and so it didn't happen. I didn't think about the bad when he was locked in the box.

The day after we came back from our first family holiday, he got me in the park when I was trying to run straight through. He gave me a necklace made of curled-up shells, the crinkled-up ones that are supposed to carry the sounds of the sea when you hold them up close to your ear. I heard the noise rush in my head, and I couldn't help it, it just came from my mouth like a bit of sick. I told him I was going to tell. His eyes looked at me, dark dark eyes like the bottom of the wishing well.

His mouth twisted into the kissing lips and he smiled and said, 'Shush, my little darling. I'm only loving you. What is there to tell?'

'I don't … I don't want you to do it anymore,' I whispered. I squirmed and gritted my teeth and they ground together like they might break. I closed my hands tight, as tight as I could make my fists.

'Now stop that nonsense. I'm not hurting you. And you like it. Don't you?' he said, telling not asking. 'Don't you?'

I told him. 'No.'

'Your mamma knows me, and she knows I wouldn't hurt you. She'll believe me when I tell her that you're telling lies. Like the time she caught you stealing a biscuit. You're very naughty and she will believe me when I tell her it's just your funny little girl lies.' His voice was like thick custard and it curdled in my stomach.

I'd never stolen anything. He was bluffing me. Yes, I took a biscuit, but didn't everyone take biscuits? That's not stealing. I didn't know if he was guessing or if he had seen me, watching me in my house. He scared me.

'She knows you tell little porky-pies. She won't believe you. She'll believe me. You naughty, naughty girl. I think you deserve to be punished. Tut-tut. What a naughty girl you are, my little Ness.'

Only Da called me that, 'my little Ness' and he had been there when Da had said it.

He whispered and told me to think about what I'd done by saying 'No' and he told me that nobody says 'No' to him, and I was very naughty, a very bad girl and I should keep thinking about it.

Then he left.

I breathed deep, all the cold air inside my body making me freezing inside and out. I was glad he was gone. I'd stopped him that day. I knew I could say 'No' and I thought that maybe I didn't have to tell, not yet, not unless he did it again.

I was seven and I was sleepwalking and wetting the bed, something that only happened on days I saw him, but nobody knew or wondered or asked why. I cried but couldn't speak, I pleaded with my eyes but couldn't tell, until I did, and then what happened next tortured me for a very long time.

The day after I said I was going to tell, he came to find me. He told me he was building a go-kart. He said it was a present and we were going to have the best time ever, better than going round and round on the roundabout, or the witch's hat, or sliding fast down the shute. It would be so much better than that. He didn't hurt me, and I didn't wet the bed that night.

Not many days after that he said he'd finished the go-kart and took me to Whinny Brae. He said it was a great place to try it out. He asked Ma if I could go with him and she said yes, of course even though I willed and willed her to say no. She told us to watch out for the main road and said we had to be back in time for tea. I was excited for the go-kart, but I didn't want to go with him. He might do something if it was just the two of us.

We had practice turns and then it was time for the big one, from the very top to the very bottom. It was fun, a bit. He told me to have the first go, even though I didn't want it. I watched him looking out at the busy road that ran across the bottom of the brae. It was always a dangerous place to play. He grinned as he stood next to me and put his thumbs up, and said, 'Ready, steady, we're going!'

My long hair flew behind like it might pull out from my head. We went faster and faster and I heard myself squealing 'Wheeeeeeee' as he pushed. me. I'll never forget the feeling when he let go, it was like flying through the air. We tramped back up the brae and he had a turn. He went faster than me. It was fun and I liked travelling fast. I saw the glee on his face when he said it was my turn again. I took my seat, settled in, and we were off. This time he didn't let go and kept pushing me. He pushed me nearly all the way down the brae and it wasn't as fast as the last time because he was still holding on.

I shouted, 'Faster, faster!'

Just before we reached the bottom, I felt him push me harder as he swerved to change our direction.

I saw it. I could see straight ahead and saw the big big lorry and there wasn't time for me to change direction back to the other way and he wasn't changing either.

He pushed me really hard ... and then he let me go.

I was holding tight onto the rope and twisted it tight, fast, to the right. The kart turned and nearly lifted me up.

I heard him yell behind me, 'Oi!'

I pulled all my strength and threw myself from the kart, and rolled onto the gravelly path, rolling, rolling as far as I could onto the grassy patch near the kerb.

As I was rolling, I saw his leg fly up as he kicked the back of the kart and he tripped right over the top of it, like he was doing a roly-poly. When I got to the grass, my rolling slowed, and I heard him scream. I saw him falling ... I heard the lorry blast his big horn ... then I couldn't hear him scream anymore because the horn was long and loud and the lorry was screeching, and braking, and trying to stop as it rolled right over him. The driver tried to swerve but couldn't do anything to stop his lorry as he was caught right under the wheels.

I screamed, and screamed, and kept screaming.

The police came and the lorry driver and the people who saw it happen all said the same thing. There was nothing that could have been done to stop him going under the truck. They saw him pushing me and thought it was going to be me under the wheels, but it wasn't because I threw myself off the kart and it was him that was run over as he kept tumbling and tumbling, because he tripped and there wasn't any time to stop anything from happening.

They said he died instantly. I cried, and I cried, and they all thought I was crying for him, but I wasn't. I cried and cried, and I thought, I really believed, that I had killed him.

When Ma asked me the question, 'Why do you think you killed him?' I told her. I didn't stop telling her until I'd had told her everything and I couldn't cry anymore.

SHE'S NOT THERE

My Da was so upset that they said he died of a broken heart. He blamed himself that this thing, this big bad thing, had happened to his little girl, his little Ness. But he hadn't known. He blamed himself because he was the one that had got him the job working for the council and they had given him an apprenticeship. Everyone thought he was okay. But he was not okay. He was never okay. He had fooled everyone, my Da and my Ma and everyone, but not me.

The night the police came and knocked on our door, the day that my Da died of a broken heart, hanging from a tree in the woods by Glendargie, that was the last night I remember of Ness. That was the night she died, too.

It was the night I became somebody else. Forever.

Chapter 46

When Kat arrived at the restaurant Jed was already there. They had the same table at the same place, the little Italian on the High Street. The lupin centrepiece had been replaced with a chunky pink peony.

Jed stood as she approached. He took her wrap and handed it to the waiter. He sat down once she had. They were seated in opposite positions to the last time. This time he was facing the door, not her. She preferred that position but smiled, knowing he would hate having his back to the door as much as she did. There was only one other table occupied, a young couple with a baby that was asleep in a car seat beside them.

'White wine?' offered Jed.

She nodded.

When her glass was filled, they raised and clinked them.

'Cheers,' said Jed. 'It was good to meet Clarke. What a lovely young man. Has he gone now?'

'Yes, yesterday. Sorry I couldn't stay and chat. I had to get back to the office. He told me you'd had a good discussion. He was impressed ... and a tad drunk. Thanks.' She smiled.

'Ah, sorry about that. He only had three pints but looked a bit bambi-legged when I put him on the bus back into town. I hadn't noticed how it had affected him until the fresh air hit him.'

'The joys of youth.'

271

'I've given him my number and told him to call anytime. He's a credit to you.'

'Not me. His dad, definitely.' She felt the pang again, like a flick of an elastic band to her stomach. She sensed her mood dip as she laid the napkin across her knee.

As if sensing it, Jed asked, 'How are you feeling?'

'Tired,' she said. 'And sort of...I don't know ... a bit different.'

He didn't prompt, just smiled at her with a little tick quirk of his mouth.

She knew his game, waiting for her to speak. 'Hey, I'm okay, it's done, finished. Big relief. Took a little while, but we got there. I just didn't expect so many ... issues? Complications? Demons?' She shrugged.

'What will happen now? Have they been charged?' Jed sipped his wine.

'It's with the procurator fiscal. They've been given bail. I hardly think they're Burke and Hare.'

'Not a risk to anyone else, I don't suppose.'

She said quietly, 'It'll be down to the jury to decide I suppose, if it goes that far, if they go to trial. For twelve good people to agree if it was planned or not. We only have Fraser's word for what happened, and Michael to back up the rest. They could have concocted the whole story for all we can prove. The forensics at the outhouses are finished and they've confirmed Cameron's blood on the tractor. It's still there.' She shrugged. 'They could have deliberately impaled him. We've only Drew's confession. I suspect he'll plead guilty to manslaughter and they'll accept it because we can't prove otherwise. And it'll save a jury trial. He could take a punt and opt for self-defence of course, if he doesn't want to plead guilty, but if he does that then he runs the risk of a much longer stretch if convicted of murder. He could take a punt and see what happens, chance his arm at the self-defence angle, and only plead guilty to preventing lawful disposal of a body, as he's already admitted that. Depends on what they want to charge him with and the advice from his legal team. We won't ever know, or be able to prove, what really happened.'

'Interesting…' said Jed. 'You can be my police expert for my next book.'

'Real police work is boring. As I'm sure you know.'

'So, does this mean you'll be in line for the DI's job?'

'Not likely. Munro's back to work and got his head down. He's not going anywhere anytime soon. He told us this week that he's been diagnosed with MS and has been on some trial at Edinburgh Royal Infirmary, at their new unit. That's why he's been missing in action so much.'

'Really?' Jed sat up. 'Tell me more?'

'I don't know more, but his treatment is finished, for now anyway, and he's doing better than ever. Why are you so interested?' She wondered why his interest was piqued as it seemed more than a casual question and thought he must know someone personally with it. Before she could ask, the waiter brought bruschetta for Jed and prawns for Kat. He lingered, rearranging the cutlery, the tableware, topped up their glasses, and moved the peony. By the time he'd left, Jed had changed the subject.

'Those prawns look delicious and the garlic smells divine. If you can't manage them all, just let me know.'

Kat laughed, pronged a prawn, and held it out to him, holding her hand beneath the fork to catch the buttery drips.

They ate and chatted, easy and comfortable. Kat saved her last prawn for Jed and slid her plate over to him so he could soak up the remaining garlicky butter. He spooned it onto the last piece of bruschetta.

'Thank you, ma'am. You can come for dinner again,' Jed said. 'So how was it left, with the Frasers and Struans?'

'I imagine it'll take some getting used to, suddenly finding out they're brothers.'

'And Drew? How did he take it?'

'Shocked. Took a while for it all to register … that his mother and father weren't who he thought, and his aunt was his mother, that Michael Struan is his half-brother. More significant, so was Cameron. Not only did he kill a man, by accident, design or otherwise, but that man was his brother. Quite biblical.'

'Indeed.'

'Add that to that fact that his daughter is not his daughter, but the daughter by the man he killed, who he didn't know was his really his brother, and the daughter had a baby by the man who was her father, though neither he, nor she, knew it. For Lorna, the man she thought was her father killed her real father, who was also the father of her baby.'

'I think I get it.'

'Confused?'

'Bit of a head mess, isn't it?'

'Is anyone who they think they are?' She looked him in the eye. 'Are you? Am I?'

'Oh, what a wicked game we play…'

Over the rim of her glass, she said, 'Indeed.'

Over the main course of spaghetti vongole, packed with tasty, fresh clams, he told her about Cassie.

Over another glass of wine, he told her about his own diagnosis of MS.

Over fresh fruit salad and Courvoisier cream, and then a couple of sobering cups of coffee, she told him about Ness.

Kat had spent years losing herself in guilt and in grief. She'd spent the first half of her life scared and her older childhood full of pain. She wasn't catholic but guilt had tormented her like a devil on her back. It wasn't her fault, none of it was her fault, she knew that, but it had taken a long time to really believe it.

She remembered twirling and dancing, days full of music playing in her head, images of pink and crimson and yellow and flashes of other colours. There were no dance classes, not like today where stage schools filled otherwise empty warehouses in every town. The only ballet was from books filled with posh girls and ponies and boarding schools. There were plenty of boarding schools around middle Scotland, but they weren't for likes of her and ballet was a dance she could only dream of. Horses galore were stabled on almost every farm and riding them was a given if you were prepared to do the mucking out for their owners.

She stopped dreaming of stables, and horses, and frills and fancy, and there was no more dancing, in her head or otherwise. She did forget, eventually, locked it all away in solid black boxes in her head, one inside the other, secure, because that was the only way she knew to deal with it. Moving away helped. Now she'd returned, the boxes were opening.

After puking her stomach into the crematorium bin, she felt purged but rattled. It was such a long time ago, but it was there, now, staring her in the face, like it had only just happened.

Nessia. She was so named by her father. He told her it was a beautiful name for a beautiful girl. He wouldn't have her called Nessie, it had to be Nessia. Or Ness. Kat had loved Ness.

Ness had hair straight down her back, a sheer smooth drop of chestnut brown. Ness was petite and slim with pudgy knees, a family trait. When Ness was broken, it broke her daddy's heart too. It was in the papers and on the local television. Al and Mari Wallace did their best to shield their daughter, but she knew. And so did the world, or everyone in her world. She knew everything but didn't understand it all. She knew it was a bad thing and she was unable to laugh or sing or dance or twirl. Big box, little box, small box, tiny.

SHE'S NOT THERE

Alistair Wallace couldn't mend his broken heart and blamed himself for what had happened. Mari Wallace laboured on, doing everything she could to protect the child who looked just like her Da. Mari looked after her own mother and worked three jobs to keep her mind from thinking and her own heart from breaking.

When Da went up into the woods and hung himself, Ness went away and never came back; there was no unravelling, no unlocking.

Kat never wanted to be the person that people pointed out and felt sorry for or talked about in whispers behind their hands. Kat bided her time and when she was done, she left with her mother's blessing and didn't look back. She didn't know the extent of her mother's distress for her Ma had kept it hidden. There was only room for so much hurt and pain and she was suffocating and she had no room for anyone else's.

There was justice to be done and although Ness and her father hadn't had any, there were many others who she could help. If things like that could happen in Kendollich and Glendargie, it could happen anywhere. She believed in God once, and in justice, and when she moved to London she stood as tall as she could and was as proud as she dared. By the time she'd returned to her hometown she no longer believed in any God and her belief in justice was threadbare, though she still strived for good and always had a tear for Ness and Mari and Alistair Wallace.

Epilogue

Early evening sun settled on the September day; orange ribbons and scatters of deep purple glowed surreal in the sky. For once the rains didn't come.

It had been some months since she'd first stood by the tree with gnarled roots and breaking bark. She placed a fragrant posy of flowers, full of white petals, delicate and already falling, at the foot of the tree as she rested a hand on the trunk. She ran her fingers across the knobbles and notches, as if reading the history in braille. She touched the torso and felt the tree, a heart alive but broken, branches like arms stretching with hope towards the sky. The surrender of summer leaves had already started.

She traced a path in the bark. Truth. Love. Strength. Life. Had she not given up God she may have said a prayer. As the wind caught her hair, pulling curly strands away from her face, Kat tried to calm it by tucking it behind her ear. Some habits remain, like some secrets stay hidden. Maybe it was time to give up the curls, let her hair fly straight, and free.

She turned and walked the path to the cottage where Jed was waiting with a tumbler of smooth malt, a black pen, and the papers. It was decision time.

Small places were no place to hide but they're very often a beautiful place to live and Kat didn't want to hide anymore. She wanted to be who she was, who she was meant to be, who she'd locked away, hidden for too many years. She'd adopted Kat, like a stray kitty-

277

cat, and given her the name to hide behind. She could still call herself Kat, but it was time, time to remember and to bring back Ness, to let her live again.

The dead don't walk, the dead can't talk, but the living do.

Printed in Great Britain
by Amazon

40995187R00158